THE GHOST OF YOU

Healing doesn't mean forgetting.

SUMMER NICOLE

MINT
SUGAR
PRESS

SUMMER NICOLE

The Ghost of You

MINT
SUGAR
PRESS

First published by Mint Sugar Press 2025

First edition

ISBN: 979-8-9937225-0-4

Cover art by Get Covers

This book was professionally typeset on Reedsy. Find out more at reedsy.com

*To anyone who has ever suffered from an anxiety disorder or lost a loved one.
I see you, and I understand you.*

You will lose someone you can't live without, and your heart will be badly broken, and the bad news is that you never completely get over the loss of your beloved. But this is also the good news. They live forever in your broken heart that doesn't seal back up. And you come through.

ANNE LAMONT

Contents

Prologue	1
Chapter 1	3
Chapter 2	11
Chapter 3	19
Chapter 4	25
Chapter 5	33
Chapter 6	49
Chapter 7	58
Chapter 8	67
Chapter 9	74
Chapter 10	85
Chapter 11	93
Chapter 12	99
Chapter 13	110
Chapter 14	122
Chapter 15	129
Chapter 16	137
Chapter 17	145
Chapter 18	154
Chapter 19	165
Chapter 20	174
Chapter 21	186
Chapter 22	196
Chapter 23	205

Chapter 24	216
Chapter 25	227
Chapter 26	235
Chapter 27	244
Chapter 28	256
Chapter 29	267
Chapter 30	276
ACKNOWLEDGEMENTS	280
About the Author	284

Prologue

I had always hated going to funerals. I was sure everyone did, but they never really affected me because it was always some distant family member that I didn't know well or a relative of someone my parents worked with. I had never lost anyone close to me or anyone that I knew very well. I now knew just how lucky I was to have everyone I loved alive and well, but that was a privilege I no longer had.

I had always seen the dramatics that people displayed at funerals and thought how over the top it was, or how it was ridiculous to be screaming and passing out in the aisle. But that behavior didn't seem so dramatic to me anymore. I finally understood it. Sitting in that uncomfortable pew, staring at the shiny chestnut colored casket, I wanted to scream, sob, and yell at the top of my lungs that this could not be happening. It couldn't be real, you couldn't be gone. Seventeen is far too young to die.

I wanted to run out of that church, go down to our spot by the water, and see you sitting on the bench reading your favorite book, but you wouldn't be there. So instead, I sat in the church and stared at your casket as the blue and yellow flowers atop it mocked me with their stems as intertwined as our lives once were. It felt like half of my soul had been ripped away from me, and I didn't know if that feeling would ever go away.

I hated this *beautiful* service that your mom and Bill prepared. It's everything you would have hated. There was a choir singing hymns and a preacher reading verses about heaven and where your soul rests, even though your mom and Bill knew that you were an atheist. But your mom always made everything about herself, and your funeral was no exception.

They sat two rows ahead of me, your mom pretending to cry and Bill rubbing her back as the choir sang Amazing Grace. It took everything in my power not to spit in Bill's face when he greeted and thanked me for coming. He was playing the part of a grieving step-father well, but I knew better. They both made me sick, but I had to show up for you. *Poor Christy, poor Bill, how will they ever deal with such a tragedy?* That's all I heard the week after the accident. As if they even cared. They barely knew their own son, but I did. And I knew a lot more than they would have liked me to.

The funeral felt like it was going to rip me apart. The finality of it was too much for me to bear. That chapter of my life was closed, the chapter where we were inseparable, and you were everything to me. It felt impossible to accept that I'll never get another day with you, another hug, another laugh, or another inside joke. You were the person I'd go to for comfort in a situation like this, but you were gone, and I had no idea what I was supposed to do anymore.

Chapter 1

Packing up my dorm room had proven to be my least favorite part of the college experience. Everything was everywhere, and I couldn't seem to make any progress. There were only a few days left in the semester, and I felt like I still had so much left to do. Any other college freshman would be psyched about going home for the summer, but not me. I dreaded going back home. I missed my parents, of course, but without Justin there, I knew it wouldn't feel the same.

It had been almost a year since the accident, but it hadn't gotten any easier. People say time heals all wounds, but I have a hard time believing that. Missing Justin hadn't stopped for a single second. My panic attacks may not be as severe as they once were, but the gaping hole in my chest was still ever-present. I didn't know if I would ever feel whole again or if I would ever be able to go to mine and Justin's spot by the water without feeling like someone is ripping my heart out of my chest all over again. I hadn't even tried. I couldn't bear to see the empty bench that held so many memories of us.

Losing someone so young and so suddenly was very strange. One second, you were talking to them on the phone on a seemingly normal day, and the next second, they were gone from your life forever. You would never hear their voice again, never feel their embrace, never get to watch them grow old or see what life had in store for them, and it was absolutely soul-crushing to think about. It's all I had thought about for the last year, and it felt like there was this heavy weight pushing down on my chest almost every second of the day. I still hadn't been able to wrap my head around it fully, and I didn't know if I ever would.

* * *

My phone buzzed loudly on the table next to me, jerking my attention away from the book I had been reading. I looked at the screen, tapped the green button, and put the phone up to my ear.

Justin's excited voice burst through before I could even say hello. "Lia! Guess what I'm doing!"

"Hm, a day before my birthday. No idea," I said, feigning ignorance.

"I'm on the way home with your birthday present! I ordered it months ago, but it was on back order. It made it just in time." He sounded so pleased with himself, as if he personally ensured its timely arrival. Justin had a knack for charming people, so maybe he did.

"I always tell you that you don't have to get me anything." I loved giving other people gifts, but never cared too much about receiving gifts myself. Of course, I was grateful, but I never expected it.

"We go through this every year. You tell me I don't have to get you anything. I get you something anyway. You remind me that you said that I didn't have to get you anything. We've been friends for nearly eighteen years now. It's getting a little old, don't you think?"

I smiled. Justin always picked out the best gifts, which made sense because he knew me better than anyone. "I suppose it is. I should just accept it, huh? It doesn't seem like you plan on stopping."

"Yes, just accept the presents, and enjoy your day. The best friend a guy could ask for deserves a gift. And for putting up with me over the years, you deserve loads of gifts."

I laughed. "You haven't been too bad. Speaking of bad, how are you and Amber doing?"

"Nice segue. We aren't really speaking anymore. I figured it was best if we called it quits," he answered.

"What? When did this happen? Don't get me wrong, I'm glad, but when?" I honestly couldn't stand Amber because no matter how much I tried to get along with her she always gave me an attitude.

"Last week, I think. I forgot to mention it because Bill was being Bill, so I'd been trying to stay out of the house as much as possible."

"Oh, that's why you were at Brayden's so much last week?" I hated Bill. Even hearing his name disgusted me.

"Yep. But let's not ruin the good mood. We're happy and excited for your birthday tomorrow!" How he managed to always put on a happy face when he had to deal with his home life was beyond me. His infectious happiness was one of the things I loved about him, though. He made me want to be as carefree as he let everyone believe he was.

"I guess. I'm just getting older, though." I didn't care too much for birthdays. As a kid I always wanted a party, but now I was happy enough with just a cake and being with my parents and Justin.

"And like fine wine, you're getting better with age."

"Whatever you say." I grinned and rolled my eyes. He always knew how to make me smile.

"That's the right answer! And since it's whatever I say, tomorrow we will get some takeout from the Italian place downtown because I know it's your favorite, and have a little birthday picnic by the water. Then we can head over to Greenfield Park because they are putting up the big screen and showing the first movie in the park for the summer tomorrow night. I think they said they were doing some eighties romcoms, which I know are your favorite."

"Wow, it sounds like you put a lot of thought into this," I teased.

"Of course! It's a special birthday. You're turning eighteen!"

"Well, it sounds perfect. I can't wait."

"Me, either."

* * *

After that, we hung up the phone, and I never heard from him again. My mind always drifted back to Justin, but it happened more often now that it was so close to when I'd be going home. I wanted nothing more than to distract myself, so I continued tossing everything I didn't need for the week into boxes, but stopped when I heard a light knock on my door. I crossed the room and pulled it open to see Max waiting, two iced coffees in hand. He held one out to me. Smiling, I took it and stepped out of the way to let him inside.

"God, how did you know that a coffee was exactly what I needed right now?"

"My coffee senses were tingling," Max joked. "Earlier, you told me you were going to start packing, and packing is the worst, so I figured you could use a pick-me-up right about now."

"You were correct. I'm exhausted, and I hate packing. I don't even know what to do with everything," I said.

"My coffee senses are never wrong," He grinned.

I laughed. "I see that." Laughing was something I rarely did, but if I did, it was with Max. He was so easy to talk to. He never pushed me to talk about anything I was uncomfortable with, plus his smile was contagious. The hole in my chest ached slightly less when Max was around.

Max sat down on my bed and looked around at all my half-packed boxes covering the floor. "Do you want some help? I have no plans for the rest of the evening, and I'm great at organizing."

"I'd love that, actually. I'm not ready to go home for the summer." I sighed.

"Because of the anniversary?" He asked with sympathetic eyes.

"Yeah, the worst day of my life. I don't want to relive it any more than I already do. Home hasn't felt the same without Justin. He lived down the street from me for my entire life, so knowing he isn't there anymore makes the whole neighborhood feel empty." My eyes filled with tears, but I quickly wiped them away, hoping Max wouldn't notice. "I'm sorry. I didn't mean to bring the mood down."

"Amelia, you know you don't have to apologize for that. We met in a grief support group, so it's kind of what I'm here for." Max said with a small smile, trying to lighten the mood as he reached to wipe a stray tear from my face.

Max had been such an angel in my life, and I was so grateful to have met him in that first support group meeting. I don't know how I would have managed this school year without him. It's funny how we lived in the same town all our lives, but never crossed paths until then. We went to different schools, but the town wasn't that big. I always felt like maybe Justin had somehow sent him to me. I wasn't entirely sure what I believed happened after someone died, but if Justin was out there somewhere, I thought maybe he was watching over me and knew I needed a friend.

"Thank you for saying that, but also for being here for me these past months, well, almost a year now," I said as I leaned in to hug him.

He opened his arms, pulling me into a tight embrace. I genuinely cared about Max, and I wished I could give him more of me, but I didn't even feel whole. I felt like a puzzle that had been stuffed into a box in the back of the closet that was missing too many pieces, and why would anyone want that? Max deserved more than I could give him. He'd been my rock and the person I'd grown closest to. He reminded me of Justin, but not appearance-wise. He had that same infectious laugh that made you want to laugh with him and made me feel at ease, even during some of my worst days. I hadn't been that comfortable with anyone in my life other than my parents and Justin, so it was easy to rely on him. Maybe

I relied too much, but he never seemed to mind.

"It's no problem. I wasn't in the best place when we met either, and you've helped me more than you could imagine. I'm grateful to have you in my life." He pulled back from our hug and smiled at me. There was a slight moment where it looked like he wanted to say something else, but he didn't. Max had lost his girlfriend to cancer just a few months before I lost Justin, so he understood my pain, and I understood his. Losing someone you love is an indescribable pain, whether it's a girlfriend or best friend. It changes you.

Needing a distraction, I walked over to my desk, turned on the Bluetooth speaker, and grabbed my phone. I flipped through my playlists and turned on the "Feel Better" playlist to try to get the mood up. I grabbed a few boxes and handed them to Max. "I guess we should get packing so I don't keep you up too late since we have finals."

"Don't hate me, but I'm already finished with finals," he said sheepishly.

"Are you serious? How? I still have two to take this week!" I was suddenly envious of Max. I had no desire to sit through two incredibly long exams the next couple of days before a two-hour drive home on Wednesday.

"My professors gave us the option to take ours early if we felt prepared enough because we didn't have any lessons left."

"Lucky! I probably wouldn't have taken mine early, even with the option, because I don't feel prepared as I should. I feel like my brain could explode at any moment."

"Well, you've got me to help with packing, at least. I'd take your finals for you, but I doubt I could pass for you. The height difference would give it away, I'm sure." He grinned at me.

I laughed and shook my head. "Oh yeah, it's the height difference that would be what gives it away."

I stood at a whopping five feet, two inches with long auburn hair, brown eyes, and pale skin, on a slender frame. In contrast, Max was six feet, two inches of lean muscle and beautiful tan skin with brown hair that hung in his dreamy emerald green eyes. But sure, it was the height difference that really stood us apart from one another. I always appreciated Max's beauty, even if we were only friends. His warm smile drew me to him, but after getting to know him, I realized he had a big, warm heart that matched, and that was what made me thankful that he decided to stick around.

I told Max which things could be packed, and he got to work organizing and labeling all the boxes he packed. He was much better at this than I was. My packing method was cramming whatever would fit into the boxes with no regard for whether I'd be able to find anything or not once I got home. He even took time to organize and repack all the boxes I had already packed as well. We stayed up until well past midnight packing and singing every song that came on. By the time we decided to call it a night, I was in a much better mood and significantly less stressed.

"You should be getting to bed soon," Max said, looking at the time on his phone.

"Yeah, I probably should. If not, I'll be sleeping through my English final in the morning. Are you sure you can't dress up like me and take it instead?" I asked, batting my eyelashes.

Max gave me a sympathetic smile. "You know I would if I could."

I walked Max to my door, holding it open for him. He stopped in the doorway and turned to me. "Text me tomorrow and let me know how the final goes, and if you want me to help you finish packing. I have to meet someone around noon, but I'm free for the rest of the day."

"I will definitely need help with the rest of the packing. But meeting someone, huh? Like a date?" I teased.

He playfully rolled his eyes. "Not a date, just a coffee. But I'll be over whenever you need me to be. Just let me know."

He opened his arms, gave me a big hug, and kissed the top of my head before turning to leave. I'm not sure exactly when it started, but Max kissing the top of my head always made me happy. It was comforting, and I always noticed he did it on days when I had a hard time. I waved at him as he walked off, and then shut my door when he was out of sight. I quickly changed into my pajamas and got in bed, hoping I could actually sleep. It was too late to take any medicine, and it barely worked anyway.

I lay awake for what felt like hours. I always refused to look at the time when I couldn't sleep because it made me more anxious and aware of how much sleep I was losing. I went over all of the information I needed to know for my exam the following day in my head until my eyelids finally felt heavy and I drifted off to sleep.

Chapter 2

Thankfully, I made it through my English final without my head exploding. It was actually pretty easy, which made me nervous. Either I was prepared, or I was overconfident and got everything wrong. I was about fifty-fifty on which it could be. On the way to my car, I noticed I was suddenly starving. I usually ate breakfast, even if it's just something small, but I skipped this morning because I wanted to get in a few extra minutes of studying before the test. It was almost eleven, so I figured I would swing by and grab a turkey club and a coffee before returning to my room to the dreaded chore of packing. There was a Moon Dollar Cafe on campus, right on the way to my dorm. They were a popular chain restaurant with a deli, bakery, and coffee shop all rolled into one. I didn't think I had gone a day without stopping by for at least a muffin since I first got my license. It was an expensive habit to have.

Justin and I would always go there to grab coffees and sometimes sit inside and read. Most Moon Dollar Cafes had a section inside them with a small carpeted reading area with comfy chairs, a magazine rack, and a bookshelf . There was always a nice ambiance; even when it was hectic, it was still somehow tranquil and peaceful inside. It was like everyone knew you weren't supposed to be loud, like how people are in a library. The one on campus wasn't as peaceful as the one back home, but it was as quiet as you could hope for, given its almost exclusively

11

college student customer base.

It wasn't too busy since it wasn't lunchtime yet. Most students didn't start to pile in until the afternoon. I pulled into a spot right in front and parked. As I was getting out, I noticed Max's car a few spaces away. I didn't expect to see him there since his coffee date wasn't until noon. Hopefully, he didn't think I was being weird and trying to spy on his date. I grabbed my phone, threw it in my purse, and headed inside. As soon as I walked through the door, I saw Max over to the side in the reading area, a Celebrity News Weekly magazine in his hands. I never took Max for the celebrity gossip magazine type, but I suppose you learn something new every day.

There were only three people ahead of me in line, and it usually moved pretty quickly. I knew it wouldn't be too long a wait, but I grabbed my phone from my purse anyway. I decided to pull up my email to see if my English final grade was in, even though it had only been about twenty minutes since I finished it. Just as I was scrolling through my email, my phone buzzed. It was from a blocked number, but I answered it anyway.

"Hello?" There was no answer. "Hello? Who is this?" I asked. "Hello?" I asked once more and then hung up.

I had been randomly getting calls from a blocked number for the past few months. I figured it was someone messing with me because a few months back, I decided to have a girls' night out with a girl from the grief support group that Max and I met in. She lost her mom to an overdose a few months back and had been having a hard time. She wanted to go out and let loose for a bit, which was understandable. Her friends bought us alcohol, so we could drink before we headed out to the bar, since neither of us was twenty-one. Being a little tipsy, I gave my number to a random guy I'd met there. It wasn't until after I gave him my number that I started getting the blocked calls. I figured the guy was a creep. I always picked up just in case it was ever something else, like maybe my parents were in an accident and someone was calling to tell me. My mind always went negative, but I would hate to miss an important call just because it was a blocked number and I refused to pick it up. Someone tapped me on my shoulder, and I jumped.

"I'm sorry. I didn't mean to startle you," Max said from behind me. I turned to face him, trying to hide my embarrassment with a smile. I felt like an absolute moron.

"You're fine. I was a little zoned out, I guess."

"I saw you standing in line, and you looked like something was wrong, so I wanted to make sure you were okay," he said. Max was always so thoughtful and attentive to me. It was like he could read my mind at times.

"Yeah, I'm fine. Just tired. All that packing last night, and then having to use my brain much more than I wanted to this morning has been rough," I said.

Max laughed, his eyes crinkling at the corners. "I can understand that."

"So, what are you doing here this early? I thought your date wasn't until noon," I asked, stepping forward as the line moved up.

"Not a date, just coffee, but it was. The person I'm meeting texted me this morning to ask if we could move it up to eleven, but it's five past eleven now, so maybe I'm being stood up," he joked.

"Maybe she's just running a few minutes late. I don't think any girl would want to stand you up. You're a catch." I playfully bumped him with my shoulder.

He smiled down at me, "Oh, you think so?"

My face flushed, feeling the embarrassment creep up my cheeks. "I mean, yeah, of course. You're a wonderful friend, so I'm sure you'd make a great date for whatever lucky girl snags you."

Max's face dropped slightly, but I wasn't sure why. It was a compliment to him. I hoped I hadn't upset him by saying that. Just then, the bell on the door jingled, and he looked toward it. "She's here. I'll see you in a little bit, okay?"

"Okay! Have fun," I said, giving him a small wave. As I turned back to the front, the line moved up again, and it was my turn to place an order.

After I got back to my room with the food, I quickly ate my sandwich, then grabbed some boxes and continued packing. Packing took so long. I didn't even realize it had been over an hour and a half. I had gotten distracted a few times and started doing other things, so packing hadn't gotten as far as I would have liked it to. It was so dull that it made it impossible to stay focused while doing it alone. I wasn't sure how long it would be until Max came over. I assumed his date must have been going pretty well to last so long, especially since it was just supposed to be coffee. It's not like they were going out to dinner and a movie or something.

Whenever I walked out of Moon Dollar earlier, I glanced at where Max and his date were sitting. Call me curious, but I wanted to see what type of girl he went for and what he liked. We hadn't gone too much into the types we liked. I'd seen photos of his girlfriend who passed away, but he never talked about any other girls or whether he even had other girlfriends before her. Her name was Vanessa, and she was gorgeous. She had beautiful curly dark blonde hair, before the chemo took it, gray eyes, and light freckles across her nose. In their photos, she and Max matched perfectly. They made a stunning couple. I felt a pang of sadness for Max and Vanessa. He was such a wonderful person that it didn't seem fair that he had to lose the love of his life so young, and it would never be fair that someone so young and full of life had to lose their life. It made no sense to me.

The girl from the coffee shop was somewhat tall, but most people seemed tall to me. She was slender with shoulder-length brown hair. She was pretty, not as pretty as Vanessa, but honestly, who could be? He was so focused on whatever she was saying that he didn't notice me leave. He claimed it wasn't a date, but he seemed interested in her. I

14

wanted Max to be happy, but a selfish part of me didn't want to lose time with him if he got a girlfriend. I knew it was bound to happen at some point, but I didn't want it to yet, not right when summer break was starting. Summer break used to be my favorite because summer was my favorite season, and there was no school, but now it was the time I dreaded most.

As I was throwing my English textbooks and binder into a box, I heard a knock at my door. It was Max, and he had no coffee this time, but he was holding a Moon Dollar bag.

"What did you bring me this time?" I asked as I gestured toward the bag.

"A brownie. I figured a little dessert might make up for making you do all the packing yourself. My meeting ran a little longer than I expected," Max said, smiling as he held the bag out to me.

"You know you can just call it a date," I said, smiling back at him, " and you're all good. I wasn't expecting you until later since your *meeting*," I made air quotes as I said meeting, "wasn't originally supposed to start until noon."

"It wasn't a date, honestly. And if it's all good, then I guess I can eat this brownie myself," he said, pulling the bag back.

"No, no. I'll still take the brownie. Thanks!" I said, snatching the bag from him and running back into my room. He followed me inside and shut the door behind him. "I guess I can share the brownie with you since you *are* helping me pack."

"Hm, sounds like a fair enough deal to me," he said as he sat down on my bed.

I took the brownie out of the bag and broke it in half. I placed the bigger half on a napkin and handed it to Max. We ate our brownies in silence, and I watched him as he looked around my room, probably trying to decide what to pack next. He looked back at me and asked, "Did you even pack anything before I got here?"

"I did, but I also got distracted a few times and maybe didn't get as much done as I thought I did," I said, embarrassed.

He huffed a laugh and shook his head. "What distracted you?"

"Well, I found some papers I had been looking for a while back and some other things I thought I lost. I was also wondering how your date, wait, I'm sorry, your *meeting* was going," I said.

"Ah, yeah, that happens to me sometimes, too, when I go through things. It's easy to get distracted. But why were you wondering about my date?" He asked.

"HAH! SEE! You called it a date!" I said, pointing my finger at him.

"You know what I meant, but why were you so curious?" He asked.

"I haven't seen you go out with anyone since we've been friends, or not that I know of. And I've never heard you talk about anyone except Vanessa, so I was curious."

"I haven't been out with anyone since Vanessa. I haven't had any new relationships with someone of the opposite sex, except for you. I know we're just friends, but you get what I'm saying. No one has been this close to me, other than you, since she passed away," he said.

"Really? No one at all?" I asked. The selfish part of me was a little happy to hear that he hadn't been that close to anyone other than me in the last year.

"Nope, nothing emotional at all. Not even anything purely physical either," he said.

"Don't feel bad. Me neither," I said with a shrug.

"Really? I know sometimes that part can get pretty difficult, or at least for me, it does."

My face flushed red. We'd never really discussed missing the physical part of being with someone. It did get challenging, though. I mean, it's an easy distraction and a quick way to feel better, but I knew it would only make me feel worse in the long run, so I abstained from it for the most part.

"Yeah, except for a few moments of weakness before I started going to the support group. A crappy ex-boyfriend wanted to see how I was and let me know that he was there for me. He didn't even like Justin when he was alive, but I let him, um, comfort me a few nights when I was feeling lonely and extra terrible, which turned out to be a huge mistake. He was taking advantage of my loneliness and pain. I wasn't trying to make any more mistakes like that again, so I stayed away from guys for the most part, except for you," I said, feeling a little ashamed at my confession.

"I don't blame you. It's hard not to seek comfort, even from people who are bad for you, when you're feeling that down and broken. I knew it would not be good for me mentally, so I did my best to stay away. I think the only action I've seen in over a year was when we kissed a while back," Max laughed awkwardly.

My cheeks grew warm again. Max came over with some wine when I'd been having a terrible day months ago, and we talked about Justin and Vanessa. We were both feeling a little vulnerable, which led to a short but heated kiss. The kiss was amazing, but it didn't feel right to kiss him then. He had been such a good friend to me, and I was afraid to lose the person who had been helping me through the hardest time in my life. I didn't want to complicate things or make them weird, so I stopped the kiss before it went any further. We both decided that it was best if we stayed friends because neither of us was in the best mental space for more than a friendship. We'd both lost people we cared deeply about, and I still had feelings about Justin that I hadn't dealt with. I don't think it would have ended well for us.

We hadn't mentioned the kiss since it happened. I think we felt like it was almost too awkward to bring up. It was almost like an unwritten rule that we didn't speak of it again, but Max was bringing it up. I guess this was a night of firsts for conversations between us. We were somewhat talking about our sex lives, which we had never discussed before. We had grown so much closer since the school year started because we saw each other nearly every day. Sometimes it was hard not to blur the lines, but giving yourself to someone after you've felt such a heart-shattering loss feels so scary. Something terrible could happen at any time, and I didn't know if the reward was worth the risk.

I laughed a nervous laugh. "I'd have to say that's the best action I've had in over a year." I don't know what made me say it, but it came out before I could stop myself. It was true, though. The one kiss with Max was much better and made me feel better than the nights I'd hooked up with Trevor out of loneliness after Justin's accident.

"Yeah?" He asked, smiling at me. "Call me flattered." We had both been sitting on my bed, facing one another, since he arrived, as we ate our brownie and talked. Our gazes met, and there was a moment where I thought he was leaning toward me, but I quickly looked away. Max stood up and cleared his throat, "So, um, what did you want to pack next?"

And just like that, the moment was gone. It sounded terrible to say that I was relieved, but in a sense, I was. Kissing once while you're drunk and emotional was one thing, but sober and where there could be actual consequences was something completely different. I couldn't afford to mess up my friendship with Max, especially not when I had a whole lonely summer waiting for me back in Cape Falls.

Chapter 3

I woke up to the alarm on my phone ringing loudly. I had one last exam to take, and then I would be finished with my freshman year of college. It was so odd to think about because a year ago, Justin and I were talking about leaving for college and how much better everything would be once he wasn't in the house with Bill anymore. He wanted to get away so bad, and I wanted that for him, too.

* * *

We were sitting on our favorite bench facing the lake as the afternoon sun beamed down, making the water look like it was shimmering. "Are you excited?" I asked Justin.

"Excited for what?" he asked, looking up from his book.

"College and being away from Bill, all of it!" I said. I was excited that Justin would not have to live in that awful house anymore.

"Of course. I can't wait," he replied, much less enthusiastically than I expected.

"We're going to have so much fun. I'm pretty nervous about being away from my parents, though. I'm sure I will miss them a lot."

"I'll miss your parents, too. Not mine, though," he deadpanned.

"Understandably so," I said.

"It's not too far, only about two hours. Still close enough where you can visit your parents, or they can come to visit anytime," he said. "That's the whole reason we picked Branston. Far enough where I don't have to live at home, but close enough to see your parents."

"That's true. For summer breaks, you can stay at my house. You know my parents won't care, and you'll be over eighteen, so Christy can't make you stay at home," I said.

"Sounds like a plan," he said before going back to reading his book.

I could tell he was trying to seem happy, but something was off with him, and I wasn't sure what it was. It worried me, but I didn't want to push if something was already bothering him.

* * *

I had set my alarm early enough to have time to eat before my exam today, so I dragged myself out of bed, much to my body's protest, and over to the bathroom. Thankfully, my parents were willing to upgrade to the single dorm suite with a private bathroom when I started at the beginning of the year. It had been convenient not having to run down the hall and wait for a shower or sink to open up for me to use. I actually got to all my classes on time. Judging by the line I saw outside the communal bathrooms, I knew there was no way I would have if I were forced to wait in that line.

When I got out of the shower, I went to my phone to check the time. I had about an hour until I had to be in class. I also had a text from Max. He said he was heading to Moon Dollar and asked if I wanted to meet him there before class. I quickly texted back that I did and that I'd be there in twenty minutes. I dried my hair, filled in my brows, swiped a few coats of mascara over my lashes, then headed out the door to Moon Dollar.

I pulled into the free space beside Max's car. I could already see him inside at a table, and someone was sitting with him. I got out, and as I got closer to the door, I realized it was the coffee date girl from yesterday. Wow, two dates in less than twenty-four hours. Max was on a roll. I pulled the door handle, and the bell jingled as I walked inside. Max looked my way, then said something to the brunette before walking over to me.

"Hey, you ready for that exam this morning?" He asked as he stopped next to me.

"Absolutely not. Information-wise, yes, but the thought of sitting in a quiet room taking a one-hundred-question test is pretty unappealing to me if I'm being honest." I looked over to the table where he was sitting. "Is that your coffee date from yesterday?" I asked.

"It is. I wanted you to meet her. She was still in town and wanted to meet up one more time before she left this morning," he answered, looking over to the table, and then back at me. I paused, not saying anything for a second. And I must have looked confused because he continued, "She was Vanessa's best friend. She is who got Vanessa to talk to me the first night she and I met."

That made much more sense now. So, it really wasn't a date then, and I'd been giving Max crap for no reason. "Oh, I'd love to meet her," I said. I thought it would be nice to meet someone from Max's life who had known him longer. We'd only ever had our mutual friends from the group, so I didn't even know much about the friends he had before Vanessa passed away. "I'll come over there after I get my order."

"Okay," he said, smiling at me before returning to the table.

The line wasn't long, so I only had to wait a couple of minutes. I grabbed my order and headed to the table where Max sat with Vanessa's friend.

Max stood up and pulled my chair out for me, "That was quick," he said.

"Yeah, I only got a muffin and coffee, so it didn't take them long."

"This is Ari. She was Vanessa's best friend," Max said as he looked from me to Ari.

"Ah, ah. Still Vanessa's best friend. We're just long-distance friends right now," she said, smiling at him as she held her hand out to me.

I shook her hand, "Nice to meet you. I'm Amelia," I said, smiling at her as I sat down in the chair Max pulled out. Max sat down in the seat between Ari and me.

"Oh, I know. Max has told me *all* about you," she said with a grin, dragging out the word all. There was a hint of something in her voice, like maybe she knew something I didn't. It didn't seem malicious but more playful.

"Good things, I hope," I replied.

"Of course. You've made this sad lump live his life again. You should have seen him before he met you. I didn't think he'd ever smile again," she said, nudging his arm with her elbow.

"I'm glad I could help," I said, looking over at Max. "He's helped me more than I could ever thank him for."

"I'm sorry about your best friend, by the way," she said, giving me a sad half-smile.

"Thank you. It's been tough, but I know you would understand that." Unfortunately, we had that in common.

"Absolutely. Vanessa and I have been friends since preschool, so since she's been gone, I've felt like a piece of my soul is missing," she said, looking down. I saw a small tear fall, but she swiped it away quickly.

"I'm going to grab myself another coffee. Do either of you need anything?" Max asked.

"I'm good," I said.

"You can grab me a blueberry muffin," Ari said. "After seeing Amelia's, I'm craving one," she laughed.

"Got it," he said, and then turned to get in line.

I looked back at Ari. "So, what brings you to town? Do you live around here?"

"Nah, I wanted to check out Branston and see how the campus was. I also knew Max went here, so I figured I'd see how he was doing since I don't think I've seen him since last summer."

"Are you thinking of coming here next year?" I asked.

"I'm considering it. I went to Briar Glen this past year, but I'd rather go ahead and transfer to a university."

Briar Glen was a technical college about twenty minutes outside Cape Falls in Briarview. Most kids we went to school with went there for their first two years of college to save money on tuition, and then transferred to a university for the last two years. That's probably what Justin and I would have done if it weren't for Bill. Justin wanted to move as soon as possible, and I wanted him to as well, so we decided to go to Branston U instead.

"It's pretty nice here. I'm sure you'd like it," I told Ari.

"Yeah, I think so too," she replied. She looked at me seriously now, "Thank you for being there for Max. I'm so glad he's had you this year. He had a hard time after Vanessa died, and we were all so worried about him."

"Of course. Max has been an amazing friend, and he's been there so much for me, too," I said.

"And you've been an amazing friend to him. He and I occasionally speak so that I can check in on him. He's told me so much about you, and you've definitely made his life less sad. Vanessa told me before she passed that she wanted me to make sure Max would be okay. She wanted him to live his life and be happy again. She wanted him to love someone again." Her voice cracked slightly at the last part, and she looked down. I saw that her eyes had started to tear up again.

"From what I've heard from Max, she seemed like an incredible person."

"She was... is. I never like to speak about her in the past tense or like she's gone for good. She's not gone; we're just in different places right now. I know I'll see her again one day. I'm not religious or anything, but she was my soulmate, in the best friend sense, so I know the universe will make sure we're back together eventually, maybe in our next lifetime. Sometimes, I feel like she's watching over me," she said.

"I understand that. It may sound silly, but I sometimes feel like Justin somehow sent Max to me because I honestly don't know what I would have done without Max this year," I said.

She looked back up at me and smiled. "It doesn't sound silly at all. Maybe Justin and Vanessa were working together on this one, wherever they may be," she said.

Max walked back to the table, handing Ari her muffin and taking a seat between us. I grabbed my phone from my purse and checked the time. I had ten minutes until I had to be in class.

"I'd better get going," I said as I stood up. "My exam is in ten minutes, so I need to get a seat and do a quick look over my notes."

"Oh yeah, I almost forgot about that," Max said as he looked down at the time on his phone. "Do you still want me to come over after your exam to help you get the boxes packed in your car?" He asked.

"Yes, that would be great," I said.

"It was so nice to meet you, Amelia," Ari said.

"You too!" I gave her a quick smile and then headed out the door.

Chapter 4

I could barely focus on my exam. The questions seemed to blur together, and simple sentences seemed more challenging to decipher. I kept thinking about what Ari said and how Vanessa wanted Max to love again. Was Ari hinting at something to me? I don't think she was implying that the person Max would love again would be me, or was she? It was too much for my brain between this and our almost moment yesterday when he came over.

After Max and I packed everything yesterday, we grabbed some takeout and brought it back to my dorm. We ate, and then watched TV for a while. Before he left, he offered to come back by and help me get all of the boxes packed in my car, so we could leave at the same time tomorrow morning to head home. My mom and dad would be at work when we got there, so Max said he would follow me home to help me unpack my car before he went to his house. He was one of the most thoughtful people I'd ever met. It was few and far between with guys around here, but I'd hit the jackpot with Max.

I glanced at the clock on the wall. I only had about twenty more minutes to finish, but I still had fifty questions. The questions weren't that difficult once I was paying attention, but I had to read all of them more than once. I hadn't had this much of an issue concentrating since the beginning of the year, when everything was still very fresh on my mind. I guess the anniversary being less than a week away, and the conversation with Ari had gotten to me. I tried to quiet my brain and focus on the exam for the last twenty minutes.

I had cut it very close. I finished the last question right before the time was up. I walked to the front of the room, dropped my exam in the basket on the professor's desk, and headed out the door. Once in the hallway, I grabbed my phone from my bag and sent Max a text to tell him that I was headed back to the dorms and he could come over whenever he was ready. My phone vibrated in my hand, but I waited until I was in the car to check it.

Max: You hungry? I can pick up something before coming over.

Me: Sure! Whatever you're in the mood for is fine.

Max sent back a thumbs-up emoji. I locked my phone, pulled out of the parking space, and headed back to my dorm. I had only been back in my room for about fifteen minutes before Max arrived.

"That was pretty quick, considering you had to pick up the food too," I said as he walked inside.

"Yeah, I was about to get food when you texted, so I was already almost there," he said.

"So what did ya get?" I asked.

"I stopped by The Cantina Grill. Tacos, quesadillas, chips with queso, and salsa."

"My mouth is watering already. You know that's my favorite place for tacos," I said as I stood to grab the paper plates from the top of the microwave.

"That's why I got it." Max always remembered things I told him about myself, no matter how small they were. I couldn't imagine how great a boyfriend he must have been to Vanessa if he was this attentive as a friend.

"You're the best," I said as I placed my hand on his arm and gave it a squeeze. I sat down in my desk chair next to where he stood as he got the food out of the bag to sort it out onto our plates. The food smelled delicious, and I couldn't wait. We both ate until we were absolutely stuffed and couldn't bear to eat anymore. The Cantina Grill never let me down.

"We should probably start trying to get all of these boxes into your car," Max said after a few minutes of sitting in silence. I think we were both almost too full to speak.

"Yeah, probably so. I don't know how in the world we're going to get them all in there," I said as I looked around my room at all the boxes that were stacked everywhere.

"Me neither, but I love a challenge. I'm excellent at Tetris," he said with a grin.

"You deserve some sort of award if you manage to fit all of these into my car."

"If we can't make them all fit, you can put a few in my car. I don't have much stuff to take home, so I have some extra room," he said.

"I'd hate to take up space in your car, but I'd really appreciate that."

"It's not a problem. I'm going by your house first anyway," he said.

"I guess that's true," I said as I got to my feet. "Let's start moving some boxes."

I carried one box at a time, while Max carried two. We had my trunk filled up in no time. The back seat was nearly full, and we almost forgot to leave space so I could see out of the back. We fit two more boxes in the front seat, but I still had three boxes with no space left. Max's car was packed with all his boxes and wasn't anywhere near as full as mine. So I helped Max carry my last three boxes to his car, and he placed two in his front seat and one in the back so they would be easy to get to once we got to my house. I was so happy when we were finally finished loading everything up because I was exhausted. Getting up early and then getting super full from all the food had my energy levels on E.

When we returned to my dorm, I flopped down on the bed. "I'm so tired," I said as I stared at the ceiling.

THE GHOST OF YOU

Max laughed and then sat down on the bed next to me. "I can see that."

I looked over at him. "Do you have anything else you need to get done today?"

"Nope, my room is completely cleaned out, and I'm all packed up," he answered.

"What about the clothes you're wearing home tomorrow?"

"They are in a small bag in my car."

"You brought your clothes?" I asked.

"No, I always keep a bag with a change of clothes in my car because you never know what could happen. You may be out eating somewhere and spill something on yourself or fall in a puddle," he said.

I looked up at him with a quizzical expression. "How many times have you been out and about and then just fallen into a puddle?" I asked.

"More than once, for sure," Max said as he looked down at me.

"I didn't realize you were so clumsy." I chuckled.

"You learn something new every day," he replied.

"That's what I always say."

I asked Max if he wanted to stay and watch some movies since he didn't have anything else left to pack or get done. I didn't want to be alone tonight. My anxiety had started to creep up, and I was afraid the panic attacks would start again. I thought that maybe it was because I was nervous about going home and having to see my lonely street and all of the places that reminded me of Justin. It was almost too much for me to know I'd never look out my window and see Justin in his chair by the window, reading while the lamp next to him illuminated his face. I'd never walk into my room and have him sitting on my bed waiting for me to get home again. My house and Cape Falls, in general, had so many memories, and it killed me inside to think about it.

I hadn't been home since I left for school in the fall. For Thanksgiving break, my parents and I went to my grandparents' house. At Christmas, we all went to the mountains for two weeks. Then, for spring break, we all went down to the beach house in Florida. I think my parents knew that being home would be hard for me because Justin spent practically every holiday with us, so they kept planning trips to keep me out of the house for the holidays. Having to be home for summer break was inevitable, and ironically, it would be the most difficult time to be home.

Unfortunately, my parents couldn't plan a two-and-a-half-month-long trip, even with my dad's flexible work schedule, so I was stuck. I was going to have to face everything I feared. I was nowhere near okay or over the fact that I had lost my best friend, but I think not being home, where the memories of Justin and me were endless, had helped me not be as sad as I would have been. I had been away and busy with school, so I was often distracted. That was something I'd been so thankful for.

Keeping my mind occupied and my antidepressants kept the panic attacks at bay most of the time. After Justin's accident, I started having panic attacks multiple times a day. They were so bad that my parents were afraid to leave me alone in the house last summer. One of them tried to always be home with me, and once I met Max, they made sure he was there if they couldn't be.

Max and I lay on my bed. We were on our third movie when I finally looked up at him and said, "I'm scared, Max."

He looked at me, a little confused. "We can turn the movie off if it's bothering you."

"No, it's not the movie. I'm scared of going home," I said as tears filled my eyes.

He tucked one arm under me, put the other around me, and cradled me to his chest. "I know it's going to be hard, but I'll be there anytime you need me to be. You don't have to feel alone. I'll come over, or we can go somewhere to get you out of the house."

I leaned into him as tears fell down my face. They eventually turned into an all-out sob, and he held me, stroked my hair, and told me everything would be all right. I must have fallen asleep at some point because I woke up, and Max still had his arms around me, but he was out cold. I felt terrible that he had fallen asleep like that because I was sure he couldn't have been very comfortable. I looked at the time on the TV and saw that it was three-thirty in the morning. I had to admit, it felt nice sleeping while someone held me. That was something I hadn't had in a long time. I reached down as gently as possible, trying not to disturb Max. I pulled the blanket up on us, and then closed my eyes and quickly fell back asleep.

I jerked awake when I heard my alarm, and so did Max. I must have forgotten to turn it off since I had it set for seven the past two mornings for my finals. Max unwrapped his arms from me, and I sat up, grabbed my phone from my bedside table, and turned the alarm off.

"Oh my god, I'm so sorry about that," I said.

"It's okay. We get to have an early start on the day now," he said as he smiled a sleepy smile.

"Yeah, but I was not planning on a seven A.M. early start for sure," I said. "And I'm sorry I fell asleep on you. I know you couldn't have been too comfortable sleeping like that. You could have woken me up if you needed to."

"It was no problem. That's actually the best sleep I've had in a while. I think it's something about having someone next to you that makes you feel safer and sleep better, if that makes sense," Max said.

"It does. Honestly, I slept great. I was just worried that you didn't."

"Well, I did too," he said. "I should probably run back to my room to shower and change so we can get on the road."

"Since you have clothes in the car, you can shower and everything here if you want," I said. "With the private bathroom, you won't have to share with a bunch of other guys or wait for a shower to open up."

"Are you sure? I don't want to get in your way," he replied.

"Of course I'm sure. You won't be in my way at all. You can shower first, and I'll run to Moon Dollar to grab us some breakfast."

"Sounds good. I'll go grab my bag out of the car and be right back," he said as he got up and slipped his shoes on.

I got up and grabbed a makeup wipe to remove all of the mascara from around my eyes. My eyes were puffy from all the crying the night before, but I didn't care at this point. I didn't even change out of my clothes from yesterday. I just slipped my shoes on and headed to Moon Dollar. I met Max in the hallway as he was coming back inside with his bag in hand.

"There's a towel and a rag in the bathroom under the sink, and my toothpaste is on the counter if you need it. I'll be back in a little bit," I told him.

"Okay. See you in a few," he said as he headed back to my dorm.

It's funny how we never have to tell each other our order anymore. Unless we want something out of the norm, we know each other's usual order for any place we've eaten together. I guess that shows how many meals we've shared since we became friends. It seemed like our whole friendship revolved around food in some way. I don't think we've hung out once without at least some snacks involved.

When I got to Moon Dollar, there was no line at all, so I went right up to the counter. "What can I get you this morning?" The girl behind the counter asked.

"Can I get two medium mocha lattes, two bacon, egg, and cheese croissants, and one blueberry muffin, please?" I had to wait a few minutes for the bacon, egg, and cheese croissants to be made, but they came out pretty quickly, and then I was headed back to my room. Thankfully, they had given me a drink carrier to make it easier to carry everything, but I was nearly to my door when I realized I hadn't gotten my keys out of my bag. I had no hands to dig through my bag with, so I hoped Max hadn't locked the door back. I didn't want to have to put our food and drinks down to find my keys. I tried the knob, and thankfully, it was unlocked.

When I pushed the door open, I saw Max. He was bent down, digging through his bag with only a towel around his waist. I had never seen Max without a shirt on, much less in only a towel. I knew he was in good shape, but I didn't realize he was as defined as he was. His arms had lean, corded muscles that tensed as he dug through his bag. He stopped and looked toward me, and then stood up. His cheeks turned red, and he looked like he wanted to run. I noticed that he had a beautifully defined six-pack and deep-cut V lines that went down to his hips and disappeared under the towel. I genuinely wanted to look away, but I couldn't. My eyes were glued to him.

"Uh, I, I'm sorry. I should have knocked. I didn't know you'd be out of the shower yet," I stammered as I felt my face flush along with his.

"It's okay. I'm sorry that I was walking around in a towel. I left my toothbrush in my bag and just needed to grab it. I'll be back in a sec. I'm going to brush my teeth and get dressed," he said, and then hurried back into the bathroom.

I knew Max was attractive. I've never tried to deny that, but I tried my best to never think of him in that way. He was my friend and a wonderful friend at that. I couldn't complicate or mess that up, especially when he had been there for me so much. He was what held me together a lot of the time when I felt like I would crumble into pieces. I couldn't afford to lose that, but sometimes I wondered if maybe I was playing it too safe with Max. I didn't want to repeat the same mistakes I had made before.

Chapter 5

I busied myself with taking our food out of the bag. I set our lattes on the desk with napkins placed perfectly next to them while I waited for Max to finish up in the bathroom. I tried to do anything other than think about Max in my room in only a towel. I did my best to push that image as far down in my brain as I could manage and hoped I could store it away in some deep part of my brain that made it too difficult to find the image again, even if it was a very nice image. He was my friend, and that was all. I couldn't go there.

I heard the sink turn on and off a few times, which I assumed was Max brushing his teeth. I waited, hoping he was almost done because I was starving, and it felt rude to eat without him. I looked up at the door just as I heard him start to turn the handle, but I quickly darted my eyes to look at my phone and pretended to be looking at something extremely captivating. For some reason, it felt weird to be looking at the door when he opened it. I didn't want him to think I was just staring at the door waiting for him to walk through, although I kind of was.

"Hey," he said as I looked up from my phone, "uh, I'm all finished in there now if you need the bathroom." He made sure not to make eye contact with me as he spoke.

"Okay, I'll shower and get ready after we eat, and then we can leave," I said, smiling at him when he finally looked my way.

"You didn't have to wait on me to eat," he said as he gave me a small smile back.

"You know I always do."

He sat at my desk, where I had neatly laid out our breakfast while he was in the bathroom. "Are these both the same thing?" He asked as if he didn't know that we ate the same thing for breakfast all the time.

"Yeah, so you can take either. I also got us a blueberry muffin to share," I replied.

"You know I love blueberry muffins," he said as he handed me one of the croissant sandwiches and lattes.

I took my food, setting it in front of me, and set my latte on the table next to my bed. We ate mostly in silence. I didn't know if it was because of the awkwardness of our earlier interaction or because we were both starving. After I finished eating, I grabbed my clothes and went to take a shower. Max told me he was going to put his bag in the car, and then he'd be back to help me with the rest of my stuff. I honestly thought he just didn't want to be in the room when I showered to try and hopefully save us from another awkward interaction.

I showered quickly and tried to scrub away all the anxiety and sadness I felt about going home and not finding my best friend there. I hoped that somehow that hot shower would be the one that washed away the ache in my chest and made it all better. It didn't work, but at least it made me feel a little more put together. I turned the water off and reached out the curtain for my towel. I wrapped myself up and sat on the edge of the shower for a minute. I tried to prepare myself mentally for the drive back to Cape Falls.

I felt the anxiety creep up and over me. It was like vines sprouted from the ground and slithered up my legs, slowly trying to overtake my entire body to pull me down into the panic attack that I was all too familiar with. It felt like someone was squeezing my chest, making it hard to pull in a breath, and my ears were ringing. I tried to fight it back, but how hot the bathroom was and how thick the air felt from the shower made it worse. I wanted to open the door and get some air, but I was worried Max might be back in my room, and I didn't want another towel incident.

I sat, trying to calm my racing heart and slow my rapid breathing, but nothing seemed to work. I needed cool air or to lie down. I grabbed my clothes and fumbled to put my still-wet legs into my pants. It wasn't working, and the vines of anxiety climbed higher, almost completely overtaking me. I gave up, snatched my robe, which I had forgotten I had, from the hook on the bathroom door, threw it on quickly, and then flung the door open. I felt the warm air rush out of the bathroom, being replaced by cooler, less dense air.

Max was sitting on my bed, but he immediately turned to me. He looked slightly alarmed by what, I assumed, was the force at which I had thrown the door open. "Lia, what's wrong?" He asked as he got off the bed and walked toward me.

Once he realized the look on my face, he knew exactly what was wrong. When he got to me, he held his arms wide, offering comfort but not forcing it because he knew that sometimes with a panic attack, I needed comfort, but other times I needed not to be touched. I leaned into him, and he wrapped his arms around me. I breathed in his familiar scent and relaxed into him when I finally registered what he had said. I pulled back and looked up at him, "Did you just call me Lia?" I asked. I felt some sort of déjà vu because no one had ever called me that except for Justin.

He looked confused. "I said Amelia, but maybe it sounded that way because I said it fast." He was talking fast when he said it, and my ears were still slightly ringing, so maybe I heard wrong.

I shook my head. It was almost as if my anxiety started dissipating as soon as I thought he called me Lia. I didn't know if it was because I was caught off guard and it distracted me, or because the familiarity had somehow made me feel better. Justin had always called me that. Our parents told us that when we were toddlers and learning to talk that he couldn't say Amelia, so he called me Lia, and it just kind of stuck. I always felt like Amelia and Lia were two different people. Lia was the more fun version of me that Justin saw, the version that let him drag me on any adventure he wanted to go on, but now that he was gone, there was only Amelia.

I wrapped my arms around Max's waist and rested my head on his chest. "Thank you for being here."

He gently stroked my dripping wet hair with one hand, and had his other arm wrapped comfortably around me. "Of course," he said as he leaned down and kissed the top of my head.

Max was probably the most comforting person I had met in my life. It was so much easier to calm down with him around. At the risk of sounding too codependent, I wished he could be around all the time when I needed him, which lately had been way too often. I figured the anticipation of going home and the anniversary of the accident looming upon me had gotten to me these past few weeks. I guess it had been building and building until it finally exploded.

My breathing returned to normal, and my heart had slowed down to a safe pace, so I pulled back from Max. He opened his arms, letting me go, and I took a step back. "I think I'll be okay. I'll get dressed and dry my hair really quickly, and then I'll be ready to go." He looked at me with a worried expression, and then nodded and went back to sit on the bed as I turned back to the bathroom.

I was dry from the robe, so I slipped my clothes on and plugged in my hair dryer. I dried my hair as quickly as I could, considering how thick and long it was. I picked up my mascara from the counter, swiped two coats on my lashes, and figured that was good enough since I'd only be in the car for two hours and then at home. I felt a twinge of anxiety in my stomach again at the thought, but I brushed it off and gathered everything left in the bathroom into my arms so I could toss it into a bag.

When I came out of the bathroom, Max was lying on my bed, looking like he was about to fall asleep, but he quickly sat up when he saw me. I felt terrible because I knew he had to be exhausted from my stupid alarm waking us up at seven. I didn't know how he would make the two-hour drive as tired as he seemed. I moved to my desk, where I left a few extra empty bags, tossed the stuff into one of them, and then walked over to sit on the edge of my bed, where Max was.

"Are you going to be okay to drive right now?" I asked.

"No, yeah, I'm fine. I just got a little sleepy since I was lying down," he answered as he ran a hand through his almost too-long hair.

"Are you sure? You look exhausted. We can wait and take a little nap before we head back if you want to."

"I'll be fine, I promise. It will feel better to be sleeping in my own bed than a dorm bed anyway, so I'll nap when we're home," he answered, as he stood up from the bed.

The pit of anxiety in my stomach was back at the thought of being back in my room at home. I took a deep breath, trying to calm my mind. "Okay, let's grab the last few things in here, and then we can go."

Max and I finished loading up his car with the rest of my stuff, and then we were on our way. Two hours wasn't that long, but it seemed like a lifetime because I had been dreading this drive since spring break. I knew spring break was the last break I'd have where I didn't have to go home, so I had been worried about it ever since. Two hours alone in a car was plenty of time for me to get in my head and spiral into a never-ending pit of anxiety. All I could think about was Justin, his house down the street, him not in his room, his grave in the graveyard downtown. I missed him so much. There was no way that I couldn't miss him. I couldn't make my brain stop, no matter how much I wanted to. Some days, I wanted to forget him so I wouldn't be so sad, but I always felt instantly guilty at the thought because I never really wanted to forget my best friend.

He was always there. He was always the person whom I could tell anything. Of course, he wasn't perfect, but who was? He was perfect for me, though. Like everyone else, he had flaws, but he was always just a call or text away. He never strayed far, but now, he was as far as a person could get. He was gone, and I couldn't stand it. I thought about a day, a few weeks before his accident, when he was still dating Amber. She had been very clingy, but he had always made sure to make time for me, even though I was pretty positive that she had hated my guts.

* * *

I waited on the front steps of our high school for Justin. He was taking forever because he had to pick up Amber, so I brought him a coffee since I knew he wouldn't have time to stop. We only had three minutes to get to class by the time he walked up.

"Thanks for the coffee. I seriously need it this morning. I'm sorry we took forever," he said, cutting his eyes at Amber as I handed him the coffee.

"You're fine. Sorry if it's cold," I said as I looked over to Amber. "Good morning!"

"Yeah, thanks," she said back, and then looked at Justin, "We need to hurry, or we're going to be late, and you still have to walk me to first period."

I internally rolled my eyes because she could have at least tried to hide how much she hated me a little. And also because I was annoyed that she would make him late if he had to walk her all the way to her class before he went to his own. "You'd better get going, then," I said as I looked at him. I tried not to sound as annoyed as I felt.

"I know, I know. I hope you have a good day. Tell me about it later?" He said as he gave me a big goofy grin that showed all of his teeth, even the bottom ones that were slightly crooked, which he always tried to hide.

I smiled back. How could I not? Even if I was annoyed, he somehow always found a way to make me smile. That was Justin's thing, asking me to tell him about my day later. He said that to me every morning as if it reassured him that we would talk later. "You, too. And of course," I told him as he turned to walk off. Unfortunately, since high school, we barely had any classes together, so even though we were in the same school, I never saw him until after school was out. I saw Amber say something to him as they walked off. She didn't look happy, but that wasn't anything new. I honestly didn't think I had ever seen her look genuinely happy.

It was a Tuesday. On Tuesdays, Justin and I always got tacos, and then went to my house to drink virgin margaritas, and non-virgin, when we could sneak some tequila from one of our parents' liquor cabinets while we watched Gilmore Girls reruns. He had a massive crush on Lauren Graham, so he didn't mind watching it with me. School had been bad. I really needed to tell him about it. My ex, Trevor, had been strutting his new girlfriend around school. She also happened to be the girl he cheated on me with for months before we broke up the week before. I really thought that I could have loved him. He could have won an Oscar with the performance he gave me for a year. I was desperately hoping it was one of the non-virgin margarita days.

I sent Justin a quick text to let him know that I was going to go ahead and pick up the tacos, so he could meet me at my house. I knew my parents wouldn't be home for a couple of hours, so I went to the liquor cabinet in the dining room to see if the tequila was still in there. Thankfully, it was. I grabbed it, took it to the kitchen, and started making our margaritas because Justin should have been on his way.

I finished the margaritas and checked the clock. Justin should have been at my house already. I went to get my phone out of my purse so I could text him and make sure that he was okay, but when I pulled my phone out, I saw that I had a text from him.

Justin: Hey! I'm so sorry. I won't make it. Please don't hate me. Amber had something she needed me to do with her. I promise I'll make it up to you.

Of course, Amber had something she needed. Of course, the one day I needed him here, she needed him for something. Any other Tuesday would have been different, but seeing Trevor with Alana made my day go to shit. I wanted Justin to be happy, but I honestly didn't think that Amber made him happy, and she never seemed happy either, so I didn't see the point. I decided it was up to me to eat all the tacos and drink all the margaritas myself then. I sent a quick text back to Justin before I started on my drink.

Me: No problem at all! Tacos and margs another night! :)

It was a problem. So much of a problem that I had drunk nearly an entire pitcher of margaritas by the time my parents got home. I put the rest in a huge cup and took it to my room to finish. I tried to seem as sober as possible, even though I was so far from it. I told my parents that I was tired and not feeling well, so I just wanted to go to bed early. I loved my parents so much and appreciated their concern, but sometimes they were a little too concerned. My mom tried to get the thermometer and asked if I needed soup. Thankfully, after I reassured her about one hundred times that I was fine, just exhausted, she dropped it and let me go to bed.

Once I got to my room, I dropped onto my bed. The alcohol was hitting me hard, and my legs felt like jelly. I was glad I held it together long enough to make it upstairs. If I had fallen in front of my mom, she would have booked me an appointment at urgent care and had every medicine that CVS carried in our house within the hour, when nothing was wrong except I drank way too much. I lay on my bed for a few minutes, trying to decide what I wanted to do until I passed out. I grabbed my phone and realized Justin had texted me two hours ago.

Justin: Yes! Any other night this week that you pick. Just tell me when :)

I felt much more annoyed now that I was drunk, so I didn't know what to say without being grumpy, so I just sent back a row of thumbs-up emojis. It only took a minute before Justin texted back.

Justin: Are you okay?

It was a valid question. I didn't think I had ever used the thumbs-up emoji, especially not replying to him. I sat up, reached for the cup from my nightstand, and then chugged it before answering.

Me: Yuppppp, super okay

Chugging that whole cup had been a bad idea. I had put more tequila in them than I usually did when we sneaked the tequila. Hopefully, my parents wouldn't notice how much was missing. Maybe I would refill them with water later or something. I was in my own world, thinking about Trevor with Alana and Justin with Amber, and how I was here alone drinking like a fool, when I realized my phone was buzzing beside me. I grabbed it and swiped across the screen to answer.

"What?" I said as I put the phone up to my ear.

"Are you okay? Why do you sound like that?" Justin asked. I hadn't even realized it was him when I answered. Good thing it was, considering all I said was "what."

"Yah, I'm fine. What do you mean? I sound like me," I tried to say without slurring my words. I didn't think I was very successful because I heard Justin let out a big sigh.

"Lia, are you drunk?" He asked.

I rolled my eyes even though he couldn't see me. "Maybe. So what?"

"One, you have school in the morning. And two, I'm pretty sure you drank way too much considering how you sound." He sounded slightly irritated, but I didn't care. I was the one who should be irritated, not him.

"Don't worry about me. Worry about Amber. She needs you, remember?" I said. The annoyance had seeped into my voice a little too much.

I almost felt bad when I heard him sigh again. "Lia. I'm sorry. I know I bailed, but I figured it would be okay since it was just one Tuesday."

Tears started to well up in my eyes because I felt bad for being annoyed with him. I had just had a really shitty day. I took in a shaky breath and said, "I know. I'm sorry. If it were any other Tuesday-" I broke off as I felt a lump in my throat rising. A sob broke free as I tried to continue. It was almost incomprehensible, but I finally got out the words, "Trevor and Alana, today and I just," I stopped because I couldn't get any more words through my sobs.

He realized what I was trying to say and quickly replied, "Oh, Lia, I'm so sorry. I saw them at school today, but I didn't even think about that. Give me fifteen minutes, and I'll be there."

I took another shaky breath and tried to compose myself enough to speak. "Okay, my parents think I'm sick."

"Okay, I'll tell them I'm bringing you some medicine and soup. See you in a few," he said, and then hung up.

I laid my phone down and closed my eyes for what seemed like only seconds before I felt someone sit down on the edge of my bed and start to stroke my hair. I opened my eyes and saw Justin looking down at me.

"Hey, I'm sorry I wasn't here," he said apologetically and continued to stroke my hair.

"You're here now," I said as I looked at him through sleepy eyes.

My stomach suddenly flipped. I was going to be sick. I sat up quickly, and the dizziness hit me like a truck. I motioned toward the bathroom. Justin lifted me into his arms and carried me to the bathroom as quickly as he could. He flipped the toilet lid up and sat on the floor next to me. I hung my head over the edge. My mouth poured water, and I knew it was coming. Seconds later, I was throwing up what seemed like three pitchers of margaritas, even though I had only drunk one. Justin sat next to me and held my hair back the whole time.

Once I had thrown up everything in my stomach until there was nothing left but dry heaves, I leaned back against the bathtub with my head in my hands. "Why did I drink that much?" I asked out loud to myself. I knew better, but I didn't always use the logical part of my brain.

"Because I wasn't here," Justin answered. "I would have never let you drink that much. We both know you're a lightweight," he said and gave me an apologetic smile.

"It's not your fault I'm insane," I retorted.

"Maybe partially my fault," he answered. "I think a shower would make you feel better."

"Yeah, you're probably right," I said as I tried unsuccessfully to stand.

Justin quickly stood up and held his arms out to me so he could help me up. He closed the lid of the toilet so I could sit down. The toilet felt like it was rocking back and forth, and I prayed I wouldn't fall off.

"You shower, and I'll get the medicine ready for you to take when you're out," he said as he placed a hand on my shoulder to steady me.

"Wait, you actually brought medicine?" I asked, surprised.

"Yes, ibuprofen and B-complex to help with your hangover and a giant bottle of water that you have to drink at least half of before you go to sleep," he said.

"I can't promise to drink that much water, but I'll try. I'll take the medicine and B-complex, though," I said as I tried to stand again. I was still wobbly, but at least I could stand.

Justin moved around me to turn the shower on and then grabbed my towel from the back of the door to place it next to the shower. "Go shower. I'll be out here," he said as he motioned to my room.

I waved him off as he shut the door. I, very carefully, stepped into the shower, then sat down once I was inside. I did my best to wash my hair and body from the bathtub floor. I somehow managed to make it work. Getting up to get out was the tricky part. I pulled myself up on the side of the bathtub and sat on the edge so I could throw my legs over. I grabbed my towel and tried to dry myself off as much as possible while seated. I realized I didn't have any clothes in the bathroom, so I stood slowly, grabbed my robe from the back of the door, and threw it around me, tying it tightly. I held onto the bathroom counter to ensure I wouldn't fall and brushed my teeth as fast as I could.

I kept my hold on the counter as I opened the bathroom door. When Justin noticed, he got up and hurried over to me. He looped his arm around my shoulders, helping me to the bed. I sat down on the edge as he handed me the medicine and water. I tossed the pills into my mouth and swallowed. After realizing how dry my mouth felt, I took a few more big gulps of water. Justin held up the dropper of the B-complex, so I opened my mouth as he dropped it under my tongue. I was not fond of the taste, so I took a few smaller sips of water to try to get the taste out of my mouth.

"Do you want me to get you some pajamas from your dresser?" Justin asked. I assumed he had just noticed that I was only in my robe.

"No, I don't feel like getting dressed. My robe is fine," I said as I pulled my blankets back to climb into bed.

"Are you going to be okay?" He asked, sounding concerned.

"I'm sure I will, but can you stay?" I asked as I looked up at him standing next to the bed.

"Of course. I didn't know if you wanted me to or if you were still mad at me." I swore I could hear a hint of sadness in his voice.

I felt so bad for being annoyed with him earlier. "I'm not mad at you. I was just upset by everything else." I scooted over so he could climb in next to me. I'm sure it seemed weird for us to share a bed, but we had been having sleepovers since we were babies, so it seemed natural to us. We were always there for each other when one of us was feeling down or needed comfort. He climbed in next to me and held his arm out so I could cuddle up to him. I accepted his invitation and snuggled back into his arms. Justin felt like home. It was like all my problems melted away when he was near.

"Why did he cheat? I get that Alana is gorgeous, but why not just break up with me first?" I asked in an almost whisper.

Justin was lying so my back was to his front, with his mouth right next to my ear. He gently stroked my hair and whispered, "Because he's an asshole and never deserved you."

Something about his voice right at my ear made a tingle travel all the way down my spine. I turned to face him, and he looked surprised. I brought my hand up and placed it on his face. He watched me with careful eyes, not moving. It almost seemed like he was holding his breath. I didn't know if it was the fuzzy brain from the alcohol, but I leaned in slowly and pressed my lips to his. I felt his body tense; maybe he wasn't sure how to react at first.

Then he put his arm over my waist and pulled me closer to him. He moved his lips against mine slowly, hesitantly. I moved my hands to the back of his head and wrapped my fingers in his hair. I pulled him closer and pressed his mouth harder against mine. He tightened his grip on my waist and kissed me back with more need, more want. Our tongues and teeth clashed wildly. I felt the heat move through my body. It made me want to be even closer to him. Then he stopped suddenly, pulling back so quickly that I nearly gasped at the loss of his touch.

I opened my eyes to look at him. He had rolled over, lying on his back. He had his hand in his hair like he was contemplating something as he stared at the ceiling. I didn't know what to say. I realized that I had just kissed my best friend. What had I done? My brain was telling me that I'd done something wrong, but my body had a completely different reaction. It was aching for his touch. I wanted more. I moved back a little, but my eyes were still fixed on him.

I reached out and touched his arm. "I'm sorry. I don't know-" I trailed off.

He turned back to face me again. He gently placed his hand on the side of my face and stared at me for a second before he spoke. "No, don't apologize. Lia, I just- I can't. You're drunk. I can't do this like this," he said as he stroked my face with his thumb.

I tried to blink back tears. I did not want to cry. That was the last thing I wanted to do, but I felt embarrassed and rejected. "I- I'm sorry-" I started to say before Justin interrupted.

"No, no. Really. It's okay. You don't have anything to apologize for. I shouldn't have," he said. He leaned forward and placed a kiss on my forehead. "It's late, and you need to sleep, so you don't feel too bad at school tomorrow." He pulled me back into him and put an arm around me. I snuggled into him and fell asleep within seconds.

I was woken up by his phone alarm blaring. I groaned and rolled over to tell him to turn it off, but he wasn't there. I grabbed his phone and hit the stop button. I looked at the time and saw that it was only six. I did not want to be up that early. I looked around my room and noticed that my bathroom door was shut, and the shower was running. A few minutes later, the water turned off, and it wasn't very long before Justin came out fully dressed for school.

"Hey, what are you doing up?" He asked.

"Your stupid alarm," I said, pointing to his phone.

"Oh shit, I'm sorry I forgot to turn that off. I wanted to make sure I was up early enough to sneak back into my house before Bill was up to notice," he replied.

Ugh, Bill. "It's okay. Don't worry about it. I need to get up to make sure I have enough time to wallow around in bed with this hangover before I have to get ready," I grumbled.

"Take more medicine and B-complex, then finish that water before you get ready," he replied. I gave him a two-finger salute of confirmation, and he let out a breath of a laugh. "I'm just trying to make sure you feel better."

"I know, I know," I said as I rolled my eyes.

His face changed, and he suddenly looked uncomfortable. He looked down at his hands before he said, "About last night-"

At first, I was confused, but then I remembered. I didn't want to have that conversation yet. I wasn't ready for it. I didn't want anything to get weird between us, so I interrupted him before he could continue. "Yeah, I'm sorry I was so drunk and grumpy with you for no reason. That was immature. I promise it won't happen again. I feel so bad that you had to hold my hair while I puked up ten gallons of margaritas." I gave an embarrassed laugh. "You won't love me any less, will you?"

His eyebrows furrowed, and he looked a little confused himself. "No, that's- I- um, is that all you remember?" He asked.

I pretended to be confused, too. "Yeah. Was there something else? Oh god, did I say something crazy? Please tell me you didn't record it if I did." I laughed again and put my hands over my face, pretending to be embarrassed.

He opened his mouth like he was about to say something, but stopped as he looked like he was contemplating something before he spoke. "No, I was just going to say that you better count me taking care of you puking as at least part of me making up for missing taco night," he said with a grin.

And just like that, things were back to normal, and I had successfully avoided an awkward conversation. Justin leaned down, planted a kiss on my forehead, and then headed home before his parents woke up.

* * *

I shook my head and brought my thoughts back to the road. I was so lost in the memory that I hadn't realized we were back in Cape Falls. I didn't know how I had even made it. It felt like I was zoned out for the entire time, but maybe that was better than spiraling into an anxiety attack while driving. I checked my rearview mirror to see that Max was still right behind me. We turned onto my street, our street. I purposely kept my eyes fixed on the left side of the road so I didn't see Justin's house. I didn't think I could handle that yet. We drove past three houses and then turned into the driveway of the fourth house on the left. Home sweet home.

Chapter 6

I sat in the driveway, looking up at my house for what seemed like forever. Max was still in his car behind me. He knew how I felt about coming home, so I knew he was waiting until I was ready, but Max needed to get home and unpack his stuff, too. I took a couple of deep breaths, used what little motivation I could pull from deep inside, and pushed myself out of the car.

My legs felt shaky when I stood. I wasn't sure if it was from the anxiety or the two-hour drive. Either way, I held onto the car door and steadied myself. I heard Max's car door shut behind me, then seconds later, he was next to me. He placed a hand on my shoulder, whether for comfort or to help steady me, I wasn't sure, but it felt nice. I looked up at the house one more time and tried to shove down the panic building inside me. It threatened to take over, but I ignored it the best I could.

I turned to Max. "I guess we should start bringing stuff inside." He nodded and walked to the passenger side of my car. He picked up the box and bags from my front seat, then walked toward the garage.

I pressed the garage button on my key ring and started toward the garage behind Max as the door opened slowly. Inside the garage, I saw my old bike leaning against the wall and the red wagon I loved when I was younger, stacked with boxes. Tennis rackets hung on the wall next to a bag full of balls. Frisbees and baseball gloves were stacked on a shelf to the left. Everything was in the same place it had always been.

The familiarity should have been comforting, but something about it unsettled me.

I walked past Max and up the steps that led to the door into the kitchen as he followed behind me. I pressed the code into the keypad, and the door unlocked. I took one more deep breath and then pushed the door open. To my surprise, I didn't recognize the kitchen at all, which made me breathe a sigh of relief. My parents had done some remodeling since I'd been gone.

I walked into the kitchen and looked around at all the changes that mom and dad had made. The cabinets were white with a new marble countertop and brand-new stainless steel appliances. The walls were a different color, and there was new backsplash that lined the wall. On the counter was a beautiful arrangement of pink, white, and purple carnations in a clear decorative vase. My mom always had to have fresh flowers. I liked how it looked, and I liked even more that it didn't look how it did the last time Justin and I stood together in this kitchen.

Max walked in behind me. "Wow, it looks great in here. I wonder when they remodeled the kitchen."

"I have no idea. No one told me, but it's nice," I said as I sat my purse and phone on the counter. As I turned to take the boxes from Max, my phone started vibrating. I figured it was either mom or dad asking if I had made it home yet, but when I picked it up, I saw it was from a blocked number. I thought about letting it go to voicemail, but instead, I swiped the green button on the screen and put it up to my ear.

"Hello?" I waited. When no one answered, I repeated it. "Hello? Is someone there?" I didn't know what I expected from someone calling from a blocked number. I didn't believe in anything supernatural, but I always picked up because I was hoping that maybe one day it would be Justin, calling from beyond the grave or something. I knew it was ridiculous, but it was hard to think that I would never hear his voice again, other than a few voicemails I had saved from before he died. "If this is someone pranking me or messing with me, please stop. I can't-" My voice cracked as I tried to finish my sentence. I could have sworn that I heard someone breathing, then the call disconnected.

I turned to see Max; he was looking at me. "Was that the blocked number again? Are you okay?"

I sniffled and wiped a stray tear from my cheek. "Yeah, I'm good. Let's get the rest of the stuff," I said as I walked past him and back into the garage. Max hesitated for a second, and then followed after me.

We unloaded box after box. I didn't even realize I had taken so much stuff with me. I probably accumulated a few things while I was there, though. After we got everything into the house, Max picked up some boxes to help me take everything upstairs to my room. My room looked completely untouched. My bed was made neatly, like it had been the last time I was here, and my pillows were placed exactly how I always kept them across the bed. The bulletin board with pictures of Justin and me still hung on my wall. There were pictures all the way from when we were babies to spring break of our senior year. Everything looked exactly the same, but it felt so different.

Seeing my room for the first time in nine months caused such a whirlwind of emotions inside me that I needed to lie down for a few minutes. My brain swirled with the events of last summer and this past school year. It was all too much for me. Max went downstairs to get me water and bring up the rest of the boxes while I tried to calm down. I swallowed down the lump in my throat and tried hard to fight back the tears that stung at the corners of my eyes.

I was home for a while after Justin's accident since it was the beginning of summer break when it happened, but I was in such a haze that I barely noticed my surroundings. Last summer, all I did was go to the support group, go to therapy, and hang out with Max if I wasn't lying in my bed dissociating. When it was finally time to leave for college, I was so thankful because I couldn't stand to be home one more second. Last summer, I kept my curtains shut so I couldn't see Justin's house, and when I left, I never looked toward that end of the street except to quickly check if cars were coming. I questioned whether I'd be able to stand being here the whole summer, but I didn't really have another option if I wanted to spend time with my parents.

It was so heartbreaking to think about him never walking into my room again and plopping down on my bed like he owned it, never having a movie marathon with him again, never having the chance to revisit the night when we shared a kiss in my bed just weeks before the accident. I had beaten myself up for lying and saying that I didn't remember anything since the day after it happened. I was afraid it would ruin our friendship, but I realized I had wanted more from him. I think I always had, but I didn't want to admit it to myself. I was so afraid of rejection that I didn't even want to try, and now I'd never get the chance to know what it could have been. It would always be my greatest "what if," and I wasn't sure if I'd ever be able to get over that.

That thought tipped me over the edge, and the downpour of tears came fast and heavy. My shoulders shook as I sobbed into my favorite pillow. I swore that I could almost smell Justin's cologne on it. He couldn't be gone, and I couldn't deal with this all summer. I didn't want to be home and in our neighborhood, where our memories were everywhere. I got up from the bed and paced around my room, not sure what to do. I looked out of my window, and saw Justin's house and the window he would wave at me from again. It only made everything worse. I turned to my dresser and saw the small plush bear that sat on top of it. Justin had won it for me a few years ago at the summer fair.

I knocked the bear and everything else that was on top of my dresser off, causing a loud crashing sound. My decorative plants and jewelry holder fell to the floor, along with the bear. I wasn't generally a violent person, but I felt such anger inside of me. I was mad at myself that I couldn't save him, angry at him for not being here when I still needed him, and mad at Christy and Bill for being such shitty parents when he was alive. I was so angry with everyone.

I assumed Max heard the commotion because his heavy footsteps came pounding up the stairs, and he burst through my door seconds later. "Are you okay? What happened?" He asked. He looked at my tear-streaked face and everything that was once on my dresser, now on the floor, and gave me a sympathetic look before walking over to wrap his arms tightly around me.

The lump in my throat rose again with more tears just waiting to fall. I cleared my throat and forced the lump and the tears away. "I'm angry," I said to Max as I wrapped my arms around him, laying my head on his chest.

"I know," he said as he reached a hand up and stroked my hair. "I want to say it will be okay, but I know that feeling never truly goes away. I was so angry with everyone and everything after Vanessa died. You'll be less angry eventually, but you'll always miss him."

I sighed and tried practicing the breathing techniques I learned in therapy. I knew Max wouldn't let go until I did, so I held onto him for a while. I breathed in a mixture of body wash, laundry detergent, and cologne that all melded into one specific scent, which I'd grown to recognize as Max. I looked up at him to see what he was thinking. He was looking at the board on my wall with the pictures of Justin and me. He had an odd look on his face that I couldn't quite place. It looked like sadness, but also something else. Once he noticed that I was looking at him, he looked away from the board and focused on my bookshelf like he'd been scanning the titles of my books the whole time.

I pulled back and looked at him, "Hey, are you okay?" I asked.

He looked down at me. "Oh yeah, I'm fine. I've just been worried about you. With coming home and all..." he trailed off, leaving the sentence unfinished.

"I'm okay. It's just a little overwhelming," I said as I walked toward my window. I sat down on the window seat and looked around at the results of my temper tantrum. Max followed my eyes to everything lying on the floor.

"Do you want me to pick that up for you?" He asked.

"No. It's my mess. You've already helped me so much today, and I don't even know how to thank you for everything," I answered with a smile. "I guess I'd better let you get home to get yourself settled."

He looked almost disappointed. I didn't want him to leave. I surely wasn't thrilled with the idea of being left alone with only my thoughts, but I thought he would have liked to get home and see his family, too. "If you want, you can come over for dinner. I know my parents would love to see you. They ask about you every time they call. Unless you have plans with your family, then we can do dinner another day."

"My parents won't be home for two days. They're gone on business, so no plans until then at least," he replied. "My brother is home but will most likely go out with his boyfriend for dinner, so I'm all free."

"My parents should be home and ready for dinner around six if you want to come back then."

"That works for me. Are you sure you'll be okay alone until your parents are home?" He asked, concerned.

"I don't think I'll throw myself off the roof before then if that's what you're asking," I said with a grin, trying to lighten the mood a little.

"Okay, I'll be back at six," he said hesitantly. I could tell by his face that he was trying to decide whether or not he actually needed to be worried about me flinging myself off the roof while he was gone.

"I'll walk you out," I said as I started to stand.

"It's okay. I think I remember how to get back out to my car," he said with a playful smirk.

"Fine. Drive safe," I told Max as he turned to leave my room.

"I will," he said. I knew by the seriousness in his eyes when he answered me that he meant it and that he knew how serious I was when I said that to someone.

I was still sitting by the window when Max pulled out of the driveway. I looked down toward Justin's house again. The garage was open, and there were no cars in the driveway. I assumed Bill was at work, and Christy was probably out shopping. I rolled my eyes. I didn't always dislike Christy. I actually used to like her when we were younger. We'd have sleepovers at Justin's, and Christy would make us snacks and help us build pillow forts in the living room, but that version of Christy was long gone.

Christy brought Bill to my tenth birthday party. That was the first time I'd met him. Justin had told me that she had a new boyfriend, but she hadn't brought him around anyone before then. She and Justin's dad, Alan, had been divorced for about a year. Even as a child, I had a bad feeling the first time I saw Bill. Something didn't seem right about him to me, and I knew Justin felt the same way. Around that time, I stopped going to Justin's for sleepovers. He always wanted to come to my house instead. A year after that, Christy and Bill were married, and he was officially Justin's stepdad.

My parents never really liked Bill either, but they were always pleasant with him because Christy was their friend at the time. I didn't know why I hadn't liked him when I was younger because he hadn't given me a reason to dislike him yet. At least not until a couple of years later, when I was twelve. Justin had come over to swim one day during the summer before seventh grade. He didn't take his shirt off before getting in the pool, which was odd for him, but I didn't think much of it.

He wanted me to watch him do a backflip underwater, so I put my goggles on and went underwater to watch. His shirt came up when he did his backflip, and I saw a huge blue and purple bruise across his ribs. I freaked out when he came out of the water and asked him what happened and if he was okay. He told me to be quiet and that I couldn't tell anyone. I told him if he was hurt, he needed to tell someone. He told me it was okay because he'd just made Bill mad, but he wouldn't do that anymore. I couldn't understand because my parents had never even spanked me. Christy had never spanked Justin before, and neither did his dad when he was still married to Christy.

I told him we could tell my parents so they could tell Christy, but he said no because his mom already knew. Bill told him that if he told anyone else that someone would come to take him away and make him live with strangers because his dad didn't want him either. I was so confused and scared for Justin after that. I always tried to get him to stay for sleepovers and have him to come to my house to play as long as our parents would let him, so he wouldn't have to be at home with Bill. I wanted to protect him and make sure that he was safe. It was all I ever wanted. But I couldn't save him from Bill, and I couldn't protect him from whatever happened the night of his accident either.

My heart felt like it was going to shatter into a million pieces all over again. Thinking of everything that Justin went through since his mom married Bill lit a whole new feeling of rage inside me. His life was hell, and he didn't even get to live long enough to get out of that damn house. I stared at the house with so much disdain that I felt like I could burn it to the ground with just a look. I didn't think I could ever put into words the level of hatred I had for Bill. I wished it had been him who ran off the bridge that night, not Justin. He deserved it. Justin didn't.

Just as I was about to get up and put everything I knocked to the floor back on the dresser, I saw a black Tesla coming down the road. It drove a few houses past mine and pulled into Justin's driveway. The windows were tinted, so I couldn't tell who was inside. I assumed that now that they didn't have to pay for college, Christy and Bill must have decided to get a new car. My god, I hated them. I turned away from the window and focused on something I could control, the mess of boxes that needed to be sorted and put away.

I spent the next few hours taking everything out of the boxes and putting it in its proper place. I hung clothes in the closet, put toiletries in the bathroom, and stacked school books and binders next to my desk. I took a break to grab a snack and then returned to it. By the time I finished, it was four, which was only about one hour until my parents would be home. I decided to take my book and go to my favorite place in the house.

I walked out of my room and down the hallway to the upstairs sitting area, opening the French doors that led outside to the upper deck that overlooked the pool and backyard. The swing at the far right of the deck had green and purple cushions I had picked out the year before, and a small outdoor refrigerator next to it. I opened the fridge to see it fully stocked with Sprite, water, and bottled iced coffee, so Mom must have stocked it recently since I was coming home. I sat down on the swing sideways, leaning against the arm with a pillow behind my back and my legs stretched out in front of me.

I thought about all the campouts Justin and I had on this deck. We'd bring our sleeping bags out here and look out at the stars at night as kids. Then, when we got older, we'd sneak alcohol and sit out here, drinking and talking for hours. I'd been so sad about him being gone that I'd forgotten to appreciate all of the happy moments we shared. I'd forgotten how much happiness those memories brought me. I could still picture Justin sitting next to me on the swing, laughing hysterically about an inside joke we shared, the wind blowing his hair into his blue eyes so much that I put his hair into a tiny ponytail on top of his head to hold it back. The memory made me smile, and I whispered, "I love you and miss you so much, Justin."

Chapter 7

I was so zoned into my book that I didn't even realize my parents were home until I heard the door out to the deck open. I turned to see my mom making her way down the porch to me.

"I thought I might find you out here," she said with a warm smile. "I stocked the fridge a few days ago so you would have everything you liked when you got here."

I knew I was a bit biased, but she really was the best mom. Even when she had her moments of being a little overbearing, I always knew she meant well. "Thank you, Mom," I said as I turned and put my feet on the ground so she could sit beside me on the swing.

She sat down and stretched her arm out across the back of the swing. I knew it was an invitation for a hug, so I moved closer and laid my head on her shoulder as she wrapped her arm around me. "How are you doing, honey?" She asked in a soothing tone.

I thought about the question and truly considered how I was doing at that current moment. "I'm okay. I've been better, but I think I'm doing all right."

She patted my head and stroked my hair gently. "I remember you guys always loved coming out here to look at the stars. You were always either out here or at the park by the water."

Mom and Dad had tiptoed around me so much, trying to ensure they didn't say something that would upset me since the funeral. It was only recently that they began to gently bring Justin up. I think they must have wanted the same thing for me that I now wanted for myself, to remember how happy having him as a friend had made me, and not focus only on the sadness I'd felt since last June.

"You know, I went to his grave to put some flowers last week. It looked like no flowers had been put there since the funeral, so I wanted it to look nice. Maybe you could visit sometime while you're home," she said.

My breath caught in my throat for a second at the mention of going to his grave, but I cleared my throat quickly. "That's nice. I may do that soon. It's just hard, and it feels weird. That's not where I feel him, or I didn't at the graveside service after the funeral."

"Then where do you feel him?"

"I actually don't know. I've been so consumed with sadness and missing him so much that I can't feel anything else."

"Oh, I know, honey. The sadness won't hurt so much in time. You'll always miss Justin, but it won't always feel like you're drowning in it," she said before she planted a kiss on the top of my head.

"I know," I said quietly as I let my head rest against her shoulder.

We sat like that for a little while. I think Mom may have needed it just as much as I did. I felt bad that when I lost Justin, it probably seemed like they lost a daughter, too. I had seen them during holidays, but we were always on a trip since I didn't want to come home, and I wasn't myself last summer. I barely left my room except to eat and go to my support group and therapy. I knew they had been worried about me, but I didn't have the energy to pretend that I was okay. They understood, of course, but I knew they missed me being me.

I hadn't eaten anything since breakfast other than the small snack I grabbed when I took a break from unpacking, and I was starting to get hungry. "What are we doing for dinner?" I asked as I sat up and turned to face my mom.

"Whatever you want. What are you in the mood for?" She asked.

"I'm not sure. It's fine that I asked Max to come for dinner, right?"

"Of course! You know Max is always welcome. His parents didn't have plans with him on his first day back?" She asked.

"No, they are out of town on business and won't be home for a few days, so he's alone. I didn't want him to have dinner alone on his first night home," I answered.

"Oh no! Poor thing. If he wants to stay here until his parents are back, he can, so he's not by himself the next few nights," she said.

If I was being honest, it would be nice to have him close by. I was sure he would be okay at home, but I imagined it could be lonely since he'd been used to being in a dorm with so many people around all year. "That's a good idea. I'll call and ask him if he wants to stay for a few days."

"Okay, I'll let dad know. I'll get the guest room ready, unless he's staying in your room?" She raised her eyebrows and gave me a questioning look

"You can get the guest room ready." I shook my head at her.

"Okay, but it's okay if you want him to stay with you. Dad and I understand that you aren't a baby anymore."

"It's not like that. We're just friends," I told her. "But could you bring the air mattress down from the attic, if you don't mind?"

She raised an eyebrow at me again.

"If Max and I want to watch movies out back, or yes, if I want him to stay in my room. But just on the air mattress, like a friend," I said as I rolled my eyes playfully at her.

"Whatever you say, honey," she replied with a grin. "I'll go ask your dad what he wants for dinner and get the guest room ready. Call Max and make sure he wants to stay."

Once she was back inside, I pulled out my phone to call Max. It took a few rings before he answered.

"Hey! I was just getting ready to head out the door," he said, sounding a little sleepy.

"Were you sleeping?" I asked.

"Yeah, sorry," he said, sounding guilty. "I didn't mean to fall asleep. I can get ready quickly and be on the way."

"No, it's no rush. We haven't even decided what we're doing for dinner yet. I was calling because my mom told me to ask if you wanted to stay here the next few days since your parents weren't home. It's okay if you don't want to. She just didn't want you to be lonely. But if you want to be at home, I completely understand." I realized I was rambling, and stopped so he could answer.

"Um, yeah, that's- are you fine with that? I don't want to bother you. I'll be alright." He sounded hesitant.

"Yeah, that's completely fine with me if you want to." I didn't understand why we were both being so weird. We conversed daily, so I didn't know why we couldn't get words out.

"Do you want me to stay?" He asked. My face flushed at the question. I didn't mind if he stayed. I liked the idea of having him there, but the question felt different than him just making sure I was fine with him staying.

I hesitated, then finally answered. "Yes, I do."

It took a few seconds before he responded. "Okay, I'll pack a few things to stay."

"It's no rush. Mom is getting the guest room ready and deciding what to eat. Are you in the mood for anything specific?"

"I'm fine with anything. I'm starving," Max said.

"Same! I hope they decide soon. Maybe they will by the time you get here," I laughed.

"Hopefully." He sounded more awake than when he first answered. "I'm getting up now, so I will see you soon."

"See you in a few!"

I picked up my book and headed inside. I figured I needed to shower again since I was outside for a while. It was the South in the summer, so it was crazy humid. You were sticky almost as soon as you stepped out the door here. As I came down the hall, I saw the door to the bedroom closest to mine open with the light on. I walked past my room to the guest room and peered inside. Mom was putting fresh towels on the dresser.

"Hey, did you call Max?" She asked when she noticed I was there.

"I did. He's staying. He's just packing a few things and then he will be on his way over. Any word on dinner yet?" I asked.

"Oh, good! I was hoping he would. Your dad said he wants Italian food. I'm not sure where to order from. What's the name of the really good Italian place that's near your school?"

"Marco's? I don't think they will deliver two hours away." I looked at her with a confused expression.

"I know that. There isn't one closer that you know of?" She asked.

"No, I don't think so. I think it's just that one family-owned place. Why not that Italian place downtown?" I asked.

"It closed down a few months ago. I think a new place opened up in its place, but I can't remember the name of it. I'll figure it out and check out their menu. Any special requests for you or Max?"

"I'm fine with anything, and he's not picky, so whatever you order will be fine," I said as I turned to walk out of the room. "I'm going to go shower." She smiled at me and nodded, and then turned back to the towels.

After I got out of the shower, I looked through my closet and tried to find something comfy but also cute to wear. I settled for a mid-thigh length red dress with white polka dots that I hadn't worn since last year. It was actually a birthday gift from Justin two years before. He knew how much I loved that print. He knew everything about me.

CHAPTER 7

* * *

"Hey, birthday girl!" Justin nearly yelled as he walked into my room.

"Hiiii" I replied.

"I got you a present, something other than the flowers," he said, with a huge grin.

"Of course you did, even though every year I tell you, that's not necessary," I said.

"Yeah, yeah, whatever. Just open it!" He said as he held a pink wrapped gift box with a small silver bow on top out to me.

I got up from my bed and took the box from him. I shook it and turned it over in my hands, looking at it from every angle. "I wonder what it is," I teased.

"Oh my god! Will you just open it already?" Justin rolled his eyes, looking exasperated.

He was always so excited about giving people gifts, and it drove him crazy if anyone took their time opening it, so I made sure to drag it out as long as possible every year. I shook it one more time, took the bow off the top, and slowly started to rip the paper. He was getting more annoyed by the second. I smiled, trying to hold back a giggle because of the irritated look on his face. I finally got all the paper off, and then I slowly opened the box. I pulled back the tissue paper, reached inside, and pulled out a red dress with white polka dots.

"It's so cute! I love it!" I said as I held the dress up to look at it.

An even bigger grin spread across his face. "I knew you'd love it. Out of the two of us, I'm definitely the best at picking out gifts." He said, smirking at me.

"If you say so." I set the dress down on my bed and walked over to him. I wrapped an arm around his waist for a half-hug.

He lazily threw an arm around my shoulders and pulled me to him. "Happy Birthday, Lia," he said. He pulled away and turned to me. "Now, put it on. We have somewhere to go."

"What? I don't want to go anywhere. I have to get ready, and I really don't want to," I whined as I walked over and flopped back on my bed.

He came over to me, grabbed my hands, and pulled me off the bed. "Nope! Up! Birthday girls need to go out and have some fun!"

"Lying in bed and watching movies all night is fun," I said as I tried to pull away to lie back down.

"The summer fair just started tonight. We'll go for a little while. We can play some games, ride some rides, get you a funnel cake," he said as he raised his eyebrows at me. "I know how much you love funnel cake."

He got me with the funnel cake. That was the best part about the fair. I rolled my eyes. "Fine. We'll go, but we gotta be back in bed watching movies by ten."

"Deal!" He said with a smile. "Now, go get dressed."

We ended up riding almost every ride, getting funnel cake, deep-fried Oreos, huge slushes, and playing games until Justin ran out of money. That was the night he'd won the small plush bear for me, and we ended up not getting back to my house until nearly midnight.

* * *

I smiled as I looked in the mirror at the dress. It was a happy memory and it was nice to remember the fun times. I went over to my jewelry box and pulled out a silver necklace with a small "A" on it that my parents had given me for my birthday the year before. I unclasped it and put it around my neck. I hadn't worn it yet, but I thought it would look nice with the polka dot dress. Although getting home earlier that day hadn't started great, I was beginning to feel good for the first time in a long time.

I was so worried that being home, where all of mine and Justin's memories took place, would be so much harder than being away; instead, it was reminding me of how nice all the memories were and how grateful I was to have experienced them with him, even if only for a short while. I knew there would still be hard days, especially with the anniversary right around the corner, but I also knew that Justin would have hated to see me like this.

He would be so upset about how sad I was. He would pull me out of bed and make me have fun, and that was one thing I had always loved about him. I decided to make a promise to Justin and myself that I would try to enjoy life again and have some fun this summer, like he would have wanted me to. I didn't want all of his effort and years of trying to get me to enjoy life instead of only worrying about school to be in vain. I owed it to him and myself to try to be happy again, and I decided that I was starting immediately.

I went to the bathroom, grabbed my makeup bag, and pulled out more than just my mascara for a change. I even got my hair wand out and gave my hair a little beach wave before I headed downstairs. I could hear Max's voice before I got to the bottom of the stairs. He was talking to my mom about the new kitchen renovations, but when I came around the corner, they both turned to me.

"Oh, honey, you look so beautiful! I love that dress on you!" She said.

Max's eyes went wide, and his mouth was slightly agape. "Wow, you look amazing, Amelia."

Max had never really seen me dressed up before. Since Justin's wreck, I hadn't done more than wear mascara and blow-dry my hair or wear a ponytail. I was always only in leggings, t-shirts, jeans, or hoodies anytime I hung out with Max the past year. Even when we had gone out with others from our group, I still wore the same things. The look on Max's face and how his eyes quickly scanned me up and down made my stomach clench in excitement.

I knew my face had to be red because I felt heat in my cheeks. "Oh, stop it, but thank you," I said as I gave my mom a quick smile and then looked at Max. "Wow yourself, you look nice too," I said. And he did. He wore a button-down white shirt with dark wash jeans and brown Chelsea boots. He even looked like he had put a little product in his hair, which gave it a "messy on purpose" look. He looked incredible.

His face flushed and he smiled shyly at me. "Thanks. I haven't fully unpacked my clothes from school yet, so I just wore what I had in my closet."

"Well, I like it. You look great." I smiled back at him, and then bit my lip as nervousness pooled in my stomach. I had completely forgotten that my mom was standing there for a second because I was so focused on Max. I looked over at her, and she gave me a smirk with raised eyebrows.

"Did you already order the food?" I asked. I wanted to change the conversation to something other than Max and me seeing which one of us could stare at and compliment the other the longest.

"I did. Your dad went to pick it up. He should be back any minute. Max, will you please take this to the table for me?" She asked as she set a stack of plates and silverware on the counter.

"Yes, ma'am," he said as he walked over and picked them up.

I went into the kitchen where my mom was standing. I knew she had asked him to do that for a reason. As I got closer, she said, "You do look beautiful, honey. It's not just the hair, the makeup, or the dress. You seem better, a little more at peace. It's really nice to see you like this." She leaned down and planted a gentle kiss on my forehead.

"Thank you. I feel a little more at peace, too," I replied. It wasn't a lie. I felt more at peace than I had in a long time, and I was so thankful.

Chapter 8

A few minutes later, I heard dad pull into the garage. He came in carrying too many bags of food. It looked like mom had ordered the whole menu. I knew we would be eating leftovers for days, which was fine with me. Max and I would have plenty to eat while mom and dad were at work during the day.

Our table was long, but Max had a plate at each end of the table for mom and dad, and then our plates were in the middle across from each other. I walked over to the table where he was standing. "Which side of the table would you like?" I asked.

"Either is fine with me. It's your pick. It is your house, after all," he said.

"All the more reason for you to pick. You're the guest." I nudged his arm with my elbow.

He smiled. "I'll take the side closest to the window."

"Your wish is my command," I said, giving him a playful curtsey as I motioned toward the table.

Max looked at me hesitantly. "You seem better than when we first got here. It's nice to see you like this." That was the second time someone had said that to me in the last ten minutes.

"I feel better than I did earlier. I'm glad you're here to see it," I replied.

"I am too."

Dad walked over to where Max and I were standing, opening his arms

THE GHOST OF YOU

wide before he wrapped me in a huge hug. "I've missed you so much! I'm so glad you're home!" he said as he squeezed me tighter. My dad was the best at giving huge bear hugs.

"I missed you too," I managed to squeak out through his tight hug.

"Oh, Brian, let her go. You're squishing the girl," my mom said as she playfully slapped him on the shoulder.

He loosened his hug. "Well, that's what happens when I go months without seeing my favorite daughter," he said.

"I'm your only daughter," I replied.

"Yes, but even if you weren't, I know you'd still be my favorite," he said before he kissed the top of my head.

I smiled. "Sure, I would."

"Also, the most beautiful daughter," he said with a smile, as he took a step back to look at my face.

"Isn't she, though?" Mom chimed in.

I knew I was their only child, but it was getting embarrassing. I was not fond of all the attention on me.

"She is," Max agreed, which made my face flush a deep red. My mom and dad exchanged a look and grinned at one another.

"Alright, alright, can we eat? I'm starving," I said. I hoped that we could move on to some better subjects of conversation, like maybe politics, or the black plague.

"Absolutely," Mom answered. She arranged takeout containers on the table where they would be within everyone's reach. There was a whole array of food. It looked like she was trying to feed an army.

Max walked around the table and took his seat across from me as Mom and Dad sat at each end. We started shoveling food onto our plates immediately. They had to have been as hungry as I was because, for a few minutes, no one spoke a word. We were all too busy eating like we had never eaten before. I guess I wasn't the only one who had skipped lunch.

As we ate in silence, I caught Max sneaking glances at me from across the table. There was something different in how he looked at me since he had gotten to my house earlier. I didn't know what it was, but my parents had noticed it too because I caught them making their "Did you see that?" face at one another from across the table. I tried to bring my focus back to chewing and swallowing without choking. I ate quickly, and it would have been beyond embarrassing to have to get the hemlock maneuver from eating too fast.

It seemed like everyone was starting to get full because we had all slowed down when Dad asked, "So how does it feel to have your first year of college behind you?"

"It feels weird, honestly, but I'm glad we made it through," I answered. I gave Max a quick glance. "I don't know if I could have done it without Max."

My parents smiled at us. "What about you, Max? How has your first year been?" Dad asked.

"It's been good. A rough start, but I figured it out. It helped to have a good study partner," he said as he looked across the table at me. I looked down at my plate, a goofy smile plastered across my face.

"I'm happy you guys had each other," my mom said as she looked at us. "I know it has been a tough time for both of you."

"It has. I think it was a weird year for us both because Justin and Vanessa weren't there, and we both expected them to be, but somehow we managed to get through the year. So, I'd say it was a win." It seemed like they all stopped breathing for a second. I hadn't spoken Justin's name out loud very much since he'd been gone, so I knew it was odd for my parents to hear me say it.

Max looked at me with a sweet smile as he reached across the table and touched my hand. "I'd say so too."

My parents got quiet for a second and just looked at us. Then, my mom spoke. "If you guys aren't too full for dessert, there are some brownies on the counter and ice cream in the freezer. I'll clean up everything. You guys go relax since it's your first day home."

"Let me help clean. You're both so kind for inviting me to stay a few days. I can't leave a mess," Max said.

"Yeah, Mom. Let us at least help. It's a lot to put up," I said as I started to stand so I could take my plate to the sink.

"Nope. You both are forbidden from the kitchen unless it's to get dessert. It's really not much, just a few plates to clean and containers to put in the refrigerator. Plus, I have your dad to help me," she said, giving my dad a wink. "And Max, you are welcome absolutely anytime."

"Mom, just-" I tried to say, but she cut me off.

"Aht, aht, only for dessert," she said, waving me off. "You've worked hard and had all those finals to get through. Go enjoy being home. I promise I'll let you clean the kitchen another night after dinner."

Mom was stubborn, and I think I may have taken her attentiveness for granted at times, but I genuinely couldn't have asked for a better mom. "Fine. We're only going to the kitchen for dessert, and then straight upstairs to relax."

"Good!" She said. "Goodnight, honey. Goodnight, Max."

"Goodnight," Max and I said in unison.

"Goodnight, Dad," I said as Max and I walked toward the kitchen.

"Goodnight, Sweetie."

I cut us each a brownie, placed a scoop of vanilla ice cream on top, covered it all in chocolate syrup, and grabbed the jar of cherries from the refrigerator to put one on top of each of our desserts.

Max watched as I made our brownies. "We may not be able to sleep after all of that sugar."

I laughed. "It will be okay. Netflix has plenty of movies we can stay up and watch." Max shook his head and smiled. He looked genuinely happy. Max had such a nice smile that it made me smile even bigger.

"I almost forgot, I need to grab my bag from the living room."

"I can carry both of these. You grab your bag and I'll show you which room is yours," I told him, as I picked up both of our bowls and headed toward the staircase.

When we got upstairs, Max waited in my doorway, bag in hand, as I set our bowls on my desk. I walked back into the hall and toward the room my mom had prepared for him. It was the next door on the opposite side of the hall from my room. I walked into the room and flipped on the light switch. It smelled like lavender, and I realized that Mom had lit a candle in the bedroom and the bathroom.

"Mom made sure to leave clean towels and even lit some candles for you," I said.

"Your mom is great. She's always been so nice to me," he said as he set his bag on the bed.

"She is pretty great," I agreed. "If you want to unpack later and use the dresser or closet, feel free, but right now, you've got a brownie sundae with your name on it in my room."

"Let's go eat our stomachache in a bowl," he said playfully.

I rolled my eyes and walked back to my room as he followed behind me. I grabbed my sundae from the desk and plopped down on my bed. I patted the spot next to me as Max got his bowl and came over.

We ate our sundaes in silence for a bit before Max spoke. "This is actually pretty good. I thought it might be too sweet, but it's not."

"I'm glad you like it." I took another bite and then put my spoon down, turning to Max. "Could you do me a favor?"

"Of course. What is it?" Max answered.

I hesitated for a second. "I want to go to Justin's grave since the anniversary of the accident is in three days, and I would like you to go with me."

"Of course, I will. Which day did you want to go?" I breathed a sigh of relief. I knew Max would be there for me, but I didn't know if maybe it was weird for me to ask him to go to Justin's grave with me.

71

"I was thinking maybe tomorrow. I would go on the actual anniversary, but I don't want to risk running into his mom or stepdad there if either of them even goes."

"I'll be ready whenever you want to go. Do you want to stop and buy some flowers or anything beforehand?" He asked.

"Yeah, we can stop at Fiona's Florals downtown and get some before we go. I haven't been to his grave since the day of the funeral. I haven't even seen his headstone yet, but I think I still remember where the gravesite is." I felt a little guilty that I hadn't had the courage to go until now. I still didn't know how I would feel once I was actually there. It could end up being a terrible idea.

Max placed his hand over mine and rubbed the back of my hand with his thumb. "We'll find it."

"Thank you. I just really don't want to go alone. It scares me, well maybe scare isn't the right word. I think just seeing Justin's name in granite may make it a little too real, I guess," I said, hoping I was making sense. I was genuinely surprised with myself for not breaking down in tears or feeling panic rise in my throat as it usually would have when I spoke about Justin. This was one of the few times I talked about him out loud where that hadn't happened. Maybe after nearly a year and finally coming back home, I was starting to accept it, or at the very least be at peace with it enough to begin to function somewhat normally again.

"I completely understand. It was like that the first time I went to Vanessa's grave after the funeral, once her headstone was up. It was too much. I feel pretty guilty for not going that often, but it never feels right. That's not where I feel her presence," he said.

"That's exactly what I was telling my mom earlier today. I didn't feel Justin at the graveside after his funeral. I don't know if maybe I was still too raw from it to feel anything, but she asked me where I did feel him, and I didn't know how to answer. It's almost as if I feel him everywhere around me, but nowhere at the same time. It's like he's always there, but the second I really need to feel him, he's nowhere to be found," I said.

"It's only been a year, so the feelings are still kind of all over the place. It's as if they are just out of reach. So close you can tell they are there, but just far enough that you can't touch them," Max said as he stared down at our hands.

"Exactly," I said. I looked down and realized that at some point, I had turned my hand over without even realizing it. My fingers were intertwined with Max's. Holding his hand felt nice. It was so much bigger than mine and so warm. He gently stroked my hand with his thumb as I looked back up to see that he was looking at me.

"You know I'm always here, right? Anything you need, you can always ask," he said, a soft expression on his face.

His eyes showed me how pure his words were and that he genuinely meant it. I could never get over how beautiful his eyes were. I could get lost in pools of emerald if I looked long enough. "I know. I really appreciate that. You have no idea how much." I placed my free hand on his shoulder and leaned forward, placing a kiss on his cheek. I lingered a little longer than I meant to as I breathed in the familiar scent that had been so comforting to me this past year. He turned slightly and kissed me back on my cheek, but a little closer to my mouth than I was to his. We lingered for a second longer, our faces so close that I could feel his breath on my cheek, but I pulled back.

He smiled at me, our hands still clasped together. "We should probably finish our sundaes before they melt."

"Yeah, we should," I agreed, smiling back at him.

Chapter 9

I was woken up by the smell of pancakes and bacon wafting up the stairs. I knew mom and dad had to be at work already, so that was odd. My stomach growled, and I rolled over to grab my phone to check the time. It was ten. It felt nice to sleep in, especially since we had such an early morning the day before. After driving two hours home and then unpacking all of my stuff, I was exhausted by the time we went to bed.

Last night, while Max and I finished our sundaes, we watched a new movie that had just come out on Netflix, but then decided we should go to bed before it got too late since we were both beat. I couldn't lie, part of me wished he had stayed in my room for the night because I didn't want to sleep alone, but I figured he'd be more comfortable and get better rest in his own bed in the guest room.

I finally mustered the energy to drag myself out of bed and went into the bathroom. I brushed my teeth, brushed my hair, and threw my robe on over my pajamas. I looked toward Max's room when I opened my door and noticed that his door was open. I walked over and looked inside. The room was empty, and the bathroom door was open, also empty. He must have been downstairs already and responsible for the pancakes and bacon I smelled.

When I got to the bottom of the stairs and turned the corner to the kitchen, Max was standing in front of the stove, flipping a pancake.

There was a stack already piled on a plate next to him. He was in red and black plaid pajama pants that hung low on his hips, and a black V-neck t-shirt with his brown hair still messy from the night before. He looked good, really good. "Hey, you," I said, startling him.

He turned to look at me with a big smile. "Good morning! I hope you're hungry."

"I am. It smells amazing."

"I was hoping I'd get it done before you woke up, so you didn't have to wait, but I guess the smell woke you up," he said, and then turned back to the stove to take a pancake off the pan.

"It smelled too amazing to stay asleep," I said as I walked over to stand next to him. "You didn't have to do all this."

"I don't mind. I love cooking. I was up before your mom left, so I asked her where everything was so I could make you breakfast," he said as he turned his head to look at me.

Could this boy be any sweeter? Max was amazing. It was hard not to notice how perfect he was, not that I hadn't all year, but something was different now. I noticed him in a way I hadn't before. "You're pretty great, you know that?" I asked as I rested my head against his arm.

"No, not at all. I just thought you deserved a delicious breakfast to get your day started off right," he said as he flipped his last pancake.

"I'll get us some plates and something to drink." I lifted my head from his arm and walked over to the cabinet where we kept the cups. "Orange juice, milk, or coffee?" I asked.

"I'll take some orange juice, please," he said as he placed the last pancake on the pile with the others.

I took down two glasses from the cabinet and decided on orange juice for myself, too. I got our plates down while Max took the pan of bacon out and placed it carefully on the stove to cool. He scooped the bacon onto a plate while I filled our glasses, and then carried the pile of pancakes and bacon over to the counter.

"It looks delicious, and I'm starving," I said.

"Go ahead and grab as much as you want. I'll get the syrup," he said as he turned and walked over to the pantry.

After I placed a few pancakes and slices of bacon on my plate, I covered everything in syrup and dug in. The pancakes were amazing. They were so fluffy, and the bacon was the perfect amount of crispiness. "I'm going to need you to make me breakfast every morning," I said. "This is incredible."

"I would gladly do it," he said, smiling at me before taking another bite of his pancakes.

We both ate until we were stuffed. Between the two of us, we finished the whole plate of bacon and nearly all of the pancakes. I didn't think we could have possibly eaten any more if we tried. After we finished, we washed the few dishes we used and straightened the kitchen back up. As I was drying the last plate, I turned to Max. "I'll go ahead and get ready soon. What time would be good for us to leave?"

"Anytime is fine with me. I just need to take a quick shower and change," he said as he stacked the last glass into the cabinet.

"Okay, I should be ready to go by noon. We can stop by the florist first." I placed my dishtowel on the counter and headed up the stairs.

I looked through my closet, trying to decide what to wear. Justin was always the worst about forgetting sweaters and shirts here when he stayed, so many of his clothes were still hanging in my closet. I thought about grabbing one of his favorite sweatshirts, but I knew it would be too hot and humid for that. I finally settled on a t-shirt and shorts.

I thought it would only be right if I wore something that reminded me of Justin. I flipped through the hangers in my closet until I found a cropped tie-dye Nirvana shirt with Kurt Cobain's face right in the center. I remembered when Justin first came to my house wearing it. He had just gotten it the day before when he'd gone to the mall. I told him how much I loved it and that I needed to get a one like it. The very next week, he gave it to me. He told me that he'd gone back to the mall to get me one, but they were sold out, so he'd taken his to a seamstress and got her to crop it and take in the sides so it would fit me better.

He always did things like that. The memory made me miss him even more. He was so thoughtful, and I knew he would have done anything to ensure I was happy. I loved him, of course as a friend, but now thinking back on it, it was more than that. I tried to deny it, but it was always there. I was pretty sure that Justin was my first, if not my only, love. And what a first love that was. To have my best friend in the whole world and the person I cared about most be my first love seemed pretty lucky to me, even if I never got to tell him how I felt.

A lump rose in my throat, threatening to bring the tears with it. It made me sad when I thought about everything I never got to tell Justin and how I lied about remembering the night we kissed. I always wondered what would have happened if I had been honest when we talked about what happened that night. I always feared that he wouldn't have felt the same way about me, and I didn't want to risk the potential rejection. I guess now I'd never know.

I did my best to swallow down the lump in my throat as I went to my dresser to find a pair of shorts. I didn't want to be sad right now. I wanted to remember him and all of our good times, not think about how the hole in my chest ached when I thought about all I was missing. I picked a black pair of high-waisted jean shorts to go with the Nirvana top, and then walked over to the bathroom. I decided against shampooing my hair since it still looked fine and had some wave in it from when I curled it the night before. I piled it on top of my head with a clip and hopped in the shower.

I showered quickly, and when I got out, I decided to take the time to do my makeup again. I wanted to look nice the first time I went to his grave. I knew Justin couldn't see me, but I wanted to try to look like some semblance of what I did when he was still alive, and I was happy.

Who knew, though? Maybe he could see me. I didn't know much about the afterlife, but who's to say he wouldn't be hanging around to see who comes to visit?

If that was the case, I didn't want him judging me for coming to his grave all teary-eyed and looking like a disaster. I knew he would have hated that. If he knew how I had moped around, refusing to come home, barely hanging on by a thread, not wanting to live my life without him this past year, he'd be so angry with me. I knew he would feel terrible that he had to leave me, but he'd be so upset that I pretty much stopped living because he was gone. Growing up together, he always tried to make sure that I was okay. He tried his best to always make me happy, even with everything he had to deal with from Bill. So, if he had any idea how unhappy I had been, it would kill him all over again.

It was a little past noon when I finally finished getting ready. I slipped my black Converse on and walked to Max's room. His door was closed, so I knocked twice and waited. A second later, he opened the door, dressed in a white V-neck t-shirt and light jeans, with a rip right across the knee. He looked handsome, as always. "I'm finally ready. Sorry, it took a little longer than I anticipated," I said as I looked him over.

"It's no problem. I was just reading. You look great, by the way, and that's an awesome shirt," he said with a smile.

"Thanks. You look great, too," I said, returning the smile.

"Do you want me to drive?" He asked. "My car is behind yours in the driveway, so I can if you want me to."

"Sure. Do you know where Fiona's Florals is?" I asked.

Once we were in the car, Max asked, "Do you know what type of flowers you want to get yet?"

"I guess it depends on what the florist has right now, but I'm hoping to get some blue roses and white lilies," I answered.

"That would look nice. Is there a significance for those specifically?"

"Blue was Justin's favorite color and also one of the colors of his favorite football team. He always dragged me to games with him when they were close by and made me watch the games on the big screen in the backyard with him and my dad during football season. I always pretended that I hated it, but I didn't. The white lilies represent me. I love lilies, and when he gave me flowers for my birthday or whatever occasion, that's what they always were. "Lilies for Lia." He'd always write that on the card. So, I guess it represents him and me, and our friendship," I said, looking down at my hands.

"That sounds like the perfect choice," Max said, his eyes focused on the road. I didn't know if he was always a careful driver when driving alone, but I noticed that he always made sure to be very careful when I was in the car with him.

"I think so too."

I didn't live far from downtown, so it only took us about ten minutes with traffic to get to Fiona's Florals. Max parked in an open space right in front, and we got out. As soon as we stepped inside, my nose was filled with the aromatic scent of every type of flower you could imagine. It smelled heavenly, like walking through a flower garden in spring. I looked around at the rainbow of colors all surrounding me. The front room was filled with flower arrangements from big to small, one-color bouquets to boutiques with an array of colors and flowers. I'd forgotten just how much I enjoyed going into the flower shop.

"Amelia, is that you?" I heard a voice coming from a flower arrangement that was moving toward me. Fiona peeked her head around the huge arrangement she was carrying to look at me. Fiona was a short woman with a round face. Her skin was the most beautiful shade of brown, and her once jet black hair was now salt and pepper. She had the kindest, big brown eyes I had ever seen. "It was last summer the last time you were in here, wasn't it?" She asked.

"It was. I've been away at school. I didn't come home for any holidays this year," I said, feeling a little ashamed.

"I figured as much since you didn't come to pick up any arrangements around the holidays," she said. My mom loved flowers. She always had fresh flowers around the house for as long as I could remember. So, since I was a kid, I had always made trips with her to Fiona's. Justin would tag along with us most of the time when we went too. We had all seen Fiona pretty regularly since we were very young. Once I had my license, I always picked up flowers for mom, and Justin always got my flowers from Fiona's, too, so she was used to us visiting all the time.

"We decided to take a few trips over the holidays this past year," I said.

"It would have been tough coming home," Fiona said, giving me a knowing look.

I wasn't sure if it was meant to be a statement or a question, but I answered anyway. "It would have. I'm actually on my way to Justin's grave for the first time since the funeral and wanted to pick up some flowers."

"Of course. Anything you want, and it's on the house," she said as she finally set the huge arrangement she'd been holding on the back counter.

"I couldn't let you do that. I'll pay for them," I told her.

She waved a hand at me. "Absolutely not. Your mother buys enough flowers every month to keep me in business for a long time, and I'd do anything for you and Justin. You know how much I loved that boy. Almost as much as you did," she said, smiling at me. "It's on me. Just tell me what you'd like."

That she did. People always loved Justin, though. He was charming, and not many people could resist it, not even a woman who had been married for thirty years, like Fiona. Justin loved coming in to talk to her when he rode with me to pick up flowers for my mom. Fiona didn't have any children of her own, so she always made us treats to take home and asked how we were doing in school. I felt bad for not coming by to see her. I never even asked how she was after hearing what happened to him. I had been too busy drowning in my own pain to realize that I wasn't the only person his death affected.

"Could I do an arrangement with some blue roses and white lilies, please?" I asked.

"White lilies? I made those arrangements quite often, didn't I?" She asked.

"You did. I'm sure you miss seeing him, too."

Her eyes looked a little misty. "Oh, how I do. I've watched you kids grow up in this town. That's probably the closest thing I've experienced to what it must feel like to lose a child or grandchild."

My heart sank. "I'm so sorry I haven't been by here since it all happened. I just couldn't bear to be in town," I said.

"Oh sugar, I understand." She walked over and wrapped her arms around me, "I'm just glad I got to see you. And you haven't introduced me to your friend yet." She nodded toward Max.

I hugged her back. "Oh, I'm so sorry! This is Max. He's a good friend of mine."

"Well, hello, Max. Are you a friend from school?" She asked.

"I'm actually from here, but I didn't go to the same high school. I went to the one across town. I've driven by here so many times, but I've never been inside until today. Your shop is beautiful," he answered.

"Thanks, baby. I try to keep it looking nice. How did you two meet?"

"We both go to Branston now, but we met last summer in a grief support group," he answered.

"So you've lost someone too? I'm happy that you two were able to find each other," she said, giving Max a sympathetic smile.

"I did. My girlfriend, to cancer early last year," he replied. He looked down quickly, but not before I saw that his eyes had turned glassy.

"I'm so sorry to hear that." She placed her small hand on Max's arm and patted gently. "If you'd like me to make you an arrangement for her, let me know, and it's on the house, as well. Don't even try to argue about it," she said, matter-of-factly. "You've helped my Amelia through a tough time, so let me show my gratitude for that."

"I would love that," Max said to Fiona. "Thank you so much."

"Of course. Come back anytime and let me know what you would like," she said. She patted Max on the shoulder before she walked back toward the counter. "I'll get started on your arrangement," she told me. "It shouldn't take me too long if you just want to walk around the store while you wait."

Max and I walked around, looking at all the flower arrangements. She had some for everything from baby showers to funerals. She had them for any occasion you could think of, and they were all so beautiful. There was also a section for greeting cards to go with your flowers, and I noticed a small area with boxes of chocolate as well. That must have been new because she never had candy in here before, except what she made for Justin and me.

It only took her about twenty minutes before she walked back up to the counter from the back, carrying the most gorgeous arrangement of flowers I had ever laid eyes on. The blue roses and white lilies were intertwined perfectly in a black vase with a white ribbon tied around it. I noticed a small card sticking up from the flowers when I got closer to the counter.

"These are amazing, Fiona. They are absolutely perfect." I said.

"I'm glad you like them. I wrote a little something on the card but left plenty of room for you to write whatever you wanted to," she said as she pushed the flowers across the counter closer to me. She handed me the pen she had tucked behind her ear.

I took the card from its holder and opened it. Right at the top of the card, she wrote "Lilies From Lia." It took everything in my power to hold back the tears that were now stinging at the corners of my eyes, threatening to overflow. Of course she remembered what Justin had always written, but this time she wrote the opposite. I felt Max right behind me. He placed a steadying hand on my shoulder for support. It was like he could sense my emotions even if he couldn't see my face.

"That's perfect," I told Fiona. I smiled at her from across the counter, tears still in my eyes.

"I thought you would like it," she said with a sweet smile.

I opened the pen and tried to think of what I should write. Max moved from behind me and over to the side of the counter. He looked at some greeting cards to give me privacy as I started writing.

I never knew how much I truly needed you until you weren't here anymore, and I hate that I never got the chance to tell you. Also, I lied the next morning after you stayed when I was drunk last May. I remembered everything, and I don't regret what happened. My only regret is that I lied, and we never got the chance to see where it could have gone. I'll love you forever, and I'll miss you always. I still kinda hate you for leaving me, though, but I know you wouldn't have if it were your choice. -Lia

Part of me wanted to throw it away and leave it at "I love and miss you" because I worried that someone could come by his grave and read it, and know that it was from me. But another part of me didn't care because it didn't matter what anyone else knew or thought now anyway. I figured there was no harm in putting it out there and saying all the things I wished I had told him. I looked down at the card again and reread it in my head to make sure that I didn't make any mistakes.

I stuck the card back into the envelope and sealed it shut. I looked to where Fiona was standing near the cash register. "Thank you so much for this. I promise I'll visit more. Now that I'm home, Mom will probably be sending me here for her flowers, so I'll see you soon."

"You better! You stayed gone too long. I can't handle losing both of you at once. And bring Max with you," she scolded.

"I will, I promise," I told her as I picked up the vase of flowers and started toward the door. Max got ahead of me and held the door open. He turned to wave at Fiona, and then let the door fall shut behind us. He walked hurriedly around the car to open the door, so I could climb in. Once I was seated with the flowers firmly in my lap, he shut the door. I didn't want to sit them down because I was afraid that they would fall over and get ruined on the drive.

Max pulled out of the parking space, and we headed toward the cemetery. Justin's grave was in the city cemetery, not too far from downtown. We got there almost too quickly. We pulled in and started down the winding path that snaked around the cemetery, taking us past rows and rows of headstones. Some had fresh flowers, and some had wilted flowers that you could tell had been sitting there too long, with no visitors to clean them up. Thinking about that made me sad. I thought about how I hadn't been by Justin's grave and how he may have had flowers sitting there for a long time before anyone cleaned them up, too.

I could tell we were getting close because my heart started to pound against my ribcage as we passed a few familiar headstones I remembered seeing at the graveside service. Coming to Justin's grave seemed much easier in theory than in execution. Knowing that I didn't have to do it alone and that I had Max was there with me made me feel a little better. I honestly didn't know if I could have done it without him. I motioned with a shaky hand as I told Max we were close by and that he could pull over. He put the car in park, and I felt my chest constrict.

Chapter 10

"Are you okay?" Max asked. "Do you need a minute before we get out?"

I wanted to take a deep breath to calm my nerves, but my chest was too tight. "I think so," I answered.

"It's okay. I'm right here if you need me. Take all the time you need," he said as he reached over and placed his hand on mine, squeezing gently. I squeezed back, hoping he couldn't tell how clammy and shaky my hands were. I took slow breaths in through my nose and out through my mouth, trying to calm my racing heart and loosen, at least, some of the tightness in my chest.

After a few minutes and many deep breaths, I finally felt like I had calmed down enough to get out of the car, so I turned to Max. "I think I'm ready."

"I'll come around so you don't have to try to hold the flowers with one hand," he said as he opened his door to get out.

He pulled my door open and held his hands out to take the flowers from me while I climbed out of the car. My legs were shaky, but I thought I could manage. Max offered to carry the flowers for me, so I could look around and find Justin's grave. I let him, because I knew if I ended up dropping the flowers, I'd be upset. We walked toward where I thought I remembered his grave being after the funeral. A strange feeling washed over me the further we walked into the cemetery. It wasn't my anxiety, or at least it had never felt like that before. It felt more like a presence. Maybe that was how it felt when you walked through a place where so many people were buried.

I noticed that we weren't the only people who had come to put flowers on a grave on a random Thursday in June. I saw a sweet-looking older lady in a yellow sweater holding purple roses. She knelt at a grave and placed the roses on the headstone. Then, I saw what appeared to be a family. A lady and two young boys weaved through the headstones. Each boy was dressed in dress shorts and a white button-up shirt and held one single daisy in their hand. They followed behind their mother, who was wearing a flowing black dress that fell just below her knees. Across the cemetery, I saw someone walking toward the very edge, like they were leaving. They were wearing a black hoodie, black pants, sunglasses, and a baseball cap. That seemed ridiculous with the heat in June, but maybe it didn't bother them. They were too far away for me to tell whether it was a man or a woman, though.

I stopped walking so suddenly that I nearly caused Max to bump into me. There it was. It was black marble and so shiny from the newness of it. I felt like I couldn't breathe, like my lungs had closed up and refused to expand as I read the words.

Justin Alexander Robinson

August 15th, 2007- June 9, 2024

Loving Son

Angel wings were carved below the words. The lump in my throat rose, restricting the air that I was trying to pull into my lungs. Silent tears streamed down my face as I read the words over and over again.

Max stood next to me. He held the flowers in one hand and rubbed my back with the other. Suddenly, the strange feeling I had when we first got there washed over me again. I wasn't sure if that was what it felt like when you felt someone's presence or what. It was like I could feel Justin, but I also had a pit in my stomach that made me feel like I was being watched. I looked around the cemetery. Everyone was focused on what they were doing until I noticed the person who was dressed in all black when we first walked up. They were standing at the edge of the cemetery, and it seemed like they were looking directly at me. I turned to ask Max if he had seen them, but when I turned back, they were gone.

I couldn't shake the feeling that something wasn't right about that person, or even if it was a real person. Maybe it was my paranoid imagination playing tricks on me. I had always hated cemeteries, as most people did, and that was exactly why. Max said he didn't see anyone, but he was also focused on me crying and trying to comfort me at the time. I tried to shake off the eerie feeling and focus on what I'd come to do, but it was more difficult than I would have liked.

I reached for the flowers and took them from Max. I knelt and placed the vase in front of Justin's headstone, next to the beautiful vase with a mixture of all types of summer flowers that was already there.

"Someone else must have been here this week. Those flowers look pretty new," Max said, looking at the flowers.

"I'm pretty sure my mom brought these. She told me she'd been by here this week," I replied.

"Those are nice too. Fiona's arrangements are so beautiful."

"They are. You have to start going by there with me now," I said. I was still kneeling in front of Justin's grave, but I turned my head to look up at him. "Fiona seems to like you."

"She seemed like such a sweet lady. I don't know how I've lived in this town so long and never been there before," he said.

I finally stood back up and walked over to stand next to Max. I looked down at Justin's grave with the blue and white flowers in front of it. They looked beautiful against the black marble of his headstone. My heart ached, and I felt that gaping hole in my chest that had been ever so present since last summer. I missed him so much that it physically hurt. Yes, I wanted to live and do all the things he would have wanted me to do, but there were moments when the pain was overwhelming. Seeing a headstone with his name on it was one of those moments.

Max reached for my hand, and I took his, squeezing tightly because I thought that sometimes his hands might be the only thing that held me together in those moments. The previous night and earlier that morning had been better than I would have imagined they'd be. I hadn't felt that good since before Justin's accident, so that was saying something. But seeing his grave felt like it was going to shatter the few pieces of me that had started to mold back together.

I knew not all days would be good days, but it was hard to resist the urge to go back to how I had been. It would be much easier to go home, curl up in my bed, and let the sadness overtake me, but I didn't want to do that anymore. I didn't know how much time had passed. It seemed like forever as I held Max's hand and looked down at Justin's grave. Max cleared his throat. "Did you want to say any words, or do you need me to leave you alone for a few minutes?"

"No, please stay," I said quickly, hoping he didn't hear the desperation in my voice. "I can't be here by myself, not yet."

"I just wanted to make sure," he said.

"I want to say something. I don't know what to say. Nothing seems right."

"Just say what you feel."

I took a deep breath. I wrote what I felt like I needed to tell him on the card. I didn't want to say that out loud in front of Max. I thought about Justin and all the good times we had and how much I cared for him, and then spoke. "Justin, you were my best friend in the whole world, and you knew me better than anyone, and I'm pretty pissed at you for leaving me." I gave a weak smile and continued, "I didn't even realize I was capable of missing someone so much until now. I don't think I have any memories from growing up that you weren't in. You were just always there, and maybe I took that for granted. I will always cherish my time with you, even though it will never feel like it was long enough. I hope you're having fun wherever you may be. Watch over me. I hope I can make you proud." I took another deep breath and blew it out slowly through my mouth to calm the shaky feeling in my chest.

"That was perfect," Max said, squeezing my hand gently.

"Thank you," I said as I turned to look up at him. "I think I'm ready to go now."

He nodded and turned to walk back to the car, my hand still in his.

Max opened the passenger side door, and I climbed in. Once I was seated, he shut the door gently and walked around to his side. "Where to? Did you want to go home, or is there someplace else you'd like to go?" He asked once he was in the car.

"We can go home. I'm getting hungry, and we have all those leftovers from dinner last night in the fridge," I answered as he shifted into gear and started down the path out of the cemetery. "I don't think I'm up for much else today. That was more mentally taxing than I thought it would be."

"It was, but you did it. I'm happy you were finally able to go," he said, giving me a small smile. "Back to your house, it is then. We can eat and watch TV, or if you need to be alone today, that's fine too. Just let me know whatever you need."

I reached over, taking his hand in mine. I intertwined my fingers through his and rested our hands on my thigh. "I don't want to be alone."

I looked over at him, trying to read his expression. He looked a little surprised, but I also saw a hint of a smile teasing at the corners of his mouth. I looked down at our hands, gently stroking the back of his with my fingertips. He relaxed his arm, putting the full weight of his hand on my leg. He turned the radio up with the buttons on the steering wheel, and we rode like that the whole way home, not speaking, just listening to the music with our hands clasped together.

When we made it home, Max started heating the food while I ran upstairs to wipe my face and freshen up after the humidity and crying at the cemetery. I took a makeup wipe and cleaned away the mascara streaked down my face. I quickly swept some fresh powder across my skin and touched up my eye makeup. By the time I returned to the kitchen, Max already had everything ready to eat.

He walked around the island, pulled out one barstool for me, and then another for himself. I hopped up on mine, grabbed my fork, and started eating. Neither of us said anything for a while. Nervousness churned in my stomach. I usually didn't have that with Max. It wasn't a bad nervousness; maybe it was more like excitement. I didn't know if maybe my emotions were going haywire from earlier, but I decided to try my best to ignore it.

I glanced sideways at Max. He was nearly finished eating, and I was getting pretty full myself. I wanted to think of something that we could do together that didn't take too much mental energy since I didn't have much to spare at the moment. "Do you want to go for a swim later and maybe watch a movie on the projector screen outside?" I asked.

"Yeah, I'm down," he said as he stood to take his plate to the sink. "Are you finished eating? I can take yours if you are."

I nodded, handing him my plate. He rinsed them off and placed them in the dishwasher before turning to me. "Oh, wait, I don't have a swimsuit. I didn't even think about packing one for some reason."

"If you're comfortable with it, you can swim in your boxers. It will just be us out there, so you don't have to worry about my parents seeing you in your underwear," I said. The thought of Max in only his underwear made me feel suddenly shy.

"I can. Are you comfortable with that, though?" He asked.

I decided not to let my nervousness show. "Oh yeah, it's fine with me. Underwear and swimsuits are basically the same thing anyway, right?"

"I guess so," he answered as he turned to grab a water bottle from the refrigerator.

"We still have to wait at least thirty minutes after eating before swimming," I said.

"That's what they say," he replied, with a chuckle.

"I'm going to change and lie out in the sun until our thirty minutes are up," I told him as I hopped off the barstool.

"I'm going to call my parents to check in and see what time they will be home tomorrow, then I'll change, well, undress, I guess," he let out a nervous laugh. "And then I'll come out there."

"Sounds good," I said before jogging up the stairs.

I shut the door and walked over to my dresser, pulling open the bottom drawer to try and find a swimsuit to wear. I had so many, but I couldn't decide if I wanted to wear a bikini or a one-piece. I finally decided on a cute pink floral-print bikini. I peeled off my clothes, threw them on my bed, and slipped into the bathing suit.

I went over to the full-length mirror and studied my reflection. As I looked at myself, I noticed I looked thinner than I had the last time I wore this bathing suit. I guess stress and grieving will do that to a person. It was rough on the mind *and* the body, apparently. I grabbed two towels from the bathroom, got my phone from my desk, and went out into the hallway. I thought about seeing if Max was ready yet, but remembered that he said he needed to call his parents first. I decided not to disturb him and wait outside.

When I got outside, I spread the towels over two of the lounge chairs for Max and me. I lay down on the chair to the left, connected my phone to the Bluetooth speaker, and hit shuffle on my playlist. A soft pop song started playing, and I closed my eyes, relaxing into the melody while I waited for Max.

I heard someone call my name, and I opened my eyes. It sounded like Justin, but I knew that couldn't be right. I heard it again. This time it was clearer. It was definitely Justin's voice. "Lia, I need your help. Please," he pleaded. I sat up and looked around, but didn't see anyone there. "I need you, Lia," he said again.

I whipped around to look where the voice had come from, but there was no one there. It was just my empty backyard. I was starting to get freaked out, so I tried to stand up to go inside, but I couldn't move. I was stuck and couldn't get up from the chair. Justin called my name again and again, but I didn't know how to help him.

Chapter 11

"Amelia? Amelia?"

I opened my eyes to see Max standing over me. "Are you okay?" He asked as he looked down at me.

"I think so," I said. I was still trying to process that it had only been a dream. It was unsettling, to say the least, and my heart was hammering in my chest. I took a few deep breaths, trying to steady myself. "How long have you been standing there?"

"I just got out here, so maybe a minute. It seemed like you were having a bad dream," he said.

"I was. Well, it was weird, but it's okay. I must have dozed off. I didn't even realize I was that tired," I said as I sat up.

"It's been an emotionally exhausting day," he said. "Do you still feel like swimming, or do you want to go inside and take a nap?"

"It must have been a power nap because I feel pretty energized now. I needed that." I was so thrown off by being jolted awake that I hadn't realized that Max was wearing basketball shorts with no shirt. There was nothing like a half-naked Max to take my mind off the jarring dream. I scanned my eyes all the way up to see him looking at me with a smirk on his face. I flushed with embarrassment because he had just caught me checking him out, but being the gentleman he was, I knew he wouldn't call me on it. He sat down on the chair next to mine, where I had spread the towel out for him.

I cleared my throat. "Is that what you're wearing to swim?"

"I'm going to take these off when we get in the pool, but I felt a little weird about walking through your house in only my underwear."

I laughed. "I guess that's understandable."

I noticed that his eyes darted quickly down my body before returning to my face, and I suddenly felt shy and exposed. "Should we get in?" I asked as I nodded toward the pool.

"Definitely. It's too hot not to be in the water," Max said, standing to pull down his basketball shorts.

I got up and quickly walked over to the pool, trying my best not to look at Max as he undressed. I stepped one foot onto the top step to test the water. It was cool, but not cold. I walked down a couple more steps and then sat down, turning to look just as Max was walking up behind me.

A thin layer of sweat was starting to form across his abs, and his boxer briefs hugged him tight, in all the right places. They didn't leave much to the imagination, and I didn't mind at all, but I looked away before he noticed me staring.

He stepped into the water and sat down next to me. "The water feels amazing."

"It does. I should have gotten the pool floats out of the building," I said as I looked over to the small storage building in the backyard. It was too late now. I didn't want to walk across the yard and get grass all over my feet.

I tried to look anywhere but directly at Max. Anyone with eyes could see that Max was handsome, but something was different. I noticed everything about him in a new way. His eyes were so green, like the moss that made an otherwise dull forest look vibrant and beautiful. They always softened when he looked at me, and his dark lashes made how green they were stand out even more. And don't even get me started on his body. He was in incredible shape.

His appearance aside, Max was a wonderful human being with so much depth and so much kindness in his heart. I never had anyone be there for me the way he had been. It could have been my fault because maybe I pushed everyone else away, but Max always stayed, even while he was dealing with the same pain. He was there anytime I needed him, and I didn't want to lose that.

Justin was always there for me when he was alive, but once we were teenagers, he became easily distracted by new girlfriends or boyfriends. I guess that was typical for a teenage boy, though. He wanted to live his life, be free and wild. I never blamed him for it, but there were times when I was a little jealous. He still made time for me, of course, but it wasn't the same as when we were kids. My feelings had maybe developed into more than his had at some point, but that was something I tried not to think about too much because it made losing him even harder.

"Hey, are you okay?" Max asked, gently shaking me from my thoughts.

"Huh? Yeah, I'm okay." I realized I was staring off into the backyard without saying anything. I was amazed that Max didn't think I was a crazy person sometimes.

"Are you sure? What's on your mind? If you feel like talking about..." he trailed off.

"It's nothing really, or everything, I guess," I laughed. "I'm sorry I zoned out."

"It's fine. I just wanted to make sure that you were okay."

"I am as long as you're here," I said, giving him a little smile. He smiled back, and I was sure I saw his face flush. It was hard to tell since it was hot out, but I was almost certain his already pink-tinged cheeks darkened.

I was starting to sweat, so I slid down a few steps until I sat where the water was up to my shoulders. Max followed, dipping his body further into the water. I noticed that he moved closer, his leg inches from mine. I shifted, pretending not to notice, and then let my leg rest against his. His eye darted down, and he moved his arm to rest it on the step above us behind my back. Seconds later, his fingers brushed my back. They moved back and forth, gently soothing. While someone rubbing my back was usually comforting, it now left a trail of heat where his fingertips touched my bare skin.

His fingers slipped underneath my bathing suit strap a few times as he slowly rubbed circles across my back. I stiffened, but not because I was uncomfortable. It was just the opposite. It felt so nice and natural that it caught me off guard. Max made me feel at peace, so I decided to lean into him. I shifted, angling toward him, letting my body rest against his. I placed my head on his shoulder, and he leaned his head down, resting his cheek against the top of my head.

I placed my hand on his thigh and felt him twitch beneath my touch. Slowly, I stroked the bare skin with my thumb, moving it back and forth. He shifted his arm from the step behind me and wrapped it around my back, fingers now resting on my side as he continued tracing slow circles across my skin.

Heat ran along the path where his bare skin touched mine. Max hugging me was nothing new. We had fallen asleep in the same bed, cuddled together more than once, but this felt new. I didn't know if it was the lack of clothes or how my thoughts about Max had shifted in the past few days, but this felt much more intimate. He lifted his head from mine, and I looked up to see that he was looking at me, our faces only inches apart. I tilted my chin up, lessening the distance even more. His gorgeous green eyes were looking right into mine as he tilted his face down, slowly moving closer. My heart thumped in my chest, and I wanted nothing more than to close the space between our lips and twist my fingers in his hair, but I was afraid.

I knew that if we did this, we couldn't go back to how we were. This wasn't a drunken kiss when we were both sad and needed comfort. This was a sober, deliberate decision that would mean so much more. Max made me happy, and having him in my life was everything to me. What if something happened and this didn't work out the way we wanted it to? I didn't want to think about that possibility because part of me was still terrified that I would crumble into a million pieces without Max. He was the glue that held me together this past year, and I couldn't lose him. I didn't know if it was worth the risk.

A loud, blaring noise from the Bluetooth speaker startled us, and we both jumped back from each other as we looked toward the sound. It took me a second to realize that it was my phone ringing. I scrambled to my feet and quickly got out of the pool. I ran over to grab my phone and saw it was my mom, so I tapped the green button on the screen.

"Hello?"

"Hey, honey! Did you have any special requests for dinner tonight?" Her voice blared over the Bluetooth speaker.

"Not really. I'm fine with anything," I answered as I tried to disconnect my phone from the speaker.

"Ask Max then and see if he wants anything specific." I looked over to Max, and he shook his head, mouthing that anything was fine.

"He said he's okay with anything, too." I gave up on disconnecting my phone because the phone wouldn't do anything. The screen was frozen; it had probably overheated in the sun.

"Okay, I'll figure something out and stop by the grocery store on the way home. Tell Max he's welcome to stay as long as he likes, even once his parents get home. He can stay anytime. I'm so happy you have a friend like him. I think he's good for you. I may be wrong, but from dinner last night, I kind of got the feeling that he may like you-"

"I'll tell him, Mom, and yes, he's great," I cut her off before she could say more. "Also, you're on speaker phone," I said, hoping she would end this conversation.

"Oh," she chuckled. "I didn't know. I'll let you get back to whatever you guys were doing and see you when I get home. Text me if there's anything either of you needs from the store."

"Will do. Love you," I said, quickly.

"Love you too, honey," she said before I hit the end button. Oh, *now* the phone screen was unfrozen. Of course.

I walked over to the covered portion of the patio and set my phone on the table so, hopefully, it wouldn't overheat anymore. As I turned to walk back to the pool, Max was looking at me, a slight grin on his face.

"I'm sorry about her," I said with an apologetic smile.

"It's fine," he chuckled. "I like your mom. She's..." he stopped for a second like he was searching for the correct word, "intuitive," he finished.

"Is she?" I asked with a raised eyebrow.

"I'd say so," he answered.

"Interesting," I said as I decided to run straight for the deep end and jump in, both physically and metaphorically.

Chapter 12

I t was almost eight-thirty, and the sun would be setting soon, so Max and I could finally watch a movie outside. I lay on my bed, still in my robe, studying the ceiling while I tried to decide what to wear. I'd never put this much thought into what I would be wearing around Max before, but now, for some reason, it mattered. I was starting to feel nervous, but not in an anxiety or panic attack way. It was a giddy nervousness at the thought that Max and I would be lying next to each other, possibly cuddled up while we watched a movie.

It was exciting. I had been a little wary of the idea because I was afraid to lose his friendship if we didn't work out, but I could be missing out on something that could be amazing because of fear. I didn't want to make the same mistake twice. Max wasn't like everyone else, and the more time we spent with each other, the more I knew that. I felt like I knew him reasonably well since we had spent most of the school year together, but it seemed like maybe we were growing closer in a way we hadn't before. He'd been more flirty, or maybe I was just more open to it than I had been before. I knew that Max wasn't only there for me because we were at the same school, and it was convenient for him. He genuinely cared, and I was pretty sure that he wasn't going to drop me because he was back home where his friends were. He wanted to be here, and I hoped that wouldn't change.

Earlier, we swam, talked, laughed, and had the best time. I needed that much more than I thought, especially with how our day started. After we'd swum until our arms and legs were jelly, we relaxed on the pool chairs to dry off until we heard Mom pull into the garage. Thankfully, Max was able to dart upstairs before she came inside. Although it would have been hilarious, it would have embarrassed Max to have my mom see him in just his boxers running through the house.

Dad grilled steaks that Mom picked up on her way home. Then after dinner, we came up to shower since we had been in the pool earlier. I lay there, trying to mentally go over what clothes I had without getting up and looking. Maybe something comfortable and cute would be best since we were just having a movie night in the backyard. I finally got up and walked over to my closet. I flipped through my clothes before settling on a floral print cropped tank and a pair of cute pink boho-style joggers. It was comfortable, but also didn't look like pajamas.

I dressed and went to the bathroom to quickly blow-dry my hair before swiping mascara over my lashes. I looked myself over in the mirror. I looked decent, acceptable for a movie in the dark. Max had seen me looking way worse, so this was at least mildly put together. I looked around my room to make sure I wasn't forgetting anything, and then decided to see if Max was ready. We still hadn't picked out a movie or gotten out the screen and projector yet, so I figured we should get that set up while there was still a little light out.

I walked over to Max's door, knocking twice. When he opened the door, he was wearing black basketball shorts and a grey V-neck t-shirt. He had also decided on cute but comfortable for his outfit, which made me feel like I had made a good choice with my own. His hair was still damp, sticking to his forehead. He reached up and brushed his hands through it so it was out of his face. Such a mundane gesture had never made my heart speed up the way that one did. His cheeks were tinted red from a little too much sun, which made his eyes stand out even more.

Max looked me up and down. Even though he tried not to make it noticeable, I saw. I had been so focused on his eyes, so of course, I caught him. I cleared my throat to speak. "You almost ready?" I asked, still looking up at him.

"Yeah, I'm ready. I was doing a little reading while I waited." He motioned to the book that was lying on the bed behind him.

"We can set everything up since the sun is almost down. Any ideas on what to watch? Has anything good come out recently?" I asked.

He walked out into the hall as he closed his door. "Not that I know of, but we can see. I'm fine watching anything."

"You're the guest, so you can pick," I said, bumping into him with my shoulder.

We rounded the corner into the kitchen, and I noticed that the screen and projector were already set up. The tall air mattress was blown up and sitting in front of the screen with a couple of pillows and blankets thrown across it. I mentioned at dinner that we were going to watch a movie, so Mom or Dad must have gotten everything ready. My parents were the best, even if they were a little embarrassing sometimes. Mom was at the sink rinsing the last of the dishes from dinner, but she turned around when she heard us come into the kitchen.

"Dad got everything set up for the movie for you guys. Do you want drinks or popcorn before you head out?" She asked.

"Tell Dad I said thank you. I would have gotten it," I said apologetically.

"It's no problem. Honestly, I think he missed doing things for you since you've been away all year. You know your dad likes to feel needed," she said with a chuckle.

I smiled thinking about my dad and how he never hesitated to help me with anything, whether it was building my LEGO sets, building furniture, to rearranging my room every six months for all three years of middle school. "I know he does. I've missed him helping me with everything just as much," I said. "And I don't want popcorn or anything right now. That steak was huge, so I'm stuffed." I looked at Max. "Do you want anything?"

"I'm fine. I'm still full from dinner, too," he answered.

"Okay, honey. If you change your mind, there's popcorn and candy in the pantry. And don't worry about taking everything down tonight. It's not supposed to rain, so it will be fine if it's left up overnight," she said as I headed toward the patio doors with Max behind me. "As soon as I finish up these dishes, I'll be going upstairs, so I won't be long."

I thought it was weird because where she decided to be in the house didn't have anything to do with me. I turned around to look at her, and she winked at me. I realized that she was saying I didn't have to worry about her being in the kitchen, where she could see us. I didn't know what she thought Max and I would be doing in the backyard. We were just going to be watching a movie and *maybe* some cuddling. I furrowed my brow at her, and she smiled, "Goodnight, love you," she called out.

"Love you too." I shook my head as I turned to go outside.

The air was cooler than I thought it would be, considering how hot it had been earlier. Max looked toward the air mattress and then glanced up at the screen. I had considered just dragging the pool chairs into the yard and throwing a blanket over them, but the air mattress would be more comfortable.

"Are you cool with the air mattress, or did you want a chair?" I asked Max.

"I'm fine with the air mattress," he answered quickly. "Are you fine sharing it?"

"Of course. I think it's big enough for both of us, unless you're planning on hogging it," I laughed. "Have you decided on a movie yet?"

"Not exactly, but I say let's not do something new. Let's do something we both already know we like," he answered. Like something that we didn't need to pay attention to? I guess that made sense. That way, we could talk if we wanted to and not miss anything important. Or possibly if we happened to be distracted by each other in another way. I must have thought about it for too long because Max spoke again. "Unless you wanted to watch something new, that's fine with me too," he added.

"No, I think that's a good idea," I said with a grin. "What are you thinking? Horror? Comedy? Romance? Specific decade? Eighties movies are always great."

"I don't know about horror tonight. We can do romance or comedy. Any decade is fine with me as long as we're not going back too far," he laughed.

"What about a classic? The Breakfast Club? Pretty In Pink? Top Gun?" I asked.

"I love Top Gun," he replied.

"It's such a good one, right? And the soundtrack," I said as I walked over to the projector to pull the movie up.

"The soundtrack is so good," he agreed as he walked over to the air mattress and sat down, grabbing a pillow to hold in his lap as he waited for me.

After I pressed play, I walked to the opposite side of the air mattress and plopped down on my stomach, facing the screen. Max followed suit, lying down on his stomach next to me. We both focused on the screen as the credits started.

We watched for a while, not speaking, but I noticed as he inched his body closer to mine. I glanced sideways at him, but his attention was on the screen, or so he made it seem. I reached behind me, grabbed a pillow, and placed it under my chest so I was propped up slightly. When I moved my arms back, I left them spread out further, so my elbow rested against Max's. I saw him look at me from the corner of my eye, but I played dumb, pretending my attention was also on the movie. We watched, in silence, until the beginning of the scene in the bar where they sang "You've Lost That Lovin' Feeling."

"I love this part and the song," Max said.

As Tom Cruise's character picked up the microphone, I turned to Max.

"You never close your eyes anymore when I kiss your lips," I sang, grinning at Max.

His smile grew wide. "And there's no tenderness like before in your fingertips," he sang back.

"You're trying hard not to show it," I sang.

"But baby, baby, I know it," we sang together. "You've lost that lovin' feelin'. Whoa, that lovin' feelin'. You've lost that loving feelin'. Now it's gone, gone, gone, whoa-oh."

We both fell into a fit of laughter. It felt good to be silly. I'm sure he wasn't expecting me to sing along. I realized that while Max and I had nice times together, a lot of the time, I was sad and not in the best place mentally. The past two days, I had laughed with him so much and felt like I could let go and be happy, and, honestly, it felt so good to feel almost normal again. We lay on our sides, facing each other, trying to catch our breath.

"I wasn't expecting a performance," Max said, his eyes crinkling with a smile.

"Me neither," I said, returning the smile. "But it felt right."

"It did," he said. "You know, it's been different the past two days."

I knew it had, but I was curious what he had to say about it. "Different how?" I asked.

"You've seemed happy, and I've enjoyed seeing you smile so much."

"Have I really been that mopey at school?" I asked, playfully.

"No, no. That's not what I'm saying-" he said.

I cut him off, "I'm kidding. I know what you mean. I've felt happier since I've been home. I was so scared to come back, but maybe it's what I needed the whole time." I thought of Justin as I said that. I felt that familiar pull in my chest. I would always feel that missing piece, but I had been working on managing how much it hurt. Justin would want me to be happy, so I was trying to do that, not only for him but for myself as well.

"I'm glad you have. I know it was hard coming home. I was really worried about you and how it might affect you. So, to see you this happy has been nice. It makes me happy when you're happy," he said as he reached a hand out to brush my hair back from my cheek.

My face grew hot at his words and the touch of his hand on my cheek. He let it linger there for a couple of seconds, resting on the side of my face. As he started to pull back, I reached up, grabbing his hand to place it back, leaving my hand resting on top of his. He kept his eyes locked on mine as I stared back at him. It felt as if he was staring into my soul. "Take My Breath Away" started to play in the background. It was my absolute favorite song from the movie.

"You make me happy," I said before I thought too hard about what I was saying. "Having you here with me makes me happy." Max stared, not speaking. Those few seconds seemed like an eternity. Had I said too much? Maybe I shouldn't have told him that. His expression softened, a flicker of adoration, maybe, but beneath it, he seemed to be contemplating something. How quiet he was being was starting to make me nervous

Then he leaned forward, his hand still cupping my face as his lips met mine. His lips were soft and he kissed me so tenderly. I kissed him back as the heat traveled from my lips down my entire body, like a flame along a line of gasoline. I moved my hand to the back of his neck, running my fingers through his hair, gripping slightly as I tugged him closer. He responded, gently pressing his body against mine.

His kiss was still gentle but more intense at the same time. His tongue grazed my bottom lip, and I let out a small gasp, parting my lips, letting his tongue meet mine. He groaned quietly. That sound awakened something inside me that had been stagnant for a year. Heat pooled low in my belly, and I wrapped my other arm around him. I tugged at him gently, signaling for him to move on top go me. He pulled back for a second, an "Are you sure?" look in his eyes. I nodded, wrapping my hands in his hair, pulling him back to my lips.

Then, he was above me, kissing me like I hadn't been kissed in such a long time. Max had always been a gentleman, and even as he kissed me, running his tongue along mine, gently gripping my hair, he was still holding his body up, so as not to press against me too closely. I wrapped my legs around his waist, pulling him down until our bodies were flush. He groaned against my mouth again as I gently bit his lip, pushing his body more firmly against mine.

I moved my hands down his sides and slipped them under his shirt, feeling his warm skin. I ran my fingertips up his back and felt a shiver run through his body. I lifted the hem of his shirt and pulled it upward. He pulled back from my lips, yanking the shirt over his head. I admired his shirtless frame for only a second before he was back against me. His lips found my jaw, then my neck, nibbling and sucking gently, leaving sparks of electricity along his path. Then his attention was back on my lips, kissing me like he had been waiting forever for this.

His left hand tightened in my hair while his right hand made its way to my hip, his fingers gripping my skin. He ground down against me, and I arched up to meet him. He took in a shaky breath, and I tightened my legs around him. My mind was foggy with desire. I never knew I needed Max this badly, in this way, but it felt so right, like my body already knew but was waiting for my brain to catch up.

Max pulled back from my lips, and it felt cold, a loss I didn't want to feel. We were both breathing heavily, and he was holding himself up on his hands, looking down at me. His eyes had a look that I had never seen from him before, almost primal. I wondered if he felt the same way I did. He must have, with everything that had just happened.

He brushed my hair away from my face and then sat back on his heels, grabbing a pillow to sit on his lap. I huffed a small laugh, knowing why he needed to hold that pillow. I pushed myself up, leaning back on my elbows, as I looked over at him. He looked back at me with an awkward smile. Neither of us could figure out how to start a sentence, so we sat in silence for a few long seconds.

My normal, not foggy with desire, brain started to come back into focus right as Max cleared his throat to speak. He sat on his butt with his legs out in front of him, pillow still on his lap, as we both started to talk at the same time. "Was-"

"I-"

"I'm sorry," we both said in unison. My god, what was wrong with us?

"You go," I said, quickly.

"It's fine. You can go," he said, smiling.

"I was just going to say that I enjoyed the movie," I laughed, and then bit my lip.

"Oh," he laughed. "Was it as good as it's always been?" He asked.

"I think it was better this time."

He smiled, looked down at his hands, and then back up at me. "I'd have to agree with you on that one."

"Should we go inside?" I asked as I looked toward the house.

"I guess so. I think I already have a few mosquito bites on me," he answered, finally taking the pillow off his lap, and laying it to the side. He stood up and stretched his arms high in the air as I went to turn the projector off. Max grabbed his shirt and slipped it back over his head. "Do we need to take any of this stuff inside?" He asked.

I thought about what my mom said earlier. "I'll grab the projector, but everything else can stay outside for the night," I answered. I unplugged the projector and picked it up as Max walked over to me, holding his hands out to take it.

He followed me inside to the kitchen. "Where do you want me to sit this?"

"You can just set it on the counter. Mom or dad will put it up in the morning."

He placed the projector on the counter before walking to the refrigerator. "I'm going to grab some water. Want one?"

"Yes, please."

He grabbed two bottles and walked over to where I was standing, holding one out to me. I opened the bottle and took a long swallow. "It was cooler when we first went out, wasn't it? It seems like it got hotter," he said after he had downed the entire bottle of water.

"Yeah, I noticed that too," I said with a smirk as I bumped him gently with my hip. We headed upstairs, and when we got to my room, I stopped, turning to Max. "Well, this is me," I said, suddenly feeling awkward.

He smiled. "I had to make sure you got to your door safely."

"And I greatly appreciate it. Are you sleepy?" I asked.

"Not really, but it's probably best that we get to bed. We did have an eventful day."

"I guess you're right," I agreed, pouting a little. I wondered if he wanted to avoid talking about everything that had just happened. That didn't seem like Max. Maybe he just wanted to save that discussion for the next day since it was getting late. I was still reeling from everything because I honestly didn't want it to stop. I wasn't sure if I'd even be able to sleep, but I figured I'd try to or at least lie in bed and try to sort out my thoughts for when we did have that conversation.

He opened his arms for a hug, and I leaned into him, resting my head on his chest. I squeezed my arms tightly around him as he leaned down, pressing a soft kiss into my hair. "Goodnight," he said, running a hand down my back.

"Goodnight," I replied, holding him a moment longer. Once I let go, he stepped back and smiled at me one last time before turning to walk to his room. I opened my door, went over to my bed without even turning the light on, and flopped down on my back.

I thought about how the day had started. Anxiety-ridden from visiting Justin's grave for the first time since the funeral, and then ended with Max and me watching a movie and everything that went with that. It was such an odd string of events, but it somehow worked out. I felt good. I felt happy, like truly happy for the first time in a very long time. I knew I still had the most challenging days ahead of me on Saturday and Sunday, but in that moment, I felt at peace, and I wanted to soak that in as much as I could.

Chapter 13

I woke up to light knocking on my bedroom door. I fluttered my eyes open and looked around the room. What time was it? I could see the sun coming in from the window, so I knew it wasn't too early. I rolled over and reached toward the bedside table to grab my phone. It was nine, so not terribly early, but I felt like I still needed a couple more hours of sleep. I heard the knocking again. "Come in," I called out, my voice cracking. I cleared my throat. "I'm awake."

My door eased open, and Max peeked his head inside. "Did I wake you?"

"No, you're fine." I was lying, but I didn't mind being woken up by Max.

He walked over to my bed and sat down on the edge. "I'm sorry if I woke you up. I wasn't sure if you were awake yet, and I was going to see if you wanted to go get breakfast," he said.

"I'm always down to get breakfast," I said, giving him a sleepy smile.

I stretched, trying to relieve my body of some of the stiffness, and then sat up. I wasn't used to swimming that much anymore. It had been so long since I'd even been home to use the pool. I watched Max as he looked around my room. His gaze paused at the bulletin board hanging above my desk again. It was the one with the photos of Justin and me that I saw him looking at on our first day back home.

I realized that Max had no idea what Justin looked like this whole time, so when we got home on Wednesday, that was his first time seeing him. I didn't keep photos of Justin and me displayed in my dorm room because I didn't think I'd be able to handle someone asking who he was and me having to explain that he was gone. I had photos on my phone, and a couple printed out that I kept in a journal, but I didn't show them to anyone, not even Max.

I had seen Vanessa because Max had a photo of the two of them in his dorm room and because, for a while, a photo of her was on his lock screen. I noticed he must have changed his lock screen a while ago because it wasn't a photo of her anymore. I watched Max as he looked at the photos for a few seconds longer. "That's Justin and me, from when we were babies up until spring break last year," I said.

Max turned back to me. "I didn't mean to stare. I thought that may be who it was."

"Oh, it's fine. I realized I had never shown you a photo of him before," I said with a soft smile as I looked over to the wall where the photos were hanging.

"It's okay. I know how hard it is to do that. I almost took the photos of Vanessa and me down in my dorm room because everyone always asked if it was my girlfriend from back home, so every time, I had to explain that she had passed away. Having to say it repeatedly to people made it more difficult. There's also the awkwardness of people not knowing what to say after I told them. So I understand," he said. His head dropped, and he looked down at his hands.

I never understood how Max always held it together so well. I could tell when things were heavy on his mind, but I'd only ever seen him cry a couple of times. He'd seen me a complete mess more times than I could count. A mess had been my default state all last year. My being okay had been a rare occurrence. I reached my hand out and placed it on top of his, giving it a little squeeze.

"That would be rough for anyone to have to say over and over again.

111

That's one of the reasons I didn't have any photos of Justin in my dorm room, or at least not where everyone could see. I don't think I could have handled answering that question that many times," I said.

He gave me a tender smile, and I squeezed his hand again. My stomach growled loudly, interrupting the moment, and he looked at me with a raised brow. "Hungry?" He asked.

"I am. Where were you thinking of for breakfast?" I asked as my stomach growled again.

"We can go to The Pancake House if you like their food."

"Like their food? They have the best pancakes in the whole state, possibly the country. Of course, I like their food," I said.

"Then it's settled. Whenever you're ready, just let me know," he said as he stood up and stretched. Just as Max turned back to me, I threw the covers back to get up, and he quickly jerked his head toward the door. I realized that it was because all I had on was a t-shirt and underwear. I threw the covers back over me, embarrassed. Usually, I would say it was no different from a bathing suit, but it currently was. My underwear was very sheer lace, so it did not hide much.

"Oh my god! I'm so sorry!" I said to Max.

"No, I'm sorry," he said, still turned toward the door. "I wouldn't have looked." This was kind of ridiculous, considering how close we had been last night, but I wasn't quite ready to be that exposed. He started walking toward the door.

"I'll just be a minute," I called after him. "It won't take me long."

"No worries. Take your time," he said before he shut the door behind him.

I got up to brush my teeth and hair before applying a little concealer and mascara. Then, I slipped on a white tank top and a pair of jean shorts, adding the necklace my parents had bought me, and a pair of sandals with leopard print straps to complete the outfit. I checked over myself in the mirror once more before I threw my phone into my purse and headed to Max's room. He opened the door right as I was about to knock. "All ready to go," I said.

"Let's go," he said as he turned back to grab his keys from the dresser.

We walked down the stairs and through the kitchen. The house was quiet, like it always was when my parents weren't here. I decided to use the front door instead of going through the garage since we'd be taking Max's car, and I regretted it the second I opened the door. As soon as we walked out, a car pulled over and stopped in front of my house. It was a brand new two-door Audi. The passenger side window rolled down, and I saw that it was Christy in the driver's seat. I had hoped that I could avoid speaking to Christy or Bill for as long as possible during my break, even all summer if I could somehow manage to never be outside at the same time as either of them, but apparently, that wasn't the case.

"Hey, Amelia! I didn't realize you were back home from college already," she called out to me.

I tried my best to keep a pleasant tone. "Yeah, I got back on Wednesday, so I haven't been home long," I said, internally rolling my eyes.

"How was your first year? I remember mine; it was so much fun," she said with a huge smile.

Was Christy really that dense? How did she think my first year of college was going to be when I'd just lost my best friend, her son, the summer before? I felt the anger start to spread through my stomach, and it took every ounce of willpower not to ask her how stupid she was for asking me that question. "Oh, it was as good as could be expected," I said, trying my best to keep the annoyance from seeping into my voice.

"Well, that's good, honey. Who's your friend?" She asked, nodding to Max. I looked over my shoulder at Max. He was giving me an "Are you okay?" look. He could tell something was wrong.

"I'm sorry, how rude of me," I said, a little ice seeping into my tone. "This is Max. He's my friend from, um, college." I didn't want to say, Oh, he's from my grief support group that I had to attend because your son died, and I'm a fucking wreck, while you seem just fine in your brand new car.

"Nice to meet you, Max," she called after him. Max nodded and threw a hand up in a slight wave. "Having some other friends could be good for you, Amelia. I've wondered how you've been holding up," Christy said, and I almost believed she cared.

"Yeah, well-" I said, but cut myself off before I said any more. I cleared my throat. "Is that a new car?" I asked.

"It is! Bill got it for me last week. I guess you could say a little pick-me-up gift, considering…" she let the sentence trail off.

I don't know if I could be more disgusted with a person, except Bill, of course. Yes, a new car to help cheer you up because the anniversary of your son's death from a car accident is coming up. I don't think she could be more tone deaf. They had to be the worst people on this planet. "Ah," I said because I didn't have anything else to say. What do you say to something like that?

"Maybe you and your parents could come over for dinner one night. We'd love to see you guys and hear how everything has been going," she said with a smile.

That sounded like the worst idea I could think of. Why would I want to go to their house to have dinner? I wondered if they thought that Justin had never told me about Bill. Did she really think I didn't know what was going on all those years? I was absolutely not going over for dinner, but I just wanted her to leave. I gave her a weak smile back. "Yeah, maybe!" I decided to push her a little. "Have you heard anything new?" I asked.

I saw her jaw tighten and then release before she spoke. "No, nothing new. I'm sorry, honey, but I don't think there's anything left to look into. It was just a terrible accident," she said with a bit of annoyance in her voice.

"Well, if you hear anything, let me know," I said sourly.

"Of course," she said. "I'd better let you guys get on your way, and I've got Zumba, so I don't want to be late."

"Yeah, wouldn't want to miss that," I said.

"It was nice seeing you and nice to meet you, Max," she said as she threw her hand up and waved.

"You too," I said with a tight-lipped smile. Max threw his hand up again and nodded. She rolled her window up as she drove off. We were still standing on the front steps, and I let out a loud sigh.

"Are you okay?" He asked.

"I hate her so much," I said, not trying to disguise the anger.

"I could tell," he said.

I started toward the car with Max in tow. He clicked the unlock button and walked around me, getting to the passenger door before I did, so he could open it for me. I smiled up at him. He made the anger inside me dissipate a little. He was such a calming presence that I appreciated so much, especially in that moment.

As we started on our way to The Pancake House, I sat quietly for a couple of minutes. Max never pried. He always waited for me to speak when I was ready and felt like talking about whatever was bothering me. I loved that about him because I hated when people pushed and tried to make me talk when I didn't want to. The anxiety crept up my chest, but I took a deep breath and tried to push it away before speaking. "That was Justin's mom, Christy," I said.

"I figured it must have been someone who knew him," he said. "You said his house was close to yours, right?"

"Two houses down, on the opposite side of the road," I answered.

"Oh, I didn't realize it was that close."

"Yeah, so, unfortunately, it's a little difficult to avoid Christy," I said.

"If you don't mind me asking, why do you hate her so much?" Max asked curiously.

I hadn't told Max about Justin's parents. I only ever talked about how we had been friends since birth, and that he had passed away in a car accident. I felt like I talked about Justin a lot to Max, but I guess it was mostly about how I missed him and how much it hurt; talking about a lot of the details of everything was hard. I never shared the details when we were in the group either. I barely even spoke about it with my therapist.

"It's a long story. I don't know if I want to get into it over breakfast," I said. We were pulling into the parking lot of The Pancake House, and I didn't think it was the best place to have this conversation, especially if someone who knew them happened to overhear. Not that I cared about protecting Christy or Bill, but knowing how Bill was scared me, and I didn't know what he would do if he heard that I was telling his secret.

"I understand," he said as he parked. We got out, and as we walked up to the door, Max held it open for me. A hostess was standing at the desk, looking down at her book. She was pretty and looked about our age. Max stepped around me, walking towards the hostess desk as I followed. "Table for two, please," he said to her.

She looked up, surprised, before running around the desk and wrapping Max in a huge hug. "Maxy! I didn't know you were back in town!" She exclaimed, still holding him in a hug. He put one arm around her, giving her a half-hug back.

"I got back into town on Wednesday," he said as she released him.

"Devon and James were here last night, and they didn't say anything about you being home yet. I'm going to get them next time they're here," the hostess said, a slight southern accent coming through.

"To be fair, he probably doesn't know. I just dropped my things off at home, and I've been staying with my friend Amelia since I've been back. Mom and Dad are out of town still," he said to her. "And this is Amelia, by the way." He gestured toward me.

"Nice to meet you, Amelia," she said, pulling me into a hug I wasn't expecting. "I'm Stephanie, or Steph, Max's friend and his parents' favorite hostess, but don't tell the others that." She whispered the last part.

"Oh, your parents eat here a lot?" I asked Max.

Steph gave me an odd look and then turned to Max. "Does she not know?"

"I forgot to mention it," he said to her. "My parents-"

Steph cut him off. "His parents are the owners," she said. "They are the best bosses anyone could ask for."

"Your parents own The Pancake House?" I looked at Max, surprised.

"They do, and a few other restaurants. That's why they travel for work so much," he answered.

I had been eating here forever and never knew who owned it. It had always been the best breakfast restaurant in the state, maybe even the whole southeast. People came to Cape Falls specifically to eat here. How had I been friends with Max for almost a year and still have so much to learn about him? I had been so wrapped up in my own pain that I didn't even know these things. We always talked about our likes, dislikes, movies, books, and school, but I guess we never got into family stuff or too deep into our relationships. "Wow. I had no idea," I said to him.

He gave me an apologetic smile, then turned back to Steph. "Are there any small booths open right now?"

"For Maxy? Always!" she said with a big smile. She grabbed two menus and led us to the dining area to the right. In the back, next to a huge window, was a small unoccupied booth. She gestured toward it, and Max and I sat down across from each other. She handed me a menu and then looked at Max. "Do you want a menu, or are you getting the same thing you always get?" She asked.

"I heard mom and dad added some new things to the menu, so I'll check it out," he said.

She handed him a menu. "Your waitress will be by to get you guys' order shortly," she said cheerfully, before walking back to the front.

I looked at Max. "I can't believe you never told me that your parents own The Pancake House!"

"It never came up, I guess," he said. "It seemed weird to randomly say, like bragging or something."

"I guess I get that," I said. "Is that why your pancakes were so good yesterday morning?"

"Maybe," he chuckled. "I learned from the best."

"You definitely did."

"What are you going to order?" He asked me as he flipped open his menu.

I looked down at the menu and scanned the pancake options. "I think I'll get a little crazy this morning. Maybe the Oreo pancakes with sausage, scrambled eggs, and grits?" I answered.

"That sounds good. I think I'll get the same thing. I haven't tried the Oreo pancakes since they recently added them."

As if perfectly timed, our waitress walked up to the table. "Max! Hey! Steph said you were here. It's been forever!" She said.

"I know, I know. I feel bad that I haven't been by in so long, but I've been at school and didn't come home many weekends," he answered apologetically.

"Amelia, this is Luna. Luna, this is Amelia," he said, introducing us.

"It's so nice to meet you!" she said as she stuck a hand out to me.

I reached my hand out and shook hers. "It's nice to meet you, too."

"Max never brings anyone here because he thinks we are all too much for a new person. You must be special if he brought you to meet all of the work family," she said with a grin.

"Oh wow, really?" I said, looking across the table to Max.

His face flushed. "Well, I mean-"

Luna cut him off. "Are you guys ready to order?" She asked as she gave Max a wink.

"We are, actually," he answered. "We'll both have the Oreo pancakes, sausage, scrambled eggs, and grits, please."

"Nice! The Oreo pancakes are so good. Your parents added them to the menu a few months ago, and they've been a hit. What about drinks?" She asked.

"I'll just take a water," Max answered.

"I'll take a water too, please," I said, smiling at her.

"No problem! I'll put this in, and it should be out shortly!" She said, turning to walk toward the kitchen.

"Everyone who works here is so nice," I said to Max.

"They are. Almost everyone has worked here for a long time. They are like a second family to us," he said. "My parents believe having happy and taken care of employees is the secret to having a successful business."

"It seems like they must be right about that," I said.

He smiled. "They do all right." I could tell he didn't like to brag or have people brag about his life. It was sweet how modest and humble he was.

Talking about his parents reminded me that I never asked when they were coming home after he called them yesterday; it was supposed to be today, but I wasn't sure what time. Truthfully, I didn't want him to go home yet. I enjoyed having him there when I woke up every morning. It had been so nice not having to be alone all day while my parents were working, and I loved Max's company. Of course, he needs to go home and spend time with his parents at some point. I couldn't keep him to myself all summer, no matter how much I wanted to. "Speaking of your parents, I never asked what they said when you called them yesterday."

"They were supposed to be coming home today, but the new restaurant they are working on getting open had a few setbacks, and they need to stay a few extra days. They said hopefully they'd be home by

Monday evening," Max answered.

"Aw, that sucks." I felt bad that he'd been home a few days and still hadn't been able to see his parents yet.

"It's okay. I'm used to them having to travel so much. Once they started expanding and opening more restaurants, they had to do a lot of traveling."

"You know you're more than welcome to stay at my house for as long as you want to," I said.

"I don't want to impose," he said, looking down at the table.

"It's not a problem at all. My parents don't mind. They love you," I said with a smile.

"I don't want to drive you crazy being there all the time either," he said, giving me a playful smile back.

"You could never." I reached across the table and placed my hand on his. "It's the opposite. I want you there. I just don't want you to feel like I'm holding you hostage," I laughed.

"If you're holding me hostage, then Stockholm Syndrome doesn't seem so bad," he said and winked at me. He flipped his hand over and laced his fingers with mine.

I blushed as heat crept across my skin where our hands touched. We sat like that, holding hands across the table, until we saw Luna making her way back to us. We both pulled our hands back at the same time. When Luna walked up, she looked back and forth between us, eyes squinted, a smile playing at her lips. She lowered her tray to the table, setting our plates and drinks in front of us.

"Do y'all need anything else right now?" She asked.

"I'm good. Thank you," I said as I looked down at the plate. "This looks amazing."

"Max?" She said as she looked over at him.

"I think I'm good for now, too. Thanks, Luna," he said, smiling quickly.

We started eating immediately, and the food was terrific. I glanced at Max as he ate and wondered how I had gotten so lucky to have Max as my friend, or possibly more now. We still hadn't talked about last night or where we wanted to take this, but I didn't think it was the best breakfast conversation, especially since most of the people in this restaurant knew Max. It was a conversation that I was looking forward to having, though.

Chapter 14

After we finished breakfast, we ran a few errands. I needed to stop by the store for some essentials, and Max wanted to buy groceries to cook dinner for my parents when they got home. He said it was the least he could do, considering they'd been letting him stay and feeding him. I told him that it wasn't necessary, but he insisted. I enjoyed cooking, so I thought it could be fun to help him make dinner for my parents. It was also a plus that it kept my mind off what the next day was as well.

Last night and this morning had been so nice. I was feeling much better than I expected, but as it got later in the day, my mind drifted to what tomorrow was. Tomorrow was June the ninth. It was the date of Justin's wreck, and it's what was written on Justin's headstone as the date of his death. Technically, I didn't find out until the morning of the tenth because he'd wrecked late that night, but that was the night my life changed forever, even if I didn't know it until the following day.

The thoughts swirled in my head, and I tried to stay focused on anything but that. We had been home for a while, hanging out and watching TV to pass the time. We didn't feel like swimming much because we had been in the sun too much the day before. It was starting to get close to time for my parent to be home, so I thought we should probably start cooking soon to ensure everything would be almost done by the time they were home.

Max got the bags from the refrigerator and put everything on the counter. He decided on one of his favorites since I said my parents weren't picky. We bought everything to make Cajun chicken breast with peppers and onions, and some asparagus and rice on the side. It wasn't too much prep, but we did have to get a move on if we were going to get everything done. I knew my mom would make a big fuss over Max cooking dinner. She already loved him, but this would solidify it further.

I got out the cutting boards, knives, and a couple of plates. "Chicken or vegetables?" I asked as I handed Max a cutting board and a knife.

"I can prep the chicken if you want to cut the vegetables. I know how much you hate touching raw meat," he said.

He wasn't wrong. I enjoyed cooking, but that was the one thing that I hated. I could prep the chicken if I had to, but it still grossed me out. "Yes, please," I said with a laugh. "Did you want them diced or just sliced?" I asked as I got the rice cooker from the cabinet.

"Sliced would be good," he said.

It didn't take long to get everything prepped and cooking. We had about fifteen minutes until my parents would be home, so while Max cooked, I set the table and lit a couple of candles. I found the nice serving dishes and set them out so Max could put the food in them when everything was done.

I hadn't realized how hungry I was, but the food smelled amazing, and my stomach was starting to growl. I walked over to the stove, where Max was, because I wanted to peek at the food to see how much longer it would be. Max scooped a small piece of chicken up on the spatula and held it out to me. "Taste it and let me know what you think," he said.

I went to grab the chicken with my fingers, not thinking about the fact that it had just come out of the pan. I yelped and dropped the chicken on the floor. "You could tell it was that bad without even tasting it?"

Max asked with a laugh.

"Yes, I just knew it was so terrible that I couldn't bring myself to try it," I said as I nudged him with my elbow before grabbing a paper towel and bending down to pick up the chicken from the floor.

Max picked up another small piece with the spatula and brought it to his mouth. He blew on it for a few seconds, then held it out to me again. I started to reach for it, but he pulled it back. "You know what, maybe I should do it just to be safe," he said as he gave me a teasing grin. He picked the chicken off the spatula with his fingers and held it out to me.

I rolled my eyes playfully and opened my mouth. He placed it in my mouth, gently brushing his fingers against my bottom lip. The chicken was so tender and had the perfect amount of spice. Max could cook; I'd give him that. "It's amazing," I said after I finished chewing.

"Yeah?" He asked, eyebrows raised. "Is it too much spice, or is the chicken tough at all?"

"No, it's perfect just how it is," I said. I watched him take a bite of his own. He chewed for a few seconds with a contemplative look on his face.

"It's decent. It could be a little better, though," he said.

"It's delicious, I promise."

He smiled. "I'm glad you think so. Hopefully, your parents think so too."

"They will," I said as I heard the garage door open. "Speak of the devil," I said with a laugh. A few moments later, the door from the garage swung open as my parents came bustling through.

"Hi, honey!" Mom said as she walked in. "What are you guys up to? And what smells so good?" She asked as she looked over to the stove where Max was finishing up.

"Max made you guys dinner, well, all of us dinner," I said, leaning against the counter next to the refrigerator.

"Oh, Max, you are the sweetest! You didn't have to do that," she said, setting her purse down on the bar. "Brian, isn't he the sweetest?" Mom said to Dad.

"That is very nice, but you're the guest here," my dad added.

"You guys have been so kind to me, letting me stay here and feeding me, so I wanted to show my gratitude," he said, still stirring the chicken in the pan.

"You owe us nothing, honey. We love having you here," Mom said as Dad nodded his head in agreement.

"I like to cook, so I don't mind," he replied.

"Just don't feel like you have to." Mom smiled at him. "I'm going to put my bag up and change clothes, and we'll be right back down."

Max and I got everything into serving dishes, arranging them perfectly on the table, and then took our seats across from each other. I felt his foot brush my leg. I wasn't sure if it was an accident or on purpose. I looked up at him, and he gave me a quick grin. On purpose. I rubbed my foot up his leg, and he looked at me with a raised eyebrow. I blushed, looking away just as my parents returned to the dining room.

"So what's for dinner, Max?" Mom asked, looking to him with a smile.

"It's one of my personal favorites. Amelia said you guys liked almost anything, so it's Cajun chicken breast with peppers and onions, asparagus, and rice on the side," he said as he looked between them.

"That sounds amazing. Earlier, I was saying I was in the mood for something with a little spice," Mom replied.

"If it tastes half as good as it smells, then it's going to be great," Dad said as he scanned the table, looking at all the dishes.

After a few bites, Mom asked, "What did you guys do today?"

"We went out for breakfast this morning," I answered.

"Where did you guys go?" Dad asked.

"We went to The Pancake House," Max replied.

"I just love The Pancake House," Mom said. "Their breakfast is unmatched, but it's been a while since we've been."

"We could all go to breakfast there sometime," Max suggested.

"That would be lovely!" Mom said.

"You know, Max knows the owners," I said, looking across the table at him.

"You do? If it's the same people that still own it, Amelia's dad and I went to high school with them."

Max flushed before he replied. "My parents are the owners."

"Your parents are Ana and Steven?" Mom asked.

"They are," Max answered.

"I had no idea! We should all have dinner together sometime," she said to Max excitedly. "We need to have them over."

"Mom," I said, giving her a "not right now" look. I didn't know where Max and I's friendship or relationship was going right now, and I hadn't even met Max's parents yet. I was worried that she might freak Max out.

She got the message I was trying to send, thankfully, and continued, "If that's okay with you guys."

"That would be great," Max said. "I'm sure my parents would love to." He seemed genuine and not freaked out, or he wasn't showing it, so I assumed that was a good sign.

"Did you guys do anything fun?" She asked, changing the subject.

"Not really. We just watched TV until we started cooking."

"That's good, though," Dad chimed in. "You guys need to have that time to relax and do nothing while school is out. I remember how stressful college could be."

"This year was stressful for more reasons than one," I said as I pushed the last few pieces of chicken around the plate with my fork. My mood dropped slightly, and Mom gave me a sympathetic look. "I almost forgot, I saw Christy today. She was driving down the road and stopped to speak just as Max and I were leaving to get breakfast."

A sour look came across Mom's face for a second before she spoke.

126

"Oh? What did she say?"

"Nothing important. Bill got her a new car to help make her feel better or something stupid, and she hasn't found out anything new about the accident," I said before I realized how angry I sounded when I spoke about them.

"That's a little tone deaf, don't you think?" Mom said to no one in particular.

"I'll say," Dad replied. I could hear the annoyance in both of their voices when they spoke of her. I knew why I hated Christy and Bill, but they didn't know about what happened to Justin while he was growing up. I wish I had told them, but Justin didn't want me to tell anyone, and I was a dumb kid who didn't want to lose my friend. I was curious where their hatred of Christy and Bill came from, considering they all used to be friends when Justin and I were little.

"Tone deaf is an understatement," I said.

I glanced at Max. He was watching us, just listening, and taking in the conversation. I'm sure it confused him, but he never pressed me for information. Funny enough, that quality made me want to tell him everything. I felt like I could confide in him about it all. I didn't realize I had been staring until he nudged my leg under the table and smiled. I smiled back, embarrassed, and darted my eyes down to my plate.

"Max, that was the best Cajun chicken I think I've ever had," Dad said.

"It was," Mom agreed.

Max's face flushed. He was not good at taking compliments. It always made him blush. "Thank you. I'm glad you guys liked it," he said.

"Now, you guys go do whatever. Your dad and I will clean up since you cooked," Mom said.

"I can clean up. I use so many dishes when I'm cooking," Max argued.

"Nope," my father said, matter-of-factly. "You go enjoy your evening. We've got this."

"Go on, now," Mom said, getting up from the table, playfully pushing me up and out of my chair.

"Fine," I said, holding my hands up in mock surrender as I backed away from the table.

"Thank you," I called out to my parents as Max and I headed up the stairs.

"Of course," Mom said.

It was only about six-thirty, so it wasn't anywhere close to bedtime yet. I thought Max and I could watch another movie or play a game or something for a while. I wanted to talk to him about last night, but I was a little nervous to bring it up. I was looking forward to knowing how he felt, but this would be a turning point in our friendship, and although I was pretty sure of what I wanted, it didn't make me any less nervous because it wasn't just about how I felt.

It depended on how Max felt and what he wanted, as well. He hadn't dated anyone since Vanessa that I knew of. So, I wasn't sure how ready he was to potentially start dating again. He kissed me back and was just as into it as I was last night, but that didn't necessarily mean he was mentally ready to jump back into a relationship. When we got to my room, I stopped and turned to Max. "It's still pretty early, and I'm not really tired yet. Do you want to play a game?"

He chuckled.

"What?" I asked.

"You sounded like the puppet from Saw asking, 'Do you want to play a game?'" he said, deepening his voice and laughing again.

"Oh, shut up," I said, laughing and playfully swatting at his arm.

"Yeah, we can play a game as long as I don't have to dig a key from behind my eye or something," he said, giving me a wide-eyed look. I rolled my eyes and pushed my bedroom door open.

Chapter 15

Max and I had played a round of Monopoly and were sitting on my bed while I flipped through Netflix, trying to find something to watch. Monopoly had taken us a couple of hours, so we didn't have the energy to play another game. I looked over at Max to see him looking at the pictures of Justin again. I wondered what intrigued him so much about them.

"Ever since I saw these pictures, I have been trying to figure out why Justin looked so familiar to me," Max said out of nowhere.

"Oh? Why do you think so?" I asked.

"Do you remember Justin dating someone named Devon? He looks like someone my brother brought to the house a couple of times."

I thought about it, trying to see if the name rang a bell. It was hard to remember unless it was someone he brought around a lot. "I think I remember Justin telling me about someone named Devon that he met at a concert the fall before his accident," I said.

"Yeah, that sounds right. That was a couple of months before Devon met James, so I think that's when I remember seeing him," he said, still looking at the pictures.

"Small world. This town isn't huge, so you're bound to see most people in it, but it's funny that my best friend and your brother dated, and now you and I..." I trailed off.

He looked over at me. "You and I?" He asked.

"That you and I are friends now," I finished.

"Oh." A look of disappointment flashed across his face.

"Like, we are right this second, but we could be... I don't know, something else eventually," I continued. "I say that because I'm not exactly sure what we're doing. It's different, and I wanted to ask you where your head was at."

"What do you want?" He asked.

"I don't know. I mean, I do know, but I don't know, you know?" I said, looking over at Max. He looked back at me with a confused expression. "What do you want?" I asked, repeating his question back to him.

"I like you and enjoy being with you and around you," he started. "I don't want to push you if you're not ready for anything yet. I don't want you to feel any pressure at all. I love being your friend, and I'm happy to keep it that way if that's what you want," he answered.

My heart melted at his words. He was the kindest and most considerate person I had ever met. It made me even more sure that what I wanted was the right choice. "I like you too," I said. "I'm nervous, to say the least, because it's a big step for me, but I think I would like to try this if you're up for it."

The most adorable grin I had ever seen spread across his face. "I would love that."

We still had things we needed to talk about, and I felt it was best to get it out of the way sooner rather than later. "Are you sure you're ready for that, too? It's no rush from me either if you're not ready," I said.

"I am. It has taken a while to process everything and get to where I am now. When I first lost her, I didn't think I'd want to try again for a very long time. Losing someone you love is traumatic. That's something you also know very well, but you've helped me so much. I know I didn't show it all that much, but I was in a terrible place when we first met in the group. My parents were really worried about me, and so was everyone else. Therapy and our friendship helped pull me out of a hole, and I'll always be grateful for that. I feel like I'm at a place now where I want to try again, with you," Max said. He looked different, younger. He was so vulnerable in that moment with me, and I could tell how nervous he was to say those things.

The tears welled in my eyes as he spoke, but I blinked them away. He made me want to try again, too. I knew Justin and I weren't dating, but a lifelong friendship being suddenly ripped away put a scar on me that I didn't think would ever fully mend; but Max had been my rock and had helped glue a few pieces of my former self back together. I felt like I owed Max the truth about my feelings for Justin, even if it didn't make a difference anymore. It was something that I needed to tell him, but I wasn't sure how to start.

"I'm glad that I could help you in some way. You've helped me more than I could ever explain, and it feels good to have someone who understands. Not many people do, or at least not many people in my life. It feels like someone ripped a hole in my chest and never sewed it back together," I said.

"I don't think that feeling ever fully goes away," Max replied.

"I don't think so either."

"Can I ask you something? You don't have to answer if you don't want to," Max said.

"Of course. You can ask me anything."

He glanced back at the wall where my pictures hung, then back to me. "Did you love him? I know you grew up together, so of course, you loved him like a friend, but was it ever more than that?" I hesitated for a second, deciding what to say or where to start, and if I should mention the kiss a few weeks before his accident. "It's okay if you don't want to talk about it," Max added quickly.

"I don't mind," I said. "I'm just not sure how to answer it. I always tried to ignore or push those feelings away because I didn't want to ruin our friendship, so if I ever had those feelings, I tried to pretend that I didn't. I watched Justin go through many relationships, and there were times when I'd get jealous, but I did my best to never show it. I think deep down I always loved him in that way, but I was worried it wouldn't be reciprocated." I looked at Max hesitantly. I wasn't sure what his reaction would be to that new information.

"You never told him how you felt?" He asked curiously.

"No, not exactly," I said, thinking back to the drunken night I'd kissed him when he came to check on me.

"Not exactly?"

"One night, a few weeks before his accident, I got very drunk and he came over to make sure I was okay, and I kissed him. We kissed. I don't know if that counted as me telling him how I felt, though," I said. It felt good to tell someone that out loud.

"You guys didn't talk about it?" He asked.

I looked down at my hands. "The next morning, I think Justin started to mention it, but I pretended I didn't remember anything that happened because I was drunk, so he never brought it up again, then he..." I trailed off.

"Oh man, that's got to be tough. I'm so sorry," Max said. He was so sincere, which was kind of ironic since he liked me and he was genuinely sorry that I didn't get to tell another guy how I felt about him. But that was just how Max was. He was kind and always put others' feelings above his own.

"It's my fault. I got scared and didn't take the chance, so now I'll never know," I said. "I don't want to live my life scared anymore. Some risks are worth taking because the outcome could be something great, but you never really know until you try. So, I want to try."

"It is really scary at times," Max said. "It just depends on who's worth the risk of getting hurt for."

I smiled at him. "I don't want to make the same mistake twice."

"I'll do my best to make it worth the risk," he said, smiling back at me.

I moved closer to him, placing a gentle kiss on his lips. It was so easy with Max. It never felt forced or unnatural, and we just fit. I pulled back and placed my head on his shoulder, letting my body relax into his. I felt him shift, and then he cleared his throat.

"I know that tomorrow is the anniversary of Justin's accident, and I was wondering what you needed from me. Do you want me to let you be alone, find something to do to distract you, or just be there with you?" He asked. "I don't want to make the day any worse. I know the anniversary of losing someone is always a tough day, so I want to do whatever you need me to, even if it's leave you alone and let you lie in bed all day."

I wasn't sure how I would feel tomorrow or if tomorrow would affect me as much as my birthday, since that's the day I found out about the accident. I didn't know if I'd want a distraction or if I would want to stay in bed.

"I'll let you know in the morning. Right now, I'm not sure what I'll need, but I will definitely let you know," I said as I lifted my head from his shoulder and looked at him. "June the ninth is the day that he wrecked, well, the night he wrecked, but I didn't find out until the next morning when I woke up, so I don't know how I'll feel yet. It's all so surreal. I know he's gone, but it being a full year since I've talked to or seen him, it's just so strange, you know?"

"It is weird. That's how I felt in April. It seemed to really sink in on that one-year mark. Loss is strange. It's almost like you never fully process it. You're always expecting to hear their voice when you answer your phone or for them to walk through your door eventually, but it never happens. I don't think the disappointment of that never happening again ever goes away," Max said.

He was right. Every time my phone rang, I expected to see Justin's name pop up, or when I looked out my bedroom window, I expected to see the light in his room on or hear him yelling "Lia" from downstairs.

I missed him. No matter how much I'd been distracted the last two days or how happy I was hanging out with Max, I still missed Justin and felt that emptiness down to my core. A tear ran down my cheek, and I looked up to see Max looking at me with a worried expression.

"I'm sorry. I didn't mean to upset you," he said.

"No, it's okay. I was thinking about what you were saying, and it's true. You never really get over it," I said as I wiped the tear away. "I think all the unanswered questions make it that much worse."

"Unanswered questions?" Max asked.

"They still aren't exactly sure what happened to Justin," I said as I played with my hands in my lap.

"I thought it was a car accident," he said with a curious expression.

"It was, but they never figured out what caused him to wreck. I think they assume he over-corrected, but he was usually a very careful driver."

Max's eyes went wide. "They didn't?"

I shook my head. "He wrecked coming over Ashbury Bridge and broke through the barrier. His windshield was busted out, so he was ejected from the car, but it just all seems so strange to me."

"That's terrible. I'm so sorry. I remember that bridge being blocked off at the beginning of last summer while they fixed the barrier, but I had no idea that was where he wrecked," Max said.

"Yeah, I think they could have investigated more, but Justin's mom gave up so easily," I said.

"Is that why you dislike his parents?" He asked.

"That, among other things. The hate for Christy and Bill goes back pretty far," I said.

"What happened?" He asked. "If you don't mind me asking," he added.

"When Justin and I were younger, his parents divorced, and Christy married Bill. It wasn't long after they'd gotten married that I noticed bruises on Justin one summer when we went swimming, and he told me that Bill had been hitting him," I said, not meeting Max's eyes.

"He never told anyone?"

"No, and he made me promise not to tell anyone. Bill told Justin that he had better not tell anyone, and he was scared. I was a kid, too, so I was scared to lose my friend or cause it to get any worse if I told. I wish I had done something, but I didn't know what to do," I said as tears ran down my cheeks.

Max moved closer, pulling me into a hug. I let him hold me while the tears fell. This was the first time I had told anyone about what happened to Justin. I trusted Max and didn't feel like I had to keep anything from him. He made me feel safe. I wish I could have kept Justin safe from the abuse, from the wreck, from everything.

Sometimes I felt like I failed as a friend. Realistically, I know there was nothing I could have done about the wreck, but I could have possibly kept him from Bill at the very least. I always tried to get him to stay the night at my house as much as our parents would allow, but it was still never enough.

Max stroked my hair gently as he held me. I wrapped my arms around him and rested against his body as I waited out the tears. We stayed like that for a few minutes, not speaking, just holding each other.

When the tears finally stopped, I sniffled, hoping to keep my nose from running, and pulled back from Max. "Thank you for being here."

"Of course. I'll be here as long as you want me to be," he said with a soft smile.

"I think I want to lie down. Having too many emotions makes me tired," I said with a chuckle, trying to lighten the mood.

"Okay, I'll go so you can get some rest," Max said as he moved to stand up.

I put my hand out, placing it on his arm. "Will you stay with me tonight?" I asked.

"If you want me to," he answered.

I stood up, pulled back the blankets, and climbed into bed. Max turned the light off and joined me as I clicked on a random show to play while we fell asleep. He lay on his back, arms folded behind his head. I wiggled closer, resting my head on his chest. He unfolded one arm, tucking it around me as he pulled me in.

I looked up at him. His eyes were so beautiful that I could have stared at them all night if I weren't so exhausted. Being cuddled up to Max calmed all the thoughts and emotions that danced around inside my head just enough for my eyelids to get heavy. Max looked at me and placed a small kiss on my forehead. I gave him a sleepy smile and then turned my attention to the TV as I drifted off to sleep.

Chapter 16

When I woke up, the sun was peeking through my window. I looked over to see Max still fast asleep next to me. He was lying on his back, arms up by his head. He looked so peaceful that I didn't want to get out of bed and disturb him, so I decided to grab my phone to check the time and scroll while I waited for him to wake up.

It was ten-thirty. We had slept in, and I actually felt rested and ready for the day for once. Having Max in bed next to me definitely made me sleep better. Most days, I slept enough hours, but never felt like it was enough. I clicked on Instagram, and the first post was Amber's, Justin's ex-girlfriend. It was a picture of her and Justin smiling on a boat out on the lake. The caption was *Can't believe it's already been a year. The world doesn't seem as bright without you in it *Heart emoji**.

I wanted to vomit. Although I agreed with her caption, I hated reading it from her. She was always so nasty to me and had an attitude with Justin almost anytime I was around them. She didn't get to play the mourning girlfriend. They had broken up before his accident, so she wasn't even his girlfriend anymore, and I heard that she was already seeing someone else before he died. She didn't have the right. No one knew him like I did. No one was as close to him as I was, and no one else had their heart ripped out of their chest a year ago like I had.

Of course, everyone was sad. They lost an amazing person. But some of the people posting weren't even there for him when he was alive. They wanted the attention of losing a friend, but never had the friend in the first place. I lost my lifelong friend. We had been friends since before I could even remember, since birth, and nothing compared to the hurt I felt this past year. Even Justin's own mother didn't seem as bothered by it as she should have been. It seemed like everyone had moved on and put this behind them. I just didn't understand.

I knew I was trying to be happy and find some ounce of peace to get back to a normal life, but it was a year later, not fifteen minutes later. It took me a year to even try to start doing those things. Everyone else was back to business as usual, not even a week after the accident. I scrolled past Amber's post only to come to another post a few more down. Justin and Brayden were shotgunning beers, and both were covered in sweat.

I could deal with Brayden's post. Brayden had been a good friend to Justin and let him stay at his house a lot whenever Bill was at his worst. Brayden didn't know what Bill had done, but he knew Justin didn't like being around him often. Brayden's post was captioned *I know you're shotgunning beers and being the life of the party wherever you are. You'd better practice up before I get there if you want to beat me. RIP Buddy.*

A tear rolled down my cheek. Brayden texted me a few times throughout the year, asking how I was and checking if I was doing okay. He was Justin's closest friend other than me, so I thought he and I probably felt it the hardest. I double-tapped his post, liking it. As if on cue, a text popped up across the top of my screen from him.

Brayden: Hey. How are you doing today?

Me: I just woke up a few minutes ago, so right now, I'm okay. How are you?

Brayden: I'm alright. Definitely been better.

Me: Yeah, same. It's weird that it's been a year already.

Brayden: It's still hard to believe. I keep waiting for him to pull into my driveway.

Me: Since I've been home, I've been waiting for him to walk into my room. It's hard to believe that it will never happen again.

Brayden: It's insane. Do you have anything to do today to keep you distracted?

I looked over at Max, still sleeping, and smiled. I was happy to have him here; I guess I needed him more today than I thought I would.

Me: A friend is staying with me, so I have them here.

I knew that Max and I weren't just friends anymore, but I didn't know what to call him yet. The term boyfriend felt too official since we had just decided to try and see how this goes the night before.

Brayden: I'm glad you have someone there with you. I've been thinking about you all week. I knew it would be a tough few days.

Me: It sure hasn't been easy.

Brayden: Tell me about it.

Brayden: If you ever need some company or someone to talk to about everything, you know you can always text me, or since you're home for the summer, we could grab lunch sometime.

I had only ever hung out with Brayden with Justin, but he was never anything but nice to me, so I didn't see why not. Besides, he was the only friend of Justin's who had texted to ask if there were updates on his accident or how I was doing.

Me: That would be nice. Let me know when you're not working.

Like many others from our high school, Brayden went to Briar Glen Tech. He had been working around his school schedule since the start of the year, and I figured that since school was out, he would probably have more hours.

Brayden: Will do. Let me know if you need anything today or tomorrow. Don't hesitate to text or call if you're having a hard time.

Me: Thank you. I appreciate it. And you too.

Max began to stir beside me, and I looked over as he rubbed his eyes. He looked so cute with his hair disheveled and his eyes still puffy. I rolled onto my side to face him. "Good morning, sleepyhead."

"Good morning," he said with a sleepy smile as he stretched his arms up over his head.

"How'd you sleep?"

"Better than I usually do," he answered. "What about you?"

"I slept pretty well, too."

"Good," he said, rolling onto his side so he was facing me, too.

"Maybe I just need to sleep with you to sleep better." The words left my mouth before I realized how they sounded.

His eyebrows shot up. "Oh?" He said, giving me a grin.

"You know what I mean," I said, rolling my eyes. I liked playful Max. I think I had mostly seen solemn Max or comforting Max because of how I had been all year. Of course, we joked around with each other. It wasn't all sadness while we were at school, but it had been more playful between us since we had come home. It felt new and exciting. It made me happy, even when the sadness was looming just overhead.

"Do I?" He asked playfully as he put his arm around my waist, pulling me closer.

"I think so," I said, blushing as I looked at him, his face just inches from mine.

He smiled and kissed my forehead. "How are you feeling today?"

"I'm okay," I said. "I've been better."

"What do you need from me today? To stay here, go away, get you food, buy a gallon of cookie dough ice cream? Anything?" He asked as he looked at me with caring, still puffy eyes.

"I want you to stay, but that gallon of cookie dough ice cream does sound good," I said with a smile.

"You got it. Do you want me to go to the store, or would you like to ride with me?" He asked.

"I can ride with you. I don't feel like going inside the store, though." I did not feel like getting ready. I kind of felt like today was going to be a 'pajamas all day' kind of day.

"That's fine. You can wait in the car if you want," he said.

"Deal," I said. "There is one more thing I think I need, though."

"And what's that?"

I moved my face closer, pressing my lips against his. He seemed surprised at first, but then he gently tightened his arm around me, kissing me slowly as I moved my hand up to cup his face. I had so many emotions swirling inside my head. So much sadness, grief, and hurt, but Max coaxed a tiny shred of happiness out to break through all the pain.

I pulled my body closer, moving my hand from his face to intertwine my fingers in his hair. His lips parted, and his tongue ran along my bottom lip, causing a shiver to run down my body. He deepened the kiss, but still kept a steady pace. I wanted to wrap myself in his arms and stay in bed all day, not even getting up to eat.

His hand was warm on my waist, the heat of his grip sinking through my shirt. He moved his hand to my back and pulled me flush against him; his lips never leaving mine. I threw my leg over his hip, wrapping around him. I pulled my lips away, trailing kisses from his mouth, up his jawline, and back down his neck. He took a shaky breath in as I made my way back to his lips.

His kiss was rougher now. I could feel the want and need in the way he held me and pressed his lips into mine. I wanted him just as much. I wanted to numb my pain and escape from this day almost as much as I wanted Max. If I could get lost in him, then maybe I wouldn't have to think about every emotion this day brought up. And I knew that if today was bad, then tomorrow would be even worse.

I tried to bring my thoughts back into the moment, back to Max's hand in my hair, back to his lips, his scent, his emerald eyes. Max moved his lips to my neck, kissing and sucking gently as he went. I quietly gasped at the sensation, and then gripped my hand into his hair, and tugged. His body pressed harder against mine as he peppered kisses up to my ear, nibbling on my earlobe.

I tightened my leg around his waist as he made his way back to my lips. His lips were much more gentle on mine now, and the fiery, needing kiss from seconds ago had slowed down. He kissed my cheek and my forehead, and then pulled back to look at me. His face was flushed, and his eyes had the same look in them as the night that we watched Top Gun.

"Why did you stop?" I asked shyly.

"I know it's an emotional day for you. I don't want you to do something you may regret later," he said as he brushed my hair back from my face.

"I wouldn't regret being with you," I said, hoping that he couldn't hear the neediness in my voice. "But I understand what you mean. Maybe not the best idea right now."

He smiled and kissed my forehead again. "Are you hungry?"

"I could eat. I want more Oreo pancakes."

"I can call in an order, and we can stop by while we're out and pick it up," Max said.

"That works. We can go anytime you're ready. I'm not changing out of pajamas today."

"I'll go change clothes and meet you downstairs," he said as he sat up and stretched again.

While we were on the way to the grocery store, Max called and placed an order at his parents' restaurant. I waited in the car while Max ran in to get the ice cream. He returned with a gallon of cookie dough ice cream, waffle bowls, chocolate syrup, whipped cream, and sprinkles. He told me that nothing cheers a person up like a sugar high. I planned on making myself a huge bowl and seeing if that was true.

Max said he needed to stop by one more place before we picked up the food. Thankfully, we had an insulated bag with us, so the ice cream wouldn't melt with the extra stops. We stopped at Walgreens, and while Max was inside, I scrolled through Instagram again to see if anyone else had posted about Justin. A few more people we went to school with had. The pictures were of Justin sitting in the stands at a football game, posing with some guys he hung out with, standing on the bank of the lake with a beer in his hand, sitting on a cooler on the beach, just random snapshots of Justin with other people doing everyday teenage things.

It made me happy and sad at the same time. Happy, because it was nice to see him smiling and having a good time. I liked remembering how he was the life of every party. But it was sad because that's over, and there will be no more lake days, beach days, football games, nothing. Death was just so final. Any of these photos could have been the last time he ever did any of those things, and it was soul-crushing to think about. He didn't deserve to die. He had a full, vibrant life ahead of him. He was almost out of here. Just one more summer, and he would have been free from Bill and able to heal from all the trauma Bill caused. He was so close.

The tears flooded my eyes, and there was no holding them back. I didn't want to cry in a Walgreens parking lot, but apparently, I didn't have a choice. I knew how desperately Max was trying to do whatever he could to make this day as bearable as possible. My shoulders shook as I let the sobs overtake me. I opened Max's glove compartment, hoping he'd have some tissues, and I was in luck because there was a pile. I grabbed a few, wiping my eyes and nose. I hated how crying made you have a runny nose. After the crying finally settled down, I was left with hiccups. I flipped down the visor mirror to see the damage. My eyes and face were red and puffy. Max would definitely be able to tell that I had been crying.

I flipped the mirror back up as Max was coming toward the car. I wished I could have hidden my tear-streaked face, but there was no use.

He opened the door and plopped down in the seat. He turned to face me as he opened his mouth to speak, but stopped when he looked at me. He set the bag down and held his arms out, pulling me into a hug. He stroked my hair with one hand and whispered, "I'm sorry." We stayed like that for a minute or two before he pulled back to look at me.

"Is there anything I can do?" He asked.

"I don't think so. I'm okay. I saw a few posts about Justin from friends with pictures of him, and it was too much. I think it's best if I stay off my phone for the rest of the day," I replied.

"That may be a good idea, or at least off social media where people may be posting about him," Max said as he put a hand on mine.

"Yeah," I agreed. "What did you have to get here?" I asked, trying to change the subject to hopefully distract myself.

"Oh," he said as he picked up the bag and looked inside. "I had an idea, but it's completely fine if you don't want to do it. I figured I'd get the stuff just in case. I got a couple of different face masks, spa headbands, a little pedicure set, a few different nail polish colors, and some lotion. I thought we could have a little spa day at home if you were up for it. Just something to keep your mind off everything and help you relax a little." He looked a little embarrassed after he said it.

I smiled. "I love that idea. Ice cream sundaes and a spa day sound perfect." I leaned over and planted a small kiss on his cheek. He looked surprised again. I didn't understand why he was shocked every time I kissed him, but it was cute. He smiled back and interlaced his fingers with mine.

We drove to The Pancake House to pick up our food, and Max didn't let go of my hand the whole drive. I hated when he had to let go to run inside. When he was back in the car, the smell of pancakes and bacon filled the car, making my stomach growl. The sadness was waiting just under the surface to take me over, so I could not wait to get home and get this day of distraction underway.

Chapter 17

Once we made it home, Max put away the ice cream, and we sat on the couch to eat our breakfast. The food was amazing, as it was the day before. Even barely warm pancakes from The Pancake House were better than most places' fresh pancakes. They were so good that neither of us wanted to stop eating, so we were so full by the time we finished that we didn't have any room left for cookie-dough sundaes unless we wanted to throw up everything we had just eaten.

We lay on the couch, waiting for all the food to digest as we watched a raunchy comedy that Max picked out. I could tell that he was trying his best to make sure that whatever we watched was something completely ridiculous and warranted no negative emotions. Even romantic comedies had twists and emotional parts, so he stayed far away from those, too. Knowing how careful he was being with me made me appreciate him even more. But it wasn't just today, it was every day.

He'd always been so attentive and cautious of how I was feeling, and I think I was too wrapped up in my own self-pity to notice how much he took into consideration how I felt. I cared for Max so much, and I had for a long time, but I didn't think I ever fully appreciated just how good to me he was. It was like I had been wearing blinders the whole year.

I had never allowed myself to feel the way I felt about him now, but these feelings couldn't be new. Maybe I was pushing them away because I wasn't ready or felt like no one wanted someone who was such a mess. But Max never left. He never got tired of having to comfort me while I was crying or having a panic attack. He was just always there. That was more than I could say for a lot of people. I did have other friends at one point, but once Justin died and I became somewhat of a recluse, they stopped calling and trying to get me to come out with them.

I knew that was partially my fault for never going, but I was mourning. I was having the worst time of my life, and they didn't understand. They wanted me to come out with them to try to get myself to feel better, but I had just lost my best friend, so I felt like they should have understood why I wouldn't be ready to do that yet. Then, I met Max and the people from the grief group, and they understood me. They got why I didn't feel like going out just weeks after I lost my friend. And when I finally agreed to go out with a few people from the group, they understood why I needed to leave when everything got to be too much, and the anxiety of it all overwhelmed me. Max was one of those people.

I looked over at Max. He was leaning back on the couch, feet propped up on the coffee table. The word love terrified me, but I couldn't lie and say that it didn't flash through my mind a few times when I was with him. It had been almost a year of seeing Max nearly every day. We had spent so much time together, and I guess I would say I loved him as a friend, but there was more there now. I don't know if I would say I romantically loved him yet, but I felt like I could love Max. Max turned to look at me. I realized the movie had finished while I was staring at him, lost in thought.

"Are you okay?" He asked.

Yeah, just a crazy person staring at you, trying to decide if what she was feeling for you was love. Of course, I couldn't answer that, though.

"Yeah, I'm fine," I answered, with a nervous laugh. "I zoned out."

"Oh, well, feel free to stare all you need when you zone out," he said with a grin.

"Will do," I said, grinning back.

"Do you want to start our spa day before I turn on another movie?"

"Sure, I'm ready for a face mask," I said. I needed one since my face was still puffy from crying earlier.

Max went to grab his spa day supplies and brought them over to me. He reached into the bag and pulled out a tube of charcoal face mask and a couple of sheet masks. I looked them over, seeing what each sheet mask was for. There was a tea tree mask to refresh tired skin and reduce signs of strain and fatigue. That sounded like the one for me. I set that one in my lap and handed the others to Max. He chose an avocado mask to retain moisture and keep your skin radiant and shiny.

"Should we turn on the oil diffuser? Get some relaxing scents in the air?" I asked.

"That's a good idea," Max said. "Where is it?"

I pointed to the table against the wall where my mom had knick-knacks and candles. "It's over there. The oils are in the drawer," I answered.

Max got up, walked over to the table, and opened the drawer. "Which oil should I pick?"

"I'd go with a few drops of lavender and eucalyptus for maximum relaxation," I said. I loved how lavender and eucalyptus smelled when my mom had the oil diffuser on. I always felt so calm when the smell filled the living room.

Max walked back over to the couch and picked up his mask, flipping it over to read the back. "So, it says we should leave this on for at least twenty minutes," he said, before tearing open the package.

I opened mine, holding the mask up to see how to place it on my face. I laid it over my face, ensuring the eyes, nose, and mouth holes were lined up correctly. I looked over at Max and noticed he was struggling, so I took the mask from him and laid it on his face correctly. I set a timer as Max leaned over and grabbed the remote, keeping his head back so the mask wouldn't slide off. It was a ridiculous sight that made me giggle. He turned on another movie, and we sat with our heads leaning against the back of the couch, feet propped up on the coffee table as we watched Jay and Silent Bob.

My phone buzzed, and I held my phone up where I could see it without moving my head to see a message from my mom. She was on her break, and I knew she'd be worried about me today. She was probably a little less concerned than she would have been because Max was here, but still concerned, nonetheless. She asked how I was feeling and if I needed anything, and said that she was sorry she had to work this Saturday. She only worked one Saturday a month, which happened to be this one.

I texted her back quickly to let her know that I was as okay as I could be and that Max was doing his best to keep me distracted. She told me she'd be leaving work in a couple of hours and would pick up food on her way home. Thinking of food still made me want to puke, but maybe by the time she got home, I'd be able to eat again. I set my phone back down and turned my attention to the TV. A few minutes later, my alarm rang, making me jump. I peeled my mask back, balled it up, and then stuck it back in the package, gently tapping the remaining product into my skin.

"Is that what we're supposed to do?" Max asked, watching me.

"Yeah, just gently tap the product into your skin, so it soaks it all up," I said, looking at him as he followed my instructions. "Pedicures next?" I asked.

"Sure! If that's what you want." He grabbed the bag and took out the pedicure set, all the colors of polish he bought, and the lotion.

I scanned the bottles of polish. They were red, black, mint, light purple, and neon pink. "Quite the selection," I said playfully.

"My options were limited," he laughed. "I thought you would probably like the mint or light purple the best, but I got a few others just in case.

I love the neon pink," he said.

"Then you can paint your toes neon pink," I said with a big smile.

"I'm cool with that." He smiled back.

"So are we doing our own or each other?" I asked.

"We can do each other if you want, or I can do yours and mine, so you don't have to touch my feet," he laughed.

"I don't mind. Hopefully, they don't smell too bad," I joked.

"Thankfully, I've never had a problem with that," he said confidently.

I grabbed polish remover, Q-tips, and cotton balls in case we messed up, and a big towel to protect the couch. I persuaded Max to let me do his first because I was excited to paint his nails neon pink. He propped his feet on the couch next to me, and I went to work. I painted them carefully, and when I finished, I added some black polka dots to his big toes.

"A masterpiece," I said as I gestured to his toenails.

"I love them!" He laughed.

"I'm glad. My turn now!" I said.

I turned sideways and leaned back, so my feet were propped up on the couch next to Max. He scooted closer, sat my feet in his lap, and grabbed the lotion. I didn't know I was getting a foot massage before he painted my nails, but I was not complaining. It had been forever since anyone had rubbed my feet. "I get a foot massage too?"

"Yeah, that's part of the spa day package," he answered as he squeezed some lotion into his hands. He rubbed his hands together, making sure lotion was on both palms.

"I didn't give you a foot massage, though," I said.

"I don't need one. This is your day of relaxation," he said as he picked my foot up, rubbing lotion up and down it. I let my head fall back against the couch and closed my eyes. He made circles on the bottom of my foot with his thumbs, and I let out a huge sigh.

"That good?" He asked, humor in his voice.

"It is. Foot massages are my favorite. I don't think there's anything more relaxing."

"I had no idea, or I would have been giving you foot massages this whole time," he said.

"It would have been a little weird if I were randomly like, hey, wanna rub my feet?" I laughed.

"We've spent almost every day together. I don't think it would have been *that* weird," he replied.

"Maybe not, but now you know," I said. "I'll be hitting you up for foot massages all the time."

He laughed. "I'm cool with that."

Suddenly, I'm standing on Ashbury Bridge, the sun is setting behind the trees, and I can feel a gentle breeze blowing even though it's humid and sticky. I look down to see that I'm holding a single lily and a picture of Justin and me. I have on the black dress I wore to Justin's funeral and a pair of black sandals. I walk to the barrier of the bridge and look over. It's about thirty feet down. I hold the lily out over the water and let it fall.

Just as I turn to walk away, I hear someone yell "Amelia!" I turn back, and the barrier is gone. Justin's car is in the water. His window is cracked but won't roll down any further. The car is filling up with water, and he can't get out. He's yelling to me for help. I look around for my car or phone to call the police, but there's nothing on the bridge but me. There isn't much time. I take a huge breath of courage, run straight for the broken barrier, and jump. It feels like I'm falling forever, like I'm never going to reach the water to help him in time. I hold my nose and brace for impact, just as I jump awake.

I looked around. Max was still sitting at my feet, but a different movie was playing on the TV, and I heard my mom's voice in the kitchen. My heart was racing, and my body felt shaky. I rubbed my eyes and tried to take long, slow breaths to calm my body and hammering heart. I felt uneasy. That was the same dream I had been having since right after Justin's funeral, but it had been a couple of months since the last time.

It never got less jarring, no matter how many times I dreamed it.

Max turned his head toward me. "How was your nap?"

I hadn't told Max about the dreams and wasn't up for discussing them, so I went with the easy answer. "It was good. I must have needed it. I don't even remember falling asleep."

"You fell asleep before I even finished massaging the first foot," he said.

"Aw, man! I didn't even get to enjoy the massage because I was asleep," I said, flopping my head back.

Max laughed. "I can give you another foot massage so you can be awake to enjoy it."

"I'd love that. I see you still painted my toenails even though I fell asleep," I said, wiggling my toes.

"Yeah, I took some creative liberty since you were knocked out," he said.

"I see that," I said as I looked down at my toes. Every other toe alternated between mint and light purple, and he added some neon pink dots to my big toe. "I love them."

"I'm glad. I figured I'd add in some neon pink dots, so we matched a little," he said.

I smiled and shook my head at him. He did a surprisingly good job, considering he didn't usually paint nails, as far as I knew. There was barely any nail polish on my skin. I'd call that a win because even I always got polish on my skin, and I've been painting my nails since I was a kid.

"Mom is home? I must have slept a while," I said as I looked over the back of the couch toward the kitchen.

"You did," he said. "I finished Jay and Silent Bob, and now this movie is almost over, too."

"I'm sorry I fell asleep on you. You could have woken me up." I felt a little bad for falling asleep during our spa day.

"No, you needed the extra rest. It's been a rough day," he said as he slid closer, putting my legs in his lap, and rubbing my feet again.

"You're going to make me fall back asleep," I said.

"It's fine. Get all the rest you need," he said as he made circles on my feet with his thumbs again.

"You're the best, you know that?"

"Not the best, but I'm all right," he said with a shrug and huff of laughter.

"More than all right," I said, giving him a flirty smile. His eyebrows shot up, and he smiled back.

Mom walked into the living room and came around the couch to where I was sitting. My first reaction was to pull my feet away from Max, but I decided it didn't matter. I thought he might stop rubbing my feet when she came in, but he didn't. "You're awake now. Are you guys hungry?" She asked. "I picked up some Chinese food on the way home."

"I'm a little hungry," I said, then looked over at Max. "Are you?"

"I could eat," he said. "After I finish your food massage, of course."

Mom looked at me with raised eyebrows and a smirk. I rolled my eyes. "Aren't we spoiled?" She said jokingly. "What did you guys do today?"

"Got breakfast, had a little spa day, and watched movies," I said. "Well, I napped through the movies."

"A spa day? That must have been nice," she said. "What did you do for your spa day?"

"We did some face masks and painted each other's toenails," I answered.

"Max, you got yours painted too?" She asked.

"I did," he said, then lifted his foot to show her.

"I love them. Amelia did well," she said with a laugh.

"She did," he agreed.

"I'm going to get the food set out on the table, so you guys can come eat when you're ready," she said, walking back to the kitchen.

After Max finished, we ate dinner with my parents. Everyone tried to keep the conversation light. They tried to avoid any direct mention of what today was while still trying to slide in a few questions to check how I was dealing. I appreciated that they had been so gentle with me since I'd been home, but I was ready for everyone to start treating me normally again. I wanted to be at the point where I could talk about Justin without it making me so sad. I wanted to talk about the good times, the fun things we did, and remember how great a friend he was, without feeling like someone had punched a hole through my chest.

The rest of the evening was pretty uneventful. After dinner, we went to my room, ate our cookie dough ice cream, and watched some more movies. I let Max pick the movies again, and he made sure to still go for comedy, which had us laughing until we cried. He had done such a great job of keeping my mind off everything. The day went better than I imagined it would, but tomorrow would technically be a year since I found out. I started to get anxious thinking about it, no matter how hard I tried to focus on what we were watching. I snuggled up to Max, hoping to calm my mind, and we both eventually fell asleep.

Chapter 18

The sun shone through the windows, and I blinked my eyes open. It felt like it was still early. I grabbed my phone and saw that I had a text from Brayden wishing me a happy birthday and telling me to let him know if I needed anything. I tapped his message and sent a quick text to tell him thank you and that I would. It was seven-thirty, which was earlier than I wanted to be awake today, but not as early as I was woken up a year ago.

* * *

Someone was gently shaking me awake, but I was still so sleepy. I knew there was no way it was time to get up yet. I opened my eyes to see that my room was still completely dark.

"Amelia," Mom said, as I rolled over to look at her.

"What's going on? What time is it?" I asked. I was straining my eyes to see her face in the dark. When my eyes finally focused, I could see that she had a pained expression on her face. I sat up quickly and faced her. "What's going on?" I asked again. She hesitated and bit her lip. That only made me more nervous. If this was some sort of birthday surprise, then it was a terrible way to surprise me. "Mom?" I said.

"Honey, there's been an accident," she said as she placed her hand on mine.

"An accident? What kind of accident? Is Dad okay?" I asked frantically.

"Your dad is fine," she said.

I breathed a sigh of relief. "Oh, good. Was it not a bad accident then? Why was Dad out so late?" I asked.

She looked down at our hands. "Your dad wasn't in an accident."

"Then who?" I asked. An accident was terrible, of course, but we didn't have any family that I was so close to that she'd wake me up in the middle of the night to tell me about it, except my grandparents, and they wouldn't be out in the middle of the night. What time was it anyway?

"Justin was in an accident," she finally said.

My heart started racing, and my throat felt so tight that I could barely get the words out. "Is he okay?"

Tears came to her eyes, and I knew the answer. I immediately felt sick, and the room started to spin. I didn't know whether to run to the bathroom and throw up or crawl back under the blankets and never come out. I felt like the breath was knocked out of me. I couldn't even process what I had just heard. I wanted to run away from this conversation because maybe then it wouldn't be true. Tears started streaming down my face, and Mom pulled me into a hug, holding me tight.

"I'm so sorry, honey. I'm so sorry," she said as she kept me pulled close to her. I sobbed into her shoulder. I couldn't even tell how long we sat like that as I cried. Time didn't feel real. I didn't think the tears would ever stop. I cried so long that my face was swollen, and my throat felt raw. The shoulder of Mom's shirt was completely soaked with tears and snot. When I finally calmed down enough to speak, I pulled back from her and sat back on my bed. I wanted to know, but I didn't know if I really wanted to hear the answer.

"What happened?" I asked through sniffles.

"I'm not exactly sure. Christy called me before I came in here. She said the police called her because someone saw Justin's car and called 911," she answered as she put a hand on my shoulder. Tears filled my eyes again before streaming down my cheeks. I did my best to hold back the sob that wanted to break free again.

"Where was his car?" I asked, still gasping through the tears.

"They found it in the water off Ashbury Bridge. He must have hit the barrier and broken through," she said.

"And he was-" I broke off. I couldn't say it. She looked down, and tears were brimming in her eyes.

"His windshield was busted, so they think he was ejected from the car. They are going to get a dive team to search the water," she said, barely holding back the tears.

That was it. I couldn't hold back the sobs any longer. They broke free, and I lay down, burying my face in the pillow. It felt like someone had punched me in my chest. It physically hurt. I had never experienced hurt like that in my entire life. I couldn't even process the words that she was saying. I jumped up out of bed, pushed past Mom, and ran straight for the bathroom.

I fell to the floor in front of the toilet and vomited until I was dry heaving, and my chest was so sore that it hurt to breathe. Mom stayed right next to me the whole time, stroking my hair and telling me how sorry she was. It was the worst day of my life, and I didn't know how I was going to make it through. I couldn't imagine a world where Justin wasn't in it. I couldn't imagine my life without my best friend being there with me. I wanted to die along with him.

No amount of comforting that my parents tried that day helped. The only thing that would have helped was Justin, and he wasn't there. I couldn't eat or drink. Anytime I tried, I just vomited it right back up. I had never seen my parents so concerned about me before. Every time mom came to check on me, I asked if they'd heard anything else, but no better news ever came.

* * *

I lay in bed staring at the ceiling. I didn't want to move too much because I didn't want to wake Max. He looked so peaceful. I thought about last year and how I was woken up to the absolute worst news of my life. Tears formed in my eyes. I could so easily remember the gut-wrenching pain and the shock that settled over me when Mom told me what happened. It had been a year, and I still couldn't believe it some days. My stomach suddenly felt queasy. I did not want to get sick. I hated throwing up, as most people did. I hoped that if I lay extremely still that maybe the nausea would go away.

I grabbed my phone again to try and find something to occupy my mind. I clicked on Instagram and saw I had a few new DMs. It was a couple of people from school telling me happy birthday. I had no idea how they remembered, but then I saw that I was tagged in a story from seven hours ago. It was Max's story. It was a happy birthday post with a picture he and I had taken in the photo booth from this bar we'd gone to with our grief support group one time. That must have been how the people from school knew. I replied back and told each of them thank you. I put my phone down, pulled the blankets up to my chin, and rolled over to try to fall back asleep.

I fluttered my eyes open, sleepily. It was brighter in my room, so I knew I had slept at least another couple of hours. I looked behind me to see Max. He was lying on his back, looking at his phone. He noticed that I was awake and looked over at me.

"Good morning," he said with a smile as I rolled over to face him.

"Good morning," I said, smiling back. "How'd you sleep?"

"I slept well. What about you?" He asked.

I moved closer. "I slept okay, too." I thought I should leave out that I had already woken up earlier, not feeling great.

He brushed my hair back from my face. "I'm glad." I shifted, laying my head on his chest. "Happy Birthday," he said before kissing my forehead.

I turned my head, kissing his chest, then smiled up at him. "Thank you."

When we finally got up and went downstairs, Mom was in the kitchen. She was cooking, and Dad was sitting at the bar. "Good morning," she called out to us.

"Good morning," Max and I answered in unison.

"And happy birthday," my dad added.

"Thank you." I walked over to hug him. Max sat down on a barstool next to my dad as I walked to hug my mom, too.

"What are you making?" I asked. "It smells great."

"Just making you guys some omelets."

"What's in them?" I asked.

"Spinach, mozzarella, and sausage," she answered.

"My favorite," I replied.

"Exactly." She kissed my cheek as I smiled at her.

I grabbed the orange juice from the refrigerator and poured it into two glasses before walking over to take the seat on the other side of Max. My nausea had gone away sometime between falling back asleep and when I woke up again. I was so thankful because spending the day on the floor next to the toilet was not what I had in mind.

"Do you guys have anything planned for the day?" Mom asked as she straightened up the kitchen.

"No, I don't think so," I said, looking over to Max.

"I actually do need to go somewhere really quickly after I finish eating, but it won't take long," he said.

"Oh, no worries." I wondered where he needed to go, maybe home for more clothes since he stayed longer than originally planned.

"Can you hang around for a couple of minutes after you finish eating before you leave?" Mom asked.

"Of course. It's not urgent," Max answered.

I took my last bite, and I must have been hungrier than I thought because I felt like I could eat another. Dad got up and walked over to the kitchen drawer, digging around for something, and Mom went to the laundry room and came out with a cake. I laughed.

"You hid it in the laundry room?" I asked.

"Well, I couldn't keep it in the refrigerator, or you would have seen it when you got something to drink. Dad finally found what he was looking for, a lighter, and brought it over to where Mom had set the cake in front of me. The cake had white icing and yellow trim with "Happy Birthday, Amelia" written in pink. There was a one and nine candle already stuck in the cake. Dad lit the candles as Mom started to sing, then Dad and Max joined in with her.

"Now make a wish," mom said after they finished the song.

I knew what I wanted to wish for, but it was a wish that couldn't come true. I wished that Justin were here. I wish that I had never lost my best friend. This was the second birthday he hadn't been here for. I wished I could have saved him. I closed my eyes and wished for something that was maybe possible, that he would watch over me from whatever afterlife he was in. I opened my eyes and blew out the candles. Mom and Dad smiled, clapping like I was still just a little girl blowing out my candles for the first time by myself.

"Want a piece now, or do you need to wait for your food to settle?" Mom asked.

"Are you kidding? Now, of course," I said to her. She grabbed a couple of plates and a knife. She cut Max and me a piece and set them in front of us. The cake was so good. Marble cake with buttercream icing, just how I liked it. I cut myself a second small slice after I finished the first. Apparently, I was starving, or I was eating my feelings. I wasn't entirely sure which it was, but either was fine. After Max finished his cake, he went upstairs to take a shower while I stayed at the bar and talked to my parents. Max had been here, so I had spent most of my time with

THE GHOST OF YOU

him since I'd been home, which I liked, but I needed some time with my parents, too.

It didn't take long before Max was coming back downstairs, his hair still damp. He wore a white t-shirt that hugged the muscles in his chest and arms with dark jeans. Sometimes, how handsome he was still caught me off guard. Max had always been handsome, but it was hard not to notice so much more now.

He walked over to the bar where I was sitting. "I won't be gone too long. Is there anything you need while I'm out?"

"I don't think so."

"Text me if you think of anything," he said with a smile. He took a small step toward me and then stopped. He was looking at me a little awkwardly. This was the first time we were parting ways since we decided to try to be more than friends, so I wasn't sure what the protocol was with it still being so new. I stood up, wrapping my arms around him. He pulled me in, returning the hug, and kissed the top of my head.

"I'll be back in a little bit," he said as he stepped back and headed for the door.

"See you in a bit. Be careful," I called after him. It still gave me so much anxiety when someone I cared about had to go somewhere without me. I always had that awful thought in the back of my mind, that it could be the last time I saw them. I turned back and saw my parents looking at me with their eyebrows raised. The second the door clicked shut and Max was outside, Mom spoke.

"Are you two dating now?" She asked excitedly.

"No," I answered, quickly. "Yes." "I guess." "It's new," I finally settled on.

"Aww," she gushed. "I love Max. Don't you love Max, Brian?" She said to my dad.

"He does seem like a pretty great guy," Dad answered. I loved my parents, but I didn't want to discuss my love life because I was still getting used to it myself.

"I'm glad you guys like him," I said. "But it's new, so I don't have too much to say about everything yet." They took the hint and didn't ask any further questions. "Do you want to watch a movie with me after I shower?" I asked.

"Of course," Mom called after me. "Let me grab your presents so you can open them first." I walked to the living room, sitting down on the end of the couch with the chaise lounge as dad sat down on the other end. Mom came into the room carrying two small boxes. They were both wrapped in white wrapping paper with a pink bow on top.

"You didn't have to get me anything," I said as she handed them to me.

"Just because you are legally an adult doesn't mean we're going to stop getting you birthday presents," my mom said, smiling at me. "You're our only child. You'll still be getting presents when you're eighty."

I unwrapped the first box. It had three gift cards in it, one was to my favorite clothing boutique in town, one was for a mani and pedi for two, which I assumed was for her and me to go together, and the last was for Moon Dollar because they knew how much I loved going there.

"These are awesome! Thank you!" I said to both of them.

"You're very welcome," Mom said. I picked the second box up and tore the paper off. It was a small black velvet box. I opened it and tears immediately filled my eyes. It was a beautiful gold necklace with a small lily pendant hanging from the chain, housing a lime green stone in the center. It was Peridot, the birthstone for August, Justin's birthstone. The tears trickled down my cheeks. I looked up at my parents. "It's perfect," I said, sniffling. Mom sat down beside me and put her arm around me.

"I didn't want to make you cry," she said. "We thought it would be something nice that you could always have with you that would remind you of Justin."

"It's okay. It's happy and sad tears. I love it. Today is just a tough day."

"Aw, I know, honey," she said as she gave me a squeeze.

Dad came over, sitting on the other side of me, as he placed a hand on my back. Their support meant so much to me. I knew they had done everything possible this past year to make my life easier and help me as much as they could. I loved them so much for that, and this gift was everything. They knew how much it would mean to me.

"Could you put it on me?" I asked Mom.

"Of course," she answered as she took the necklace out of the box, placing it around my neck. After she clasped it, I looked down, holding the pendant between my fingers. It really was perfect. I missed him so much.

Before starting the movie, I ran upstairs to jump in the shower. When I got out, I towel dried my hair, put on some concealer and mascara, then grabbed a cute, but comfy white sundress out of my closet and slipped it on. I didn't have the energy to get fully ready today, but I wanted to dress up a little since it was my birthday, and maybe I wanted to impress Max a little too.

When I came back downstairs, my parents were on one end of the couch, cuddled up next to each other with "Labyrinth" already pulled up. It was one of my favorite movies since I was a little girl. David Bowie's voice was the best, and everyone loved the goblin king.

"How'd you know?" I said jokingly.

"Oh, I don't know. Maybe because we have watched it every single year either on your birthday or near your birthday for your whole life," she said with a chuckle.

"My favorite birthday tradition," I replied as I plopped down at the other end of the couch in my favorite spot.

We were about thirty minutes into the movie when I heard a knock at the front door. Mom, Dad, and I all looked at each other. It was odd because no one ever came to our house unannounced. I almost hoped it would be a delivery with a vase of lilies.

Last year, after mom had woken me up to tell me about the accident, I stayed in my bed all day crying, except when I had to go to the bathroom to throw up. I couldn't bring myself to get out of bed, I couldn't eat the cake my parents had already bought, I couldn't open my presents, I couldn't do any of it. All I wanted was to go back to bed and wake up to find out that everything had been a horrible nightmare and that none of it was real. Unfortunately, that didn't happen. When my mom went out to check the mail that day, there was a delivery at the front door. It was a vase full of white lilies with a card. The card said *Lilies for Lia. Can't wait for our picnic this afternoon. Happy Birthday.*

Justin had already set the delivery up for my flowers before his accident. In a way, it was comforting because it was like a last message, letting me know that he was still with me even if he physically wasn't anymore. I had cried so much that day that I didn't think I could have any more tears left, but when I saw those flowers and read the card, I did. I kept the card and one of the flowers. They were both tucked away inside one of Justin's favorite books on my shelf upstairs. I doubted that Justin had my birthday flower deliveries set up more than a year in advance, so I knew it couldn't be that, but part of me wished it was.

Mom paused the movie and got up to answer the door. "Oh, come in. I was worried it would be a man with a Jesus pamphlet," she laughed as Max walked in the door past her. He was holding a colorful bouquet of flowers that were in a crystal vase. I was pretty sure that they were from Fiona's. He was also carrying a cute pink gift basket filled with something I couldn't quite see from where I was sitting. He set his keys down on the bar, and walked over to where I was, holding out the flowers and gift basket to me. Mom followed and sat back down next to Dad, watching Max.

"These are so beautiful, Max!" I exclaimed as I took the vase from his hands. "I love them."

"I hoped you would," he said. I leaned forward and set the vase down on the coffee table, and he handed me the gift basket. I saw that it was filled with every type of candy that I loved. It had Kit-Kats, Twix, Crunch Bars, Sweet Tarts, Nerd Ropes, and so many others.

"This is amazing!" I said to Max. "You got all of my favorites. How did you remember?"

"I pay attention," he said with a grin. I stood up, hugging him tightly. He hugged me back, resting his cheek on the top of my head. This boy was perfect. He made me feel better and feel a little more whole. I tilted my head up and wrapped my arms around his neck to pull him down for a kiss. He hesitated, darting his eyes to the side where my parents were sitting. I had completely forgotten that we had an audience. My parents didn't care, but it still felt a little weird to show too much PDA in front of them. I lay my head against his chest as if I was just pulling him down for a bigger hug, and then let go to sit back down.

"Want to watch Labyrinth with us?" I asked.

"Of course." He said as he sat down next to me. "Bowie is great."

I pressed play, and he put his arm around me as I leaned into him. I noticed my mom look over at us a couple of times out of the corner of my eye. One time, I turned and she gave me a thumbs up. I smiled, shaking my head, and went back to watching the movie.

Chapter 19

After the movie, Max and I got more cake and added some of the cookie-dough ice cream we had the day before. My parents said they were going to the park for a walk, but I think they just wanted to be out of the house so Max and I could hang out alone for a while. After we ate our cake and ice cream, I started digging through my basket, trying to decide which candy to eat first. "I'm going to have a cavity after all of this," I said.

"I'm sure of it," Max laughed.

"Ugh, I hate the dentist."

"Really? That's something I didn't know about you," he said.

"Doesn't everyone hate going to the dentist?" I asked.

"I don't think so. I don't hate it; I actually kind of like it."

"Weirdo."

"I like how my teeth feel after they polish them," he said.

"I guess that's nice, but as a whole, I'm just not a fan of people having their hands in my mouth," I said.

Max laughed. "I get that."

"What's something else I don't know about you?" He asked.

I thought about it for a moment. "Hm, I hate needles."

"I think that's most people," Max answered.

"That's true."

"Where is somewhere you'd love to visit, like the top destination on your list?"

"I'd have to say Mykonos, Greece. It looks so beautiful. It seems like it would be so perfect and relaxing," I answered. "What's yours?"

"Probably Rome. I'd love to see the Colosseum and the Trevi Fountain," he answered.

"That would be amazing too. We should take a couple of weeks and go to all the places we want to see, staying a couple of days in each place," I suggested.

"That would be awesome," he said. "Maybe next summer break?"

Butterflies filled my stomach. That meant he was planning for us to still be together next summer. Future plans used to make me nervous, and I honestly couldn't picture my future for a while. It seemed so bleak, but with Max, the future excited me. I wanted to have things to look forward to. I wanted to feel like my life was worth living again. Justin and I used to talk about making plans to travel when we were on our summer breaks during college, and I would always carry him with me. I'd make sure to do everything that we planned to do for him.

"That would be perfect."

"What's your favorite place to go here?" He asked.

"Like in our town or just in the United States?" I asked.

"Both," he said.

"Here in town, my favorite spot to go is the waterfront park. I love to sit by the water and read or just hang out. In the US, my favorite place would have to be Hawaii. We went a few years ago, one summer, and it was incredible. You can't beat the crystal clear water at Hanauma Bay," I answered.

"I think there's a trend," he chuckled.

"I just like to be by the water, I guess."

"We will be by water when we go to Mykonos," he said.

"The pictures I've seen are breathtaking, so I can only imagine how beautiful it will be in person."

"Nowhere near as beautiful as you are," he said. Then, he scrunched his face up. "That was cheesy; I'm sorry."

I busted out laughing, and so did he. "It was, but still cute," I said.

"I've wanted to tell you how pretty you looked since I got back, but I was trying not to do too much in front of your parents. I decided I'd work it into the conversation in the most cheesy way possible, I guess. You really do look beautiful, though," he said as a blush crept across his face.

"Thank you." I smiled at him. "You look pretty handsome yourself," I replied, suddenly feeling shy.

"No, but thank you."

"Don't be so modest. You know you're cute," I said playfully.

"No, no." He said, still blushing. He got so uncomfortable with compliments. It was adorable.

"I want to take the flowers up to my room. I feel like it will liven it up some. Will you bring the basket of candy too?" I asked.

"Trying to hide a stash in your room?"

"Absolutely! Got to have my midnight snack stash in case I need a quick sugar fix." I stood, picking up the flowers. Max grabbed the basket of candy and followed behind me to my room. I looked around, trying to decide where I wanted to sit them. I finally decided to place them on my desk. I wasn't sure if they needed sunlight, so I made a mental note to call Fiona tomorrow and ask.

Max set the candy basket on my nightstand and sat down on the bed. I climbed up behind him to the middle of the bed and propped myself up on the pillows. He did the same and then turned to me. "How are you feeling?"

"Honestly, better than I thought. I've had my moments, but I've been okay, considering. You've made the day better," I said, smiling at him.

"I'm glad it hasn't been too bad. I was worried about you," he replied. I felt a pull in my chest, but it wasn't a bad thing. It was hard to explain, but I felt it when Max showed how much he cared.

"No need to worry. I'm okay."

I placed my hand on the side of his face, as he stared at me with that look in his eyes that I'd only noticed in the past few days. He leaned into my hand as I studied his face, his lips, his eyes, and how his hair fell across his forehead. He was so gorgeous. He brought his hand up, brushing my cheek with his fingertips before tucking a strand of hair behind my ear. He leaned in, planting a soft kiss on my lips, and then pulled back.

"I've been wanting to do that since this morning," he said with a soft grin.

"So have I."

I leaned in and pressed my lips to his again, kissing him slowly. My stomach fluttered. I never wanted to stop kissing him. I wrapped one hand around his neck and twisted my fingers into his hair as I brought my other hand up, lightly resting it on his chest. He moved his mouth slowly over mine, teasing his tongue along the edges of my lips. I moved my body closer to his as he put his hands on my waist, pulling me to him. I straddled his lap, holding him as close as I could, our bodies moving together, and our lips never breaking contact. I heard my phone ding with a text notification, but I didn't care.

Max pulled back. "Do you need to get that?"

"Nope," I said, urgently pulling his lips back to mine. He wrapped his arms around me, running his hands up my back. I tugged at the hem of his shirt, and he unwrapped from me long enough to pull it up and over his head, tossing it to the ground. His hands were on my hips, my dress pushed up from how I was sitting. His hands teased at the hem of it as I kissed my way up to his ear. I nibbled his earlobe gently and whispered, "It's okay."

He shuddered. "Are you sure?" he whispered back.

"I'm sure," I said before giving his earlobe another nibble. He let out a soft groan and moved his hands up my hips, underneath my dress. He pulled it over my head and tossed it to the floor, where his shirt lay, and then his lips were back on mine. The last few layers of clothing fell to the floor with the rest as our lips crashed together with a need that, until recently, I hadn't felt in a long time. Max's hands were everywhere, and his touch on my skin felt electric but careful.

He pulled back, both of us panting. "Do you have a condom?" I asked.

"I don't. I didn't know I'd need them," Max chuckled as the blush on his face deepened.

"I think I have some," I said as I moved off him to check the drawer on my nightstand. Thankfully, I did have a few. I grabbed one, tore it open, and then lay down to pull Max on top of me. He trailed kisses softly down my neck as I rolled the condom on. He let out a small gasp at the touch of my hands on him, and I grinned.

I wrapped my arms around his neck, and he stopped kissing me long enough to ask one more time. "Are you sure?"

"I'm sure," I answered, meaning it so much more than he even knew. I didn't think I had ever wanted someone so much.

He kissed me gently as he pressed his body slowly into mine until there was no space between us. I gasped at the sensation of fullness and let myself get lost in the moment. My mind swirled with total bliss, and I realized there was no one I would rather be in that moment with than Max. His careful touch made me feel a way I had never experienced, and I felt happier and more at peace than I ever had with anyone else.

Max lay behind me, his arm draped over my body. I wasn't sure what time it was, but I was sure my parents had to be back home already. Neither of us had gotten dressed yet, but I wasn't worried about them coming into my room unannounced. They weren't that type of parents, thankfully. I was so tired that I didn't even want to move, and I was pretty sure Max felt the same way.

He kissed my head, and I turned over to face him.

"How's your birthday been so far?" He asked, looking at me through hooded eyes.

"I'd say it's been surprising, but very nice," I answered, giving him a flirty grin.

"I'm glad to hear it," he said, returning the grin. "Is that necklace new?" He gestured to my neck, where the gift my parents had given me hung.

"My parents gave me my birthday presents while you were gone, and this was one of them. It's beautiful, right?" I said as I held it between my thumb and forefinger.

"It is. Is that a lily on it?" He asked.

"Yeah," I said, still holding the necklace.

"For Justin, right?"

"Yeah, and the stone is his birthstone. His birthday is in August," I answered.

"That was sweet of them," he said before planting a kiss on my forehead.

I snuggled into his chest, breathing him in. My mind drifted to Justin, and I felt guilty. I felt guilty that I was thinking of Justin with everything that had just happened with Max, but I also felt guilty that I was enjoying my birthday. I knew it was ridiculous, but the feeling was still there. Max made me happy, but there were still what-ifs in my mind. If Justin hadn't gotten into an accident, would I have ever told him that I did remember kissing him or told him about my feelings? Would it be Justin and me lying here like this instead? It's hard to know because the way he stopped us that night embarrassed me and made me think that he didn't think of me that way, so maybe I wouldn't have told him anyway. It's not like any of it mattered now, but it was still on my mind.

Max ran his hand down my back, bringing my mind back to the present. I still had the rest of my birthday left to try to enjoy, and I needed to be present for it. I decided that I wanted to take Max down to the waterfront park, where I loved to sit and read. It was mine and

Justin's spot, so it was special to me. I hadn't been in a year. I didn't even dare to come home, much less go to places that were something just between Justin and me. Today felt right, like it was the right time to go, and I wanted to share it with Max since he had been my biggest support through everything other than my parents.

"Do you want to go somewhere?" I asked as I tilted my head up to look at him.

"Sure. Where?"

"Can we go to the waterfront park I told you about a little bit ago, the one that's my favorite place in town?" I asked.

Max got out of bed first, handed me my clothes, and then went to his room. We both needed to do a little freshening up before we went anywhere. I rolled to the edge of the bed and grabbed my phone to check it before I got up. My screen was full of notifications. I had messages on Instagram and some texts all saying happy birthday. It was people from school, a couple of distant family members, and some people from our grief group. I was going through, replying thank you to everyone, when I got to the last new text.

It was from a number I didn't have saved. It just said *happy birthday*, with no capital letters, no punctuation, nothing. I didn't recognize the area code of the number. It wasn't a Georgia area code. Maybe it was someone from the group who had gotten a new number or someone from school. People did come from other states to the university, so that could be why I didn't recognize it. I just typed back *"Thank you!"* And hit send. I wanted to ask who it was, but I'd feel bad if I asked and it was someone that I definitely should have had their number saved. I hopped out of bed to get dressed and ready to go.

The sun was setting as Max and I pulled up to the park. We had gotten ready quickly, grabbed some snacks and water, and then told my parents we'd be back in a little while. I didn't want it to be dark by the time we got to the park. It looked so beautiful in the setting sun, but I felt a panic attack creeping up as soon as I was about to climb out of the car. My heart was pounding faster than normal, and my chest began to tighten. I closed my eyes and took several deep breaths, trying to ground myself and get it under control before it took on a life of its own. Max put his hand on mine, gently stroking with his thumb.

"Are you okay?" He asked, concern in his voice.

"Yeah, it's just that I haven't been here since..." I trailed off. It was always hard to finish sentences that ended in words I still didn't want to believe.

"Ah," he said, understanding. "Was this a special place for you two?" He asked.

"We used to come here to hang out and read. If one of us was stressed or needed to be away from everything, we came here. It was our spot together, but also our favorite spot by ourselves," I answered.

Usually, when I felt anxious, it made it worse when someone asked me questions, but Max's asking helped take my mind off the anxiety. I wasn't completely calm, but I was calm enough to get out of the car, at the very least. I reached for the door handle as Max did the same.

We walked up the concrete path through the park to where the benches and swings sat facing the water. I walked past a few until I got to the one that Justin and I always sat on. I stood there for a minute and looked around the park, seeing if it had changed as much as my life had. It hadn't, which made me happy. The fact that it looked the same as it always had gave me a strange feeling of comfort. I sucked in a deep breath of fresh air and sat down on the bench. Max sat down next to me but didn't speak.

"I love this park," I finally said after a minute.

"I've always thought it was nice. I just never came here much," he replied.

"You've missed out. My parents have been bringing me here since I was little. I guess they loved the view too. Maybe that's why I grew to love it so much."

"I can understand that. My parents hardly ever took me to the park," he said.

That made me a little sad. He hadn't told me much about his childhood, but I had assumed it was decent. He never said anything bad about his parents. "Why not?" I asked.

"They just worked a lot. Didn't have the time, I guess."

"I'm sorry."

"It's okay. I can drive myself to the park now," he said with a small laugh.

"That's true," I said, laughing. "Or I'll bring you to the park."

He smiled at me. "I'd like that."

I scooted closer to him, and he put his arm around me as I leaned my head on his shoulder. We looked out over the water, watching the sun set behind the clouds. The clouds and sky were streaked pink and orange. It was a view I had missed so much this past year. It was beautiful, and it made my heart feel full and at peace. I reached up to touch the necklace, feeling the lily pendant between my thumb and forefinger as I made one last birthday wish. *I wish you could be here with us, Justin.*

Watching the sunset with Max at my favorite place while holding a little piece of Justin close to my heart was the perfect end to my birthday. I wanted to soak up this feeling and keep it with me forever.

Chapter 20

It had been about a month since my birthday, and I had been feeling pretty good, all things considered. The anxiety was still there, and I didn't think it would ever fully leave me, unfortunately. The panic attacks had lessened, which I was incredibly thankful for. There were good and bad days, of course. I was sure it would always be up and down for me because I didn't think the pain of losing a loved one would ever completely go away, no matter how much time passed or what I had going on in my life.

I'd take the good with the bad, though. I had accepted that I would always miss Justin, but I knew he would always be with me because I had the memories of all the times we shared, and no one could take those away from me. I'd cherish them always and remember how great a friend he had been. The people you were around growing up shape who you are. There would always be parts of me tied directly to him, and we would always have our inside jokes and conversations that no one else knew about.

I was sure Justin would have liked Max. I wish they could have met, but if Justin were still here, I don't know if I would have ever met Max. We had lived in the same town and never crossed paths until last year, so who's to say? I still like to think that somehow Justin sent Max to me because he knew I would need someone with him gone. It made me feel like wherever he was, he was still looking out for me.

Max had been amazing the last month, and I honestly expected nothing less. He had always been great, but sometimes people changed when the relationship dynamic changed. Max hadn't changed one bit. If anything, he had become even more perfect and attentive than he already was as a friend. His parents finally came home the week after my birthday, and he went home. Even though he only stayed with me a little less than a week, I had gotten used to Max being at my house, so, selfishly, I was bummed when his parents got back.

He started helping his parents out at The Pancake House a few days a week, and I started yoga classes and therapy, so we are a bit busier, but we still saw each other pretty much every day, even if only for a few minutes. We also started going out more once my anxiety eased off a little. Max introduced me to his friends from high school, his brother, and some other people from the restaurant. We had even hung out with Ari and Brayden a couple of times, too. It felt so normal and like a summer break should. It was the complete opposite of last year's summer break, and I was genuinely enjoying living life again.

A couple of days after Max's parents came home, he invited me over to meet them. They were the nicest people. I could tell where Max got some of his features and personality traits from. When I told them who my parents were, they insisted that we all have dinner together, just as my parents had. They were always so busy that it had been tough to nail down a time when they were free. But after almost a month, it was finally happening.

I was actually excited. I thought it would be fun to have everyone together and maybe hear some crazy stories about my parents from high school. My parents had been cleaning the house all morning, as if it didn't already stay spotless. My mom even went to Fiona's to get some fresh bouquets to put around the house. We decided that the easiest thing to do for dinner was to have it delivered. Neither Mom nor Dad wanted to be in the kitchen prepping and cooking for hours when they had to entertain guests afterward.

We called a local catering company earlier in the week to have them whip up a full spread. I told Mom she might be slightly overdoing it, but she insisted that we needed enough food for a Thanksgiving-sized meal. She ordered appetizers, salads, a main course, sides, desserts, and wine. There was no way we would eat all of the food, but Mom knew how to host a dinner that people would remember.

Everything she ordered sounded amazing, so I ate very little for breakfast and skipped lunch so I could eat as much as possible at dinner. I gave Max and his parents a heads-up so that they would know to bring their appetites. Appetizers were around five-thirty, and then dinner would start close to six, so we had about two more hours until Max and his parents arrived. I told Max to invite his brother, but I wasn't sure if Devon would want to come because he and James had broken up the week before, and I knew it was tough on him.

I was lounging on the swing, reading a book while I waited for Max to let me know if Devon was coming. On days when I didn't have yoga or therapy, and when Max was busy, I was on the swing, enjoying the fresh air and reading. It was still my favorite spot in the house, and I missed it during my time avoiding home. I hoped the coming school year would be better. I wanted to come home some weekends and actually be home to enjoy the holidays, too.

It had been so nice being home with my parents, and even though it was still challenging at times, I loved going to the places that held the most memories of Justin and me. I regretted staying away for so long. I knew that I needed time to adjust, but I wondered if maybe I could have processed it and started to feel better sooner if I had just come home and faced all the things I was so afraid of. Being back in a space where I felt comfortable and had so much love around me helped me start to heal in ways that I didn't think I'd ever be able to. Max and my family truly made my heart feel as if it were almost whole again.

Thankfully, I had only run into Christy a couple of times. I tried my best to avoid her at all costs. I even decided to take yoga at the studio across town instead of the one closest to our neighborhood, so I wouldn't run into her if she had Zumba on the same day. When I was unfortunate enough to run into her, I always asked if she had heard anything new about Justin's accident. One, because I genuinely wanted to know, but also because it made her suddenly have to go to get away from the conversation. I hadn't run into Bill at all. I hated Christy, but at least she was always by herself, and I didn't have to see Bill's awful face.

My phone buzzed on top of the mini-fridge. Max was off work, and texted to let me know that Devon was coming. I knew Mom would be happy he decided to join us. She and Dad met Devon when they went to The Pancake House, and they instantly loved him. The feeling was mutual for him, too. Mom and Devon hit it off immediately, maybe because they were both artists. He was probably the most bubbly and happy person I had ever met, other than my mom, but since he and James had broken up, he hadn't been himself. I hoped that tonight would put him in a better mood.

It was about five-twenty when I finished getting ready. I heard the doorbell sound from downstairs and figured that was my cue. I stepped off the stairs and came around the corner as Mom opened the front door.

"Hi! Long time no see!" I heard Mom nearly yell.

"Marie! Brian! How have you been?" Max's mom asked.

"Oh, Ana, we're good. How are you guys this evening?" Mom asked.

Max and Devon came through the door behind their parents. I waved at Devon, and he waved back. Max smiled, walked over, and put his arms around me, pulling me into a hug. He leaned down, his mouth right at my ear. "You look gorgeous," he whispered, sending chills all over my body.

"You look pretty handsome yourself," I said, pulling his face to mine and kissing him. The kiss lingered probably a little longer than appropriate with our parents in the same room, but they were too occupied with each other to notice.

Then, I heard Devon. "All right, lovebirds. Get a room," he said. He sounded a little more like himself than when I last saw him. Max and I broke our kiss, and we both laughed. All four of our parents were now looking at us.

"Ah, young love. Do you remember those days?" Mom asked Ana.

"Oh, do I." She replied.

"You're still my young love," Dad said as he wrapped an arm around Mom and kissed her cheek.

"And where's my sweet line?" Ana asked, playfully nudging Stephan, Max's dad, with her elbow.

He smiled and kissed her on the cheek. "Now you know you'll always be my young love."

"Yuck! You all need to go get a room," Devon said with a laugh.

After everyone settled into their seats at the dining table, we ate course after course. Mine and Max's parents reminisced about their high school days and all the trouble they could have gotten in if they had ever been caught. Who knew our parents were such rebels, with how they were as adults? It was so funny to even think of them that way. I couldn't imagine my parents young, going out and partying like they said they did, but it was fun to learn new things about them. I guess that was why they were so cool about most things. They had never really made me feel like I couldn't talk to them, and I was so thankful for that. I knew people who couldn't tell their parents anything without fearing they would flip out. Our parents were all pretty chill. I guess in that way, Max and I were raised similarly.

After dessert, we went outside to the outdoor fireplace for wine and the Charcuterie board. Our parents even poured Max, Devon, and me a glass. We sat on the patio couch and chairs while our parents talked and reminisced some more. Max and I sat next to each other, his arm around me, and my head resting on his shoulder. I was tired already, and it wasn't even late yet. Devon was in the chair closest to us, and we'd been trying to figure out plans for the following weekend. Devon wanted us to come with him to see a band that was coming to town, so we were trying to decide if the Friday or Saturday show would be best.

"Doesn't Christy live in this neighborhood, too? I haven't seen her in years," Ana asked. I hadn't been paying attention to what our parents were talking about, but my ears honed in at the mention of Justin's mom. I wondered what she would have to say about her. I saw my mom and dad exchange a look.

"She lives just a couple of houses down," Mom answered.

"Do you ever see her? I heard something happened to her and Alan's son."

I stiffened next to Max, sitting up. Devon and mom glanced toward me. I tried to keep a straight face. Although I had been better, when I was caught off guard with the mention of Justin, it still affected me, especially if it was something I wasn't expecting to hear. It was also weird to hear anyone mention Justin's dad. We hadn't heard about him in years. Since his parents' divorce, Justin had only gotten gifts and cards from him during the holidays. He never really called or stayed in touch with him otherwise.

"Yes, her son, Justin, was in a terrible accident last year and passed away. He was Amelia's best friend," my mom answered carefully.

"Oh, Amelia, I'm so sorry. I didn't realize. I knew you and Max met in the support group, but I had no idea who you'd lost," Ana said, with a sympathetic look, nearly identical to Max's on her face. Max looked so much like his mother, especially in their facial expressions.

"It's okay," I said with a weak smile.

"Poor Christy must be a wreck," Ana said. I had to stop myself from

179

rolling my eyes.

"Well," my mom started, "She's been more okay than you would think she is," she finished.

"Oh?" Ana said.

"She's not the same Christy we were all once friends with anymore. She's been a bit different since she married Bill after she and Alan got a divorce," Mom said. She was trying her best to say things nicely. Mom wasn't usually one to gossip, so maybe that was why she was trying to say it without saying too much.

"Wow. It's crazy how we've all lived in this same town, but Stephen and I have somehow missed so much. I guess we haven't been able to keep up with everyone as much since we are always traveling for work. We need more off days to be home," Ana said, looking at her husband.

"I agree," he answered. "We should make this a regular thing. It's been so nice catching up with you guys."

"We would love that!" Mom said with a big smile.

They switched topics to vacations and how we should all take a trip somewhere. I relaxed back into Max, and then Devon, Max, and I went back to talking among ourselves.

"I'm sorry my mom brought that up," Max said.

"It's okay. I'm fine," I answered with a smile. I remembered that a while back, when we first came home, Max told me that he thought Justin and Devon dated for a while, and I had been meaning to ask Devon about it. I turned to Devon. "Did you and Justin date the fall before his accident?" I asked.

Devon gave a small smile. "We did, briefly. He was great. I couldn't believe it when I heard about his accident."

"I thought I remembered Justin mentioning someone named Devon, so after Max saw a picture of him in my room and said he looked like someone you dated, I was curious. I meant to ask you before, but it always slipped my mind," I said. "His accident was a shock to us all.

Sometimes it still seems like it's not real to me."

"I couldn't imagine losing my best friend or the person I was in love with, for that matter," he said, giving Max and me a sympathetic look. "I'm glad you guys found each other and were able to be there for one another. It's a crappy thing that you had in common to bond over, but I feel like you helped each other out a lot, based on what I could see on Max's end, anyway."

"It was crappy, but I feel like we did too, or at least I know Max helped me a ton." I placed my hand over Max's and gave it a squeeze.

"It was mutual," he said, kissing the top of my head.

Devon had a sad look in his eyes. I wasn't sure if it was from his recent breakup with James or something more. "What happened between you and Justin, if you don't mind me asking?"

"It was just bad timing. He and I got along great; he was fun and caring, but I know I don't have to tell you that." He smiled at me. "It just wasn't the right time for us. He said he had some things going on that would make him cancel plans occasionally, but wouldn't tell me what they were. I always felt like he held back a lot. It's hard when someone doesn't let you in. I wonder if maybe we had met at a different time when he had less going on, if it could have been something great," he said with a sigh. "I did meet James not long after he and I broke up, but we see how that ended."

My heart sank. I knew what Justin had going on, the same thing he'd always had going on since he was a kid. Bill. Justin kept it a secret from everyone but me. I remembered the times he'd come to my house with bruises on his body. I knew why he wouldn't want to be around anyone until they faded enough not to be noticeable, or where he could have explained it away as getting hurt playing a sport. I hated Bill for everything that he took away from Justin. He took away his ability to live like a normal kid and do normal things. I wish I could have fixed it for him.

"I'm so sorry. He did always have a lot going on, but I promise, it wasn't his fault," I said to Devon, hoping to reassure him, even though it didn't really matter anymore.

"I wish he felt like he could have confided in me," Devon said. "You never know, we could have stayed together."

"He very much wanted to be the only one to fight his battles," I said. "He probably didn't want to worry you."

"I guess," he sighed.

That was the first time I had talked about Justin that much to someone who wasn't a therapist, my parents, or Max. I felt so bad for Devon. He had no idea what hell Justin endured while they were together. I didn't feel like it was my place to tell him, at least not right now, especially with our parents sitting only a few feet from us. I liked Devon, and it felt nice to have someone who knew Justin that I could talk to. I knew I could talk to Justin's other friends, but I wasn't very close with them, except for Brayden. Maybe I should have kept in touch with everyone more. I isolated myself because I was sad, but maybe I would have felt better if I had people around me who cared about Justin, too, other than my parents.

After a few more glasses of wine and an entire Charcuterie board later, Max's parents were standing up to head home. Thankfully, Stephan had only drunk one glass of wine because Ana had quite a few. They would have been staying the night if his dad had kept up with her.

"Marie, let me help you clean everything up," Ana said through slightly slurred speech.

"Absolutely not. You are our guests!" Mom answered. "We'll just make sure to leave a big mess for you at your house when we come for dinner next time," she laughed as she put a hand on Ana's shoulder.

Ana and Stephen laughed. "That works for us!"

I lingered near the back door with Max while our parents and Devon were all in the kitchen. Devon and my mom were talking about new art supplies they wanted to try for different projects, so I knew I could steal a few more minutes with Max. I wrapped my arms around his neck, and he bent down to kiss me. When his lips met mine, I felt electricity, even after a month and more kisses than I could count; it still took me by surprise. I wrapped my hands in his hair, and he tightened his grip on my waist.

I pulled back. "I don't want you to leave yet," I pouted.

"I drove separately and packed some clothes so I could stay," he said, and then kissed my forehead.

"You did?" I asked. "I thought you wouldn't stay since you had to be up early in the morning for work."

"Who needs sleep?" He asked with a laugh.

"Hopefully not you," I said, giving him a flirty grin. "I'm happy you're staying. It's been almost a whole three days since you spent the night."

"I know. Such a long time. How have you managed without me?" He asked playfully.

"We're heading out, Maxy," Ana called out to him.

We walked over to join our parents at the front door as they said their goodbyes. I hugged Devon and both of Max's parents.

"Thank you for coming over for dinner. We had a great time," I said to the three of them.

"Yes, we have to do it again soon," Mom said from behind me.

"We had a lovely time," Ana said, "And of course, very soon!"

They headed out the door, and Mom shut it behind them before heading to the kitchen to straighten everything up. She was putting wine glasses in the dishwasher as Max and I walked to the kitchen to grab water bottles from the refrigerator. Mom looked up from what she was doing. "It was so nice catching up with your parents tonight," she said to Max. "I can't believe we were all friends in high school, and now we both have children who are out of high school. Time flies."

"I think they enjoyed it too. They had been talking about how excited they were since we made the plans," he replied.

"Dinner was great, by the way," I said.

"Thanks, honey. I did a great job placing the order," she laughed.

"We'll have to order from there more often."

"Absolutely," she said.

"Do you want us to help you and Dad clean up this stuff?" I asked.

"Oh no, it's fine. You guys don't have to do that. We've got it," she said with a smile.

"Okay. We're going upstairs. Max has to work in the morning, so we'll probably go to bed soon. Goodnight," I said to them.

"Goodnight," they said in unison.

Once Max and I were in my room, I changed into an oversized t-shirt with no pants and flopped onto the bed. Max took his shirt and pants off and climbed in next to me. We'd gotten more comfortable with each other in the past month and slept comfortably now, rather than trying to be fully clothed if we were sharing a bed. We turned on a show and cuddled up to one another. His arm was draped over my body, resting against my stomach.

"How are you feeling?" He asked into my hair.

"I'm okay. Why?"

"Just checking. I could tell you were a little off earlier after my mom brought up Justin," he said.

"Oh, that. Yeah, I'm okay. It threw me off a little, but I think I'm okay now. It just caught me off guard," I said.

I reached up, feeling for my necklace. I rubbed the lily pendant between my thumb and forefinger like I often did since my parents had given it to me. Max planted a kiss on the back of my head. I felt the ever-so-familiar tingle of anxiety start to creep up my back. It had been at least two weeks since I suffered a full-blown panic attack, so I didn't know where it was coming from. I squeezed my eyes shut and started counting backward, forcing myself to breathe in and out slowly.

Max realized what was happening. He could always tell, even if I didn't say anything. He backed away slightly so I could roll over and face him. I buried my face in his chest, and he cradled me gently against his body. He held me in his arms, patting my back until I drifted off to sleep.

Chapter 21

I woke up feeling cold. I couldn't remember the dream I had been having, but I knew it wasn't a pleasant one. I had the pit in my stomach that I always had after a nightmare, but I could usually remember them. I reached back, feeling the bed next to me, and realized that Max wasn't there. I pried my eyes open and saw that he was standing beside the bed, pulling his jeans on. Looking at him through sleepy eyes, I watched as he pulled his shirt over his head.

He glanced over and noticed that I was watching. "Good morning, sleepyhead. I'm sorry. I didn't mean to wake you."

"It's okay," I said, my voice sounding groggy. "I'm cold. Come back to bed." I reached my arms out to him.

"I wish I could," he said as he leaned down for me to wrap my arms around him. He kissed my forehead, my cheek, my other cheek, my nose, and then my lips. He lingered on my lips a little longer, and I wished I could hold him hostage in bed with me all day. I needed him more than The Pancake House did. Well, that probably wasn't true. They had crazy busy mornings during the summer, so I guess they needed him more, but I still pouted a little when he pulled back from the kiss.

"Then, do it. The bed is already warmed up, and there's a spot just for you," I said, patting the spot he'd just gotten up from. He leaned down again and placed another lingering kiss on my lips. I brushed my fingers through his hair as he kissed me. I didn't want to let go. He pulled back again, and I sighed.

"I know, I know. You need to go," I said, pouting again. He smiled at me and chuckled.

"I'd never leave if that were an option," he said, quickly kissing my forehead before standing back up.

"Good."

"Go back to sleep. You need the extra rest today. You tossed and turned a lot last night. Text me whenever you wake up," he said as he walked toward my bathroom.

"I will. Have a good morning at work."

"I'll try," he said. "I'm going to brush my teeth before I go. I'll lock the door when I leave."

"Okay, I lo…" I trailed off. I did not mean to say that. Thankfully, he was already in my bathroom, so hopefully, he hadn't heard what I almost said. He stuck his head back out of the bathroom door.

"Did you say something else?" He asked.

"Just that I'd text you when I woke up," I said.

"Oh, okay. Sleep well," he said before going back into the bathroom.

I rolled over, snuggling up to the pillow he'd been lying on. It smelled like a mixture of his cologne and shampoo. It was a scent that smelled like comfort to me. I took a big inhale and drifted back to sleep.

I woke up gasping for air with my heart racing. I felt like I was in the middle of a full-blown panic attack, straight out of my sleep. I jerked upright in the bed and put my hands over my heart. It was hammering in my chest. I tried to take some slow, deep breaths, but it was hard when I felt like I'd just finished running a marathon. I lay down flat on my bed, pulling the pillow that smelled like Max on top of me. I hugged it into my chest while I counted backward from one hundred as I took a few more slow breaths.

My heart rate slowly returned to normal, and breathing got easier. I had the same pit in my stomach like I'd had a nightmare, but I still couldn't remember what it had been about. I wanted to, at least, remember what was making me wake up like that. Maybe it was my anxiety flaring back up for some reason. Thankfully, the feeling wasn't any worse than it had been at the height of it last year. I was finally starting to feel calm again, so I grabbed my phone from the nightstand.

It was almost noon. I had no idea how I'd slept so long. Max and I didn't go to sleep late, so I thought I'd wake up around ten at the absolute latest. Maybe Max was right, and I did need the extra rest. Honestly, I didn't feel rested at all, even sleeping as late as I had. I guess having nightmares all night and morning will do that. I didn't want to get up yet, so I checked my messages.

Max had texted me when he got to work, letting me know he made it there safely. Then he texted me again a couple of hours later to tell me that he was on a break and that the morning rush had been crazy. I texted him back to let him know I'd just woken up and that I woke up having a panic attack, but I was okay. I also told him that I hoped he was having a good day and to text me whenever he could.

I rolled out of bed and went to the bathroom. I hoped a nice hot shower would help me feel better and a little more awake. I brushed my teeth, turned the shower on as hot as I could stand it, and got in. I let the water run over me for a couple of minutes before shampooing my hair and washing my body. After shampooing my hair, I put a hair mask on and sat for a little while before rinsing it out. Since my morning started rough and I didn't have anywhere to be, I thought I'd do a little self-care to calm my nerves.

Once I was out of the shower, I brushed my hair and looked through the drawers in my bathroom to find a face mask. I put it on, and then lay on the bed, watching TV until twenty minutes were up. I patted the excess product from the mask into my face and finished with my usual skincare routine.

It was almost two, and my stomach was growling. I threw on some clean pajamas and headed downstairs. Mom was in the kitchen cleaning out the Tupperware cabinet when I got downstairs. "You slept in today," she said. "Do you want some coffee? I just made a fresh pot a few minutes ago." Thankfully, all of us were caffeine addicts, so there was almost always a fresh pot of coffee if my parents were home.

"I'd love one," I said as I walked over to pull a mug from the cabinet. I poured myself a big cup, dumping a few teaspoons of sugar and a splash of milk in it. I took a big swallow and sighed. It warmed my soul. I knew it was probably all in my head because coffee didn't work that fast, but I started to feel less tired almost instantly.

"Did you go to bed late?" Mom asked as she was digging through the cabinets.

"Not at all. I don't know why I slept so long," I answered.

"Maybe you didn't sleep well," she said. "You could try some melatonin."

"That's what Max said. He said I tossed and turned all night," I replied. "I woke up having a panic attack too, so I don't know what's going on."

"Oh, I'm sorry, honey. Maybe it's just a little flare-up happening right now. Your cycle could affect it. It really could be anything."

"Yeah, that's possible," I answered.

"I almost forgot," she said as she stood up and looked over at the bar. "There was a letter for you this morning." She moved around all the Tupperware bowls she'd set on the counter, finally picking up a white envelope.

"A letter? From who?" I asked.

"I'm not sure. There wasn't a return address or our address, for that matter. It just had your name on it," she said as she handed it to me.

On the front of the envelope in block print, it just said Amelia, no address, no last name, nothing. That was odd. That meant that whoever it was from had dropped it off themselves. I turned over the envelope and tore it open. There was a folded white piece of paper inside. I took the paper out and unfolded it. The writing on the paper was the same block print that was on the front.

I know you've been having a tough time, and I think I may be able to help with that. Meet me at the waterfront park tonight at 9:00.

That was all the note said. I looked at it again, turning it over to check the back, and picked up the envelope, looking at it again too. Was Max trying to surprise me? I usually wasn't a fan of surprises. I'd had my fill of surprises for a lifetime, but I was sure that what Max had planned would be amazing, like anything he did. He must have left it here when he left for work earlier, or drove back to the house on his break while I was sleeping to drop it off. I almost wondered if my mom was in on it, too.

"What did the note say?" She asked curiously.

I read it to her, and she seemed genuinely surprised. I knew my mom wasn't a great actress, but it was still possible that maybe she was good at acting surprised. Mom loved Max, so she'd go along with anything he had planned for me. I was excited to find out whatever it was. He was here when I started feeling more anxious last night, and he saw how I tossed and turned all night, so maybe he wanted to do something to help me feel a little better. He knew that the park by the water was my favorite place in town.

I wondered why he wanted to wait until nine. Maybe he needed time to prepare his surprise since he was at work today. I had the rest of the day to try and figure out what Max's surprise was, but I needed to eat, or I was going to pass out and not feel up to anything. I pulled open the refrigerator and looked for something that seemed appetizing, but nothing caught my eye.

"Are you looking for something to eat?" Mom asked.

"Yeah," I answered. "But I don't see anything I want."

"There's some bacon and eggs in the microwave that I cooked about an hour ago. Your dad and I had breakfast for lunch, and I made extra because I knew you had to get out of bed at some point today, and you'd probably be hungry," she said with a laugh.

I walked over and pressed the button on the microwave to heat up the food, and then sat down at the bar and started eating. Mom was still matching Tupperware with lids and tossing any that didn't have a match in the trash. "I don't know where these lids walk off to. It's not like they have legs. It's baffling. Maybe the dishwasher eats them?" She said.

"Maybe," I replied, taking another bite of bacon and eggs. "Where's Dad?"

"He's gone to the driving range with a couple of guys from work. They were going to go play golf, but it's ninety-eight degrees outside right now, so I told him that it probably wasn't a good idea to be walking around on the golf course for hours in this heat."

"That makes sense. I wouldn't be outside at this time of day unless it were in a pool. And even that is iffy with this heat."

"Exactly," she said. "What are your plans for the rest of the day, at least until nine?"

"I'm not sure. Probably nothing. I think I'll just hang around the house until I need to get ready to go," I said.

"Want to help me sort through all of this, then?" She asked, looking up over the counter at me.

"Sure," I said. I liked hanging out and talking to my mom. I finished eating, rinsed my plate, and stuck it in the dishwasher before sitting on the kitchen floor next to her.

It took us a while to sort through everything, and after we finished, we decided we deserved a reward for our hard work. Mom made us ice cream sundaes, and we turned on a movie. Dad got home when we were almost finished with the movie. Neither he nor Mom felt like cooking, so he grabbed a pizza and some wings on his way home for us to eat for dinner. I hadn't noticed it had gotten so late. It was about five after seven. I needed to get ready if I was going to meet Max at nine. So after we ate, I went upstairs to start getting ready.

Once I got to my room, I realized I had left my phone upstairs all day. I felt so bad because Max had probably texted or called me. I grabbed my phone from the nightstand and checked the notifications.

Max: I'm so sorry you woke up like that. I wish I could have been there. I'm glad you're feeling okay now. Work has been good, just busy like always.

Max: I was going to come over after work, but Devon asked if I wanted to see a movie this evening. He seemed a little down when he came into the restaurant today, so I didn't want to say no. If it's okay with you, I can come over after and stay the night. It may be a little later, but I don't work in the morning, so we don't have to go to bed early.

His last message was from three hours ago. I felt terrible that I hadn't responded since I first woke up. Going to the movies with Devon was a nice cover to use so he had time to set up his surprise, and so I didn't wonder why he didn't come over like he usually did. I loved that he was trying to surprise me, but he had to know that I would figure it out. I decided to play along anyway.

Me: Hey! I'm so sorry I didn't see either message until now. I was helping Mom clean the kitchen cabinets, which took forever, and then we watched a movie and ate dinner. I'm so crazy, I left my phone upstairs all day. What time are you and Devon going to the movies?

It only took a minute for him to text back.

Max: We're actually at the movies now. It just started a few minutes ago. I had my phone on vibrate instead of silent, just in case you messaged back. I was starting to get worried. I'm glad you had a good day, though. How are you feeling now?

Me: I feel okay. I think it helped that I had something to do to distract me all day. I haven't had any other panic attacks. Fingers crossed it stays that way.

Max: Good. I was hoping you wouldn't have any more. Do you want me to come over tonight after the movie, or do you want to relax and go to bed early?

I don't know why he was asking when I already knew I was seeing him in less than two hours. I guess he was still hoping that I hadn't figured out about the surprise.

Me: I want you to come over. I don't want to go to bed early. And we can relax together... or not ;)

Max: Oh? I can't wait.

Me: Me neither. Enjoy your movie! Text me when you're out.

Max: Will do. :)

I wasn't sure what the surprise would be, so I was indecisive on what I should do for my makeup. I couldn't decide if I should do a full face or just my quick everyday makeup. I opted for an in-between look. I put on a tinted moisturizer and some concealer, patted a little cream blush onto my cheeks, did a quick, neutral smoky eye with tans and browns, and then swiped a couple coats of mascara on my eyelashes, and finished with a tinted chapstick.

I ran the brush through my hair and decided to spray some beach wave spray in it and leave it how it was. I let it air dry after my shower earlier, so it had a nice texture to it on its own. I didn't have much longer before I needed to leave, so I went to my closet and picked out a mint sundress and a pair of white sandals. I went to my jewelry box, put on a small pair of hoops, and then checked over myself in the floor-length mirror. I was good to go. My lily pendant hung around my neck like it always did. I rarely took it off, so I never had to remember to put it back on. Picking out an outfit didn't take as long as I thought it would, but I wanted to go ahead and leave because I was eager to get to Max. So I threw my phone and the book I'd been reading into my purse and headed downstairs.

Mom and Dad were sitting in the living room when I came downstairs.

They were watching some reality TV show and eating popcorn. I thought about Max and me sitting together years down the road and how long my parents had been together. I wanted that, and I felt like it was possible with Max. Maybe it seemed too fast to be having those thoughts when we'd only been dating a little over a month, but we'd already been there for each other for over a year.

"I'm leaving. I'm not sure exactly when I'll be back, but it shouldn't be too late," I said.

"Okay, honey. Just be careful. And when you get home, come through the garage door," Mom said as she looked over the back of the couch at me.

"I will. Love you," I said as I walked toward the door that led to the garage.

"Love you too," they both called after me.

The park was only about ten minutes from my house. It was around eight forty-five when I pulled into the parking lot, and it was nearly empty, except for two cars. I assumed one car belonged to the couple that was walking and pushing a stroller toward it. They were probably getting ready to leave the park before it was completely dark out. I watched them take their baby out of the stroller and strap it into the car seat. The other car was parked to the side, but I didn't see anyone else in the park. Max's car wasn't in the parking lot, so I assumed I must have beaten him there since I was a little early.

I decided to get out and head down to the bench by the water to wait. Max would know where to find me. I tossed my keys into my purse and strolled down the concrete path. If I were being honest, I hoped Max would hurry because being in the park completely alone this late was a little creepy. It didn't usually bother me, so maybe it was just because my anxiety had been higher all day. I checked my phone. Max hadn't said anything back since my last message to him. He was probably just going to show up.

I took out my book and leaned back against the bench's backrest. I hoped that reading would pass the time a little quicker and give me something to focus on so I didn't get any more freaked out. It had only been five or so minutes when I heard a car door shut. I figured that it had to be Max. I didn't want to ruin his surprise, so I kept looking down at my book and pretended that I didn't notice that he was there. I could hear footsteps coming down the concrete path, getting louder as they got closer.

After a few steps, I didn't hear him walking anymore, so I assumed he had gotten off the path to come across the grass and try to sneak up behind me. He was almost to me now because I could hear his footfalls again on the grass getting closer, and then he stopped. I waited for him to say something with my head still down, pretending to look at my book.

"Amelia?" he said. The voice didn't belong to Max, but it was familiar. I looked up and whipped my head around so fast to face him that I almost made myself dizzy.

"JUSTIN?!"

Chapter 22

That was the only word that I could manage to get out. I jumped off the bench and backed away from him. I was too stunned to say anything else. I suddenly felt dizzy and nauseous. I was afraid that I was going to pass out. My heart was pounding in my chest. I didn't think it had ever beaten that fast before. My legs felt like jelly, and I thought they were going to give out on me. I leaned against the small stone wall in front of the water, placing my hand on the wall to steady myself. I closed my eyes and tried to pull in a few deep breaths.

My heart hadn't slowed down, and I was worried that I'd have a heart attack at this rate. The deep breathing didn't help either. I felt like I was gasping for air, like someone was gripping my chest, squeezing every bit of air out of my lungs. I hadn't experienced a panic attack this bad or whatever this was in so long, and I couldn't calm down. I still had my eyes closed. Maybe I was hallucinating. Maybe I was having some sort of psychotic break. That would be just my luck. I decided that I'd just keep my eyes closed, and then once I opened them, either no one would be there, or Max would be.

I struggled to take a few more slow breaths. My heart hadn't gotten back to normal yet, but I could tell it had slowed down some. It couldn't be Justin. It couldn't. I had wished for over a year that it was all a dream and that he'd just walk back into my house as if he'd never been gone, but I had finally started to accept that it wouldn't happen. Because I knew that if he were okay, he would have told me. He wouldn't have let me suffer for a year, thinking he was dead. He wouldn't do that to me, so there was no way he had been okay this whole time.

I took another big breath and opened my eyes, looking at the bench I had been sitting on. And there he was, standing right behind the bench. He didn't look quite like himself, though. His facial hair was a little longer than he usually wore it, he had bags under his eyes, and he was dressed in all black a the hood up over his head. I just stared at him. I didn't even know what to say. He moved and walked around the bench. He was standing right in front of where I had been sitting.

He opened his mouth to speak. "I know this is probably a bit jarring for you-" Justin started.

"Where have you been?" I interrupted.

"It's a long story. I'd really like to explain it to you," he continued.

The more I looked at him, the angrier I got. I would have thought that I'd be happy. I had been miserable without him and went through the worst year of my life, but how could he not tell me that he was okay? How could he let me think he was dead? I felt betrayed. The nausea was back, and I felt tears sting my eyes. I went through absolute hell, and he couldn't even send me a text saying he was okay. I couldn't handle this. So, Justin had left the note at my house. Why couldn't he have done that right after the accident? I couldn't wrap my mind around what was happening. All I knew was that I couldn't be there anymore.

Justin was looking at me, a concerned expression on his face. I couldn't take his pitying look when it was all his fault that I felt this way in the first place. I couldn't hold back the tears any longer. They streamed down my face, and a sob broke free from my throat.

"Lia-" Justin said, taking a step toward me. I held up a hand to him, and he stopped where he was. I could see tears forming in his eyes. Between sobs, I was finally able to get a sentence out.

"How could you do this to me?" I nearly screamed. I was glad the park was empty. I guess that was why he wanted to meet me at night.

"I didn't mean to hurt you. I had to get away," he said with tears rolling down his cheeks.

"I went through hell! Do you have any idea how I felt?" I sobbed. "It felt like somebody ripped my heart straight out of my chest! Why wouldn't you tell me that you were okay? I was miserable, Justin! Didn't you think about that? I was your best friend, or at least I thought I was. When my mom woke me up that morning to tell me what happened, I wanted to die with you! I went to your funeral, for fucks sake!" I yelled.

He was standing in front of me, looking down, and I could see tears running down his cheeks. I felt so bad for yelling at this person I loved and had missed so much, but I was angry. I wanted to be happy. I wanted to run into his arms, give him the biggest hug, and tell him that I was so glad he was okay, but the anger from all of the stress that I had been through because I thought my best friend had died was too strong. I had been completely miserable for the last year, and he'd been okay the whole time. I just couldn't believe that he wouldn't tell me.

"I'm so sorry, Lia," he said as he wiped his eyes and looked at me. "I'm so sorry."

I didn't know how long it took for the tears to stop, but once they finally did, I was left with the sniffles. My shoulders slumped, and I let out a sigh. I moved to the side and walked around Justin to sit back on the bench. My throat hurt from crying and yelling, and I felt like I was going to lose my mind. I put my head in my hands and closed my eyes, trying to breathe. I didn't feel like speaking until I was sure my voice wouldn't shake. He sat down on the bench next to me, but made sure not to sit too close.

I finally looked up and turned to him. He was watching me carefully. It was hard not to stare when it felt like I was looking at a ghost. I couldn't believe that he was here and that I was seeing him with my own two eyes. I opened my mouth to speak, and then stopped. I sat back against the bench and looked up at the sky. I wanted to say something, but didn't know what to say. I wanted to tell him I was happy to see him, but I had a million questions. I didn't know where to start. I wasn't even sure if I was ready for that conversation yet.

My phone started ringing in my purse, and I jumped. Mom and Dad knew I wouldn't be back for a while, so I doubted it was them. I figured it was probably Max. Apparently, he was actually at the movies with Devon earlier. The movie had probably ended, and he was most likely calling to let me know he was getting ready to come to my house. I didn't think it was a good idea for Max to come over. I was sure my face was red and puffy, and I didn't know what I would tell him was wrong with me. I didn't want to lie, but I couldn't tell him it was because I ran into Justin. He'd think I was crazy. I barely believed it myself.

It stopped ringing, and I took the phone out of my purse to check it. There was a missed call and a text from Max that he'd sent a few minutes before. He was letting me know that he was leaving the movies and going home to pack a bag. I assumed he called to make sure I still wanted him to come since I didn't text back. I didn't know what to tell him. I stared down at my phone, trying to think of something.

Me: Hey! I'm sorry, I must have fallen asleep. I was more tired than I thought. You don't have to come tonight. I'm just going to go back to sleep. I don't feel good right now.

That last part wasn't a lie. I didn't feel good. I was still nauseous and a little dizzy, and I couldn't wrap my head around it all. I waited for Max's reply as Justin sat patiently beside me. He was so still that I wasn't sure he hadn't turned to stone. I glanced over to see him looking out at the water. It was odd. I was sitting on the bench with Justin, how he and I always did, but it was immensely different from how it had ever been. My phone dinged, jerking my attention away.

Max: It's okay. I'm sorry if I woke you up when I called. I hope you start feeling better. Call me if you need me, no matter what time it is.

Me: I will. Goodnight :)

Max: Goodnight :)

"I missed you so much," I said, looking out over the water. I knew there were many more important things I needed to say or ask, but I could barely form a coherent thought to figure out what I wanted to ask first. And it was true. I had missed him. I had missed him more than I could ever explain to him. It was a pain that I wish I had never felt, that I wouldn't wish on my worst enemy.

"I missed you, too," he replied.

I could feel him looking at me, so I turned to him. Tears formed in my eyes again. Just the fact that I was seeing his face in person and not in a picture or a memory in my head was overwhelming. I sniffed and blinked back the tears. I reached out toward him, brushing my fingertips against his cheek. Although I was pretty sure he was real, I still wanted to make sure he wasn't going to disappear. I sighed as my fingers grazed his warm skin.

"I do want to know everything, but I don't think I can have this conversation tonight," I said. "I need a little time to process first."

He was looking at me with sad eyes. "I understand," he said. "But I really am sorry."

"I'm not going to say it's okay because it's not. But I want you to know that I am happy to see you, and I'm so happy that you're okay, even though all of the yelling probably made it seem otherwise."

"No, it's okay. I deserved that," Justin answered.

"Regardless, it doesn't mean it was okay for me to yell at you like that. I think right now, I just need to go home, process this, and get some rest," I said, looking out over the water again.

"Take all the time you need. Could you please not tell anyone that you saw me?" he asked.

"You know I won't. Do you have a number I could call you at when I'm ready to talk, or should I wait for another cryptic letter?" I asked.

"I'll give you my phone number," he said. I pulled out my phone and went to create a new contact. In the name, I typed J and then waited for him to tell me the number. After I typed in what he said, I looked at the number. It looked familiar, and I couldn't figure out why. It wasn't the number he had before the accident because I still had that one saved, and his phone was found in his car anyway.

I looked up at him. "Why does this number look familiar?"

"I texted you happy birthday," he answered sheepishly.

That was it, the number that texted me happy birthday that I didn't have saved. I had texted thank you, assuming it was someone from school, but the number never replied after that.

"You weren't worried about me finding out it was you?" I asked.

"I doubted you would try to trace back an unknown number telling you happy birthday, but even if you did, it's a prepaid phone with no name or address attached. I wanted to tell you for a while now. I wasn't sure how to without completely freaking you out, so if you somehow found out, it would have been okay."

"Good job with that, by the way," I said sarcastically.

"I'm sorry. I gave up trying to find the perfect moment. At this point, I assumed that it would be alarming, no matter how I did it," he said apologetically.

"A fair assumption."

He gave a weak half-smile. I was finally starting to feel as close to normal as was possible, but I still needed some time. At the very least, I needed a few hours to wrap my head around it before I could hear his explanation. Although I had calmed down, I still felt angry. Not as angry as I was, but it was still there.

I stood up from the bench, picking up my purse. I dug around for my keys, finally pulling them out. Justin stood up next to me, but he seemed so awkward. It felt so odd between us, and I hated it. I mean, it was odd right now. I'd spent a year thinking he had died, and here he was, walking up to me at the park. It was a weird situation, but no matter how strange it was, he was my best friend. That hadn't changed because "he died." His place in my life was never replaced, not even by Max. I just had to figure out how to navigate this if no one could know that he was alive.

"Can I walk you to your car?" He asked.

I nodded and started walking up the concrete path to the parking lot. I saw that one car was still off to the side. Justin must have been in the car the whole time from when I first pulled up. We walked silently to the car, and when we got to my door, I clicked the unlock button and pulled the handle. I stood by my door and looked up at Justin. "I'm glad you're back from wherever you've been," I said.

"Me too."

"I'll text you," I said as I got into the car. Justin gave me a quick nod and shut my door. I turned the key in the ignition and watched as he walked over to his car and got in. He cranked the car, but he just sat there too. I assumed he was waiting for me to leave. I flipped down the mirror and turned on the inside light to check my face. I knew I had to look horrible. My eyes were red and swollen; mascara was streaked down my face. It was far from how I looked when I left the house earlier. I just hoped my parents were already in their room when I got home so they wouldn't see me.

I shifted the car into reverse, backed out of the parking space, and headed home. When I got home, my parents were not in the living room, thankfully. I didn't know what I would have told them. They thought I was out with Max, and if I came home looking like I'd been crying my eyes out, they would definitely have some questions. My parents weren't nosy or invasive people, but they wouldn't let it slide if they thought someone had hurt me.

I crept up the stairs and into my bedroom, stripped all of my clothes off, and went into the bathroom to run a hot bath. I felt sticky from being outside, not to mention awful from all the crying. I hoped a bath could help me relax and clear my head a bit. I poured lavender bubble bath and spearmint and eucalyptus bath salts into the bath while it ran. It always smelled so amazing, and the aroma alone relaxed me. I washed all of the makeup off my face while I waited. Once the water was to the top, I lowered myself into the bath and lay my head against the back of the tub.

I thought about Justin, and it still seemed unreal. I honestly couldn't believe what had just happened. Anger stirred in my chest again, but I reached up and felt the lily pendant between my fingers like I always did, and my heart sank. I thought about all the pain I'd felt this time last year and how much I would have done anything to have one more day with him. I would have moved mountains to have one more hug, one more phone call, to see his face one more time in person. And I had, but all I did was yell and tell him that I couldn't have a conversation with him.

How had I taken the one thing that I had begged for so much the last year for granted? There he was, right in front of me, and I did nothing that I had been wishing I could do. I should have run into his arms and given him the tightest hug, but instead, I backed away from him and didn't want him to touch me. What if that was the chance that I had begged the universe so desperately for, and I just blew it? The tears came again, and this time, they felt like tears of relief. I got to see my best friend again.

They quickly turned to tears of guilt, though. I knew Justin, and I knew he would never intentionally hurt me. I felt so bad for yelling the way I had. If he had let everyone think he was dead, I knew he had to have a good reason for it. I could tell he felt terrible for keeping it from me, and I knew I had made him feel worse. It hurt to cry by that point. My throat was already scratchy and aching from earlier, and crying again made it even worse.

After the crying had subsided a little, I lay back in the water, taking more deep breaths, letting the lavender, spearmint, and eucalyptus work its magic. The water was starting to cool down, so I decided it was time to get out. I dried off and slipped on an oversized t-shirt that I was pretty sure had been Justin's, and then slid under my blankets. I grabbed my phone and pulled up Justin's number.

Me: Did you make it back to wherever you were going safely?

It only took him a couple of seconds to reply.

Justin: I did.

Me: Good.

I waited. Nothing came through, so I texted again.

Me: I'm glad that you're safe.

Justin: I'm glad you came tonight. Sleep well.

Me: You too.

I couldn't go to sleep without knowing that he was okay. I locked my phone and laid it on the bed next to me. I pulled the blankets up to my chin, closed my eyes, and drifted off to a dreamless sleep.

Chapter 23

Surprisingly, I'd slept pretty well, and when I woke up, I wasn't in the midst of a panic attack. The pit in my stomach that I had the last day or two wasn't there either. I almost thought what happened last night was a dream until I checked my phone to see the texts between Justin and me were still there. I had a message from Max telling me that he hoped I felt better and got some rest. I texted him that I did and hoped he had slept well, too.

I felt terrible that I lied to him, but I couldn't tell him the truth, not yet anyway. I wanted to see him, but I was worried that he would be able to tell that something was going on with me. I could probably pass it off as being anxious, which I was, but there was more to it than I could tell him. I also worried that my parents might say something about last night since they thought I was meeting Max for some big surprise. Then, he would know I went somewhere last night and had lied. I didn't want that either.

I could only imagine how that would seem to him if I couldn't tell him what really happened. It would look awful, and I never wanted to hurt him by making him think I met up with someone and lied about it. It was all too much. When I came downstairs, my parents asked me what my big surprise was. I obviously couldn't tell them it was Justin coming to tell me that he wasn't dead, so I lied to them, too. I said Max had a little nighttime picnic set up for me and that we hung out at the park after.

Mom gushed over how sweet that was and how Max was a keeper. I didn't want to risk Mom mentioning it to Max, so he couldn't come here, at least not when they were home or awake, until I could tell Max the truth so he'd know why I lied. My brain felt too full, and I didn't even know the whole story of why Justin did what he did yet. I needed to find that out before I told Max anything. I wasn't sure I was ready for that conversation yet, but I couldn't put it off much longer.

It had only been a couple of hours and a few lies to people I cared about, and the guilt was already eating at me. I wanted to ask Justin if I could tell Max, at the very least. I knew Max wouldn't tell anyone, but I couldn't go around acting shady without some sort of explanation. I had no idea where Justin was staying or who he was staying with, or if he was even staying with anyone, or if he had been alone this whole time. I needed answers, and I hoped I wouldn't have to wait for some middle-of-the-night meeting to get them.

Max asked about coming over, but I told him I had some errands to run and was taking an extra yoga class, so I would be pretty busy until the evening. I figured if I named enough things that seemed like they would keep me busy for a large portion of the day, maybe it would seem believable. He was off work, so it would have been the perfect time for us to spend all day together, but I couldn't until I didn't have to lie straight to his face.

Max texted me back saying that one of the employees at The Pancake House had a family emergency, so he had to cover their evening shift anyway. It worked out perfectly. He'd be occupied for the evening, so that would be one less lie I would have to tell about why he couldn't come over after all of my imaginary errands were finished. I wanted to go ahead and see if Justin could meet me sometime soon so he could tell me what was going on. And if I were being honest, I really wanted to see him again.

I knew everything was real and not some twisted dream, but it was still so strange. I wanted to see his face again in person. Like, really see him, not just yell at him and tell him I needed to leave. I had missed him so much. Although I was still a little angry, I thought the explanation would help with that, and maybe he and I could get back to normal and act like we always did around each other. All I wanted for the last year was my best friend back, and maybe I could finally have it.

Me: Do you think we could meet up today?

Justin: Yeah, what time is good for you?

Me: Anytime. I'm free all day.

Justin: I can't be out where anyone could see me. Do you mind coming to where I'm staying?

Me: Sure, and where's that?

Justin: In Kingsland. It's about thirty minutes away.

Me: Send me the address, and I'll be on my way.

My parents left not long after I got up. They were going to some museum a few towns over, and I wasn't sure when they'd be back. Justin texted me the address, and I changed clothes quickly, threw my hair in a ponytail, and headed out the door.

The drive felt much longer than it was. I don't know if it was because of unfamiliar roads, since I didn't go to Kingsland for anything, or because of the anticipation, so I listened to music to pass the time. Once the GPS said I was about five minutes away, I started to get nervous with knots forming in my stomach. I wanted to see him, but I was still trying to wrap my mind around the fact that he'd been alive the whole time. How had he found a place to stay? I didn't even know what type of place I'd be pulling up to.

The houses that I passed were pretty. It seemed like a nice neighborhood, so I had even more questions. How could someone pretending to be dead have money to pay for a place at all, much less one that seemed to be in a nice neighborhood? I turned onto the road he was staying on and drove slowly because the GPS said the house was in six hundred feet.

I pulled into the driveway of a pretty white house with a two-car garage and black shutters. It was two stories with a long porch that stretched across the front. Who was Justin staying with? There was no way he was staying here alone. In the driveway sat the car that I'd seen Justin driving at the park. I wasn't sure if I should get out and knock or wait for him to come out. I decided to text him to let him know that I was outside. The garage door opened seconds later, and he came walking out to my car. I rolled down my window as he approached.

"Is it okay if I park here?"

"Actually, could you pull into the garage? In case someone you know sees your car here," he asked.

"Yeah, sure," I said. I guess I understood him wanting my car hidden. If someone I happened to know saw my car and asked why I was here, I wouldn't know what to tell them because I didn't even know who else lived here, and I couldn't say, "Oh, just meeting up with my friend that's been pretending to be dead for a year." I put the car back into drive, pulled past his car into the garage, and turned off the engine. He came in behind me and hit the button to close the garage door. I opened my door and got out, but I felt awkward just standing there. It was like I didn't know how to act around him anymore.

"You didn't have any trouble getting here, did you?" Justin asked.

"No, the GPS brought me straight here," I replied. He walked past me to the door that led into the house, and I followed after him.

"Good," he said as he opened the door and held it, gesturing for me to go inside. We were standing in a mudroom with a shelf for shoes, hooks for coats, and a big sign that said "Welcome, please leave your shoes here." Justin slipped his shoes off and set them on the shelf, and I did the same. The mudroom led into a bright white kitchen with white walls, white cabinets, white countertops, and stainless steel appliances.

"Do you want anything to drink or something to eat?" Justin asked, turning to me.

"No, I'm fine," I answered.

"Are you sure?"

I nodded my head, but he opened the refrigerator, grabbed two water bottles anyway, and walked through the kitchen. We went through a formal dining room with a long natural wood table, and then into a living room. There were two white couches with light wood end tables at each end of both, and a deep blue ottoman sitting in front of a fireplace with a huge television hanging over it.

On each side of the fireplace were built-in shelves that went all the way to the ceiling with cute knick-knacks and books covering them, but not in a way that made it seem crowded. It was a beautiful house. Whoever decorated it knew what they were doing. Justin walked into the room and sat on the couch perpendicular to the shelves. I carefully seated myself on the couch facing the fireplace and looked around the room at all the decor. After a minute of silence, I decided to speak first.

"Whose house is this?" I asked curiously.

"It's my dad's," Justin answered.

"Your dad's? I didn't even know you two were ever in contact like that," I said, a little confused. Were there more things that he had kept from me over the years?

"We weren't," he answered. "Not until the night I wrecked." He was playing with his hands and messing with the hem of his shirt. He seemed so nervous and awkward, and I hated that. We'd never been this way around each other, and it felt so unnatural.

"What happened then?" I asked.

"I was on my way home, and when I was crossing Ashbury Bridge, a car tried to run me off the road. It got so close to me that it made me hit the barrier, and I lost control. While the car was out of control, I broke through the barrier and landed in the water," he said, looking down at his hands. I waited for him to continue.

"When I hit the barrier, it broke my windshield, so when the car hit the water, I was able to climb out before the water started coming in," he continued. "I was so disoriented that it was a miracle I didn't drown, but somehow I was able to swim to the edge and climb out of the water."

"But why not call for help? Why did you stay gone?" I asked as I felt a lump rising in my throat. Hearing him recount what happened when he wrecked was getting to me. I thought I had lost him, and it was awful, but hearing him retell exactly how I almost lost him was hard. I couldn't imagine how hard it must have been for him to tell.

"I walked to the nearest store. It was the only one that stayed open that late, and I asked if I could use their phone. I called my dad and told him that I'd wrecked and asked if he could pick me up, and he did," He explained.

"But that doesn't explain why you let everyone think you were dead," I said, still confused. Justin took a deep breath and let out a huge sigh.

"I was scared. The car that ran me off the bridge was a big SUV. I'm not exactly sure what type, maybe a Tahoe or something similar. But I saw who the driver was," he said. I sat in anticipation and waited for him to finish. "It was Bill."

I gasped and put my hands over my mouth. "Bill tried to kill you?!" I asked in shock. I knew he was the literal scum of the earth from everything else he had done to Justin, but I never thought he would go as far as to try to kill him. That was insane. Justin only had one more summer, and then he'd be away at college. So I didn't understand why he would try to kill Justin when he would have been moving out so soon. I was shocked, but also not at the same time. I guess I wouldn't put anything past Bill.

Justin nodded his head. "So, I called my dad, and when he picked me up, I told him what had happened and what had been happening since Mom married Bill," he said, finally looking up at me with tears in his eyes.

"What did he say?" I asked, surprised. He had never told anyone except me, even though he should have.

"He was upset and said that he should have fought harder to have custody of me," Justin said. "I asked him why he never really came to see me or called. He said that he did, but every time he tried to, Mom would tell him that I didn't want to speak to him or see him and that I was mad at him for leaving us. I told him I never said any of that and that mom just told me that he didn't care and wasn't a good dad, so that's why he never came around."

My heart broke for him all over again. I was stunned. All this time, I thought that Justin's dad didn't want to see him because Justin would talk to me about it and say the same things his mom told him. I couldn't believe that Justin could have gotten away from Bill years ago if it weren't for Christy's lies. I didn't think it was possible to hate her more, but somehow, I did. It was her fault that Justin had to endure what he did for so many years and was robbed of a normal, happy childhood.

"I'm so sorry, Justin," I said because I wasn't sure what else to say. It was a lot to take in, even for me, so I couldn't imagine how hard all of this was for him. I felt even worse for yelling at him when I first saw him. I felt like a terrible person. I wanted to wrap him in a huge hug and never let him go.

"I'm sorry that I didn't tell you sooner, Lia. I was scared and didn't know what to do. I wanted to make sure that Bill thought I was dead, and I worried that if I told you and they saw that you weren't upset, he might know that something was up," he said as he looked down at his hands again.

"I understand. And I shouldn't have yelled at you the way I did when I first saw you. I was hurt, but I should have known that you wouldn't do something like that without a good reason." Even though I tried to keep my words even, I started to feel a little lightheaded and nauseous.

I felt a panic attack clawing its way up my chest. All the information was overwhelming, even just the fact that Justin was here, in the flesh. I needed to get to a bathroom and splash some cold water on my face to calm down. "Could I use your bathroom?" I asked quickly, hoping I could hold it off just a few seconds longer.

"Yeah, I'll show you where it is," he said. He looked at me with a concerned expression. "Are you okay?" he asked as he got up and led me down a small hallway.

"I will be. I just need a minute," I said to him, as I walked through the door he gestured to, closing it quickly behind me. I didn't even turn on the light as I leaned against the wall, trying to calm down.

"Do you need anything?" Justin asked from the other side of the door.

"No, I'm okay," I answered, trying to keep my breathing even.

"Let me know if you do."

"I will."

I heard his light footsteps retreating as he walked back down the hall. I slid down to the floor and sat, taking deep breaths and counting backward from one hundred. When I was to twenty-three, my heart was almost back to normal, and my chest didn't feel as tight. I stood up and finally flipped the light switch on. I turned on the sink and let the cold water run over my hands for a second before leaning forward to splash some cold water onto my face. I felt like I had calmed down enough, but my mouth was so dry. I needed something to drink, so I walked slowly back to the living room, running my fingers along the wall, hoping it would help me stay grounded. Justin was on the same couch he had been sitting on before.

I walked over and sat next to him instead of on the couch I had been on. He looked over at me, surprised. I didn't like the awkward distance, and I didn't want to take my time with him for granted anymore. I couldn't be upset after knowing everything he'd been through. I was just happy to have him back in my life again. I was so glad I got to have more moments with him, like the ones I had begged for since I found out he was gone.

"Are you okay?" He asked.

"I think so. I'll take that water now." He grabbed the water from the end table and handed it to me. I opened it and took a big swallow. Panic attacks always gave me the worst dry mouth. "I have panic attacks every so often now. They eventually pass, but sometimes I need to do things to help myself calm down," I said.

His eyes looked sad. "Those are new."

"Yeah. You know I've always been an anxious person, but I've never had panic attacks until..." I trailed off.

"I'm so sorry. I wish I could take back all of the problems I've caused you," he said as he looked down again quickly, but not quickly enough to hide the tears forming in his eyes.

"It's not that you caused me problems. It was just how I dealt with the grief. I thought I'd lost you forever, and it was too much. My brain had to find a way to deal with that somehow," I said as he looked back up at me. "I missed you so much. I didn't think I was going to make it through. My life, as I knew it, had ended, and I constantly felt like a huge piece of myself was missing, like there was this huge hole in my chest that wouldn't heal. I know it sounds dramatic, but I couldn't help it."

Looking at me through glassy eyes, he reached toward me and placed his hand on mine. I flipped my hand palm up, and he threaded his fingers through mine. It felt so foreign but somehow still natural at the same time. I looked down at our hands, and tears came to my eyes, too. I didn't think I'd ever be able to touch him again, and here we were, hands clasped. I was never going to take any amount of time or contact with him for granted again.

"I still feel terrible," he started. "I never meant to hurt you. I would never want to cause you pain. I think that may have been the hardest part of this all, having to stay away from you and being unable to tell you what was happening. I wanted to so bad, and I know I could have earlier, but I was so nervous and didn't want to scare you. I tried calling a few times but never had the courage to speak," he said.

I looked up at him and suddenly remembered the calls I'd received from blocked numbers where no one would speak when I picked up. "That was you?" I asked. He nodded his head.

"I always picked up because I had some strange thought in the back of my mind that maybe it would be someone with some sort of information about what happened to you, but after a while, it just made me sad," I said.

"I know. I stopped trying to call after the last time. You picked up, and you were upset. It sounded like you were crying, and I couldn't call anymore until I knew I would be able to speak," Justin replied.

I thought back to the last time I remembered getting a call. Max and I had just gotten home, and I was not doing well. "That was my first time coming home since I left for school. It wasn't a good time for me."

"You didn't come home all year?" He asked.

I shook my head. "I couldn't stand the idea of being here, where there were so many memories. I didn't think I could handle it," I said.

He looked even more sad, if that was possible. "I didn't realize it would cause you so much pain," he said.

I let go of his hand and wrapped him in a hug. He put his arms around me, and I rested my head on his shoulder. Tears streamed down my face. His embrace felt like coming home, like my comfort, my safe space. I thought I had missed him a lot, but I didn't even realize how much until that moment. I'd forgotten just how comfortable and happy Justin always made me feel. I knew it, but I think the grief took over everything and sometimes made me forget to help myself cope. Because if I didn't remember how great it was, then maybe it wouldn't hurt so bad.

His scent was so familiar. It was like a security blanket. I never wanted to leave that moment. It felt like a dream come true because I was sure it would never happen again. I breathed him in and held onto that moment for as long as I could. When we finally pulled back, I saw that he had tears running down his face, too. We both wiped our faces and sat back on the couch. I wasn't sure what else to say.

After a couple of minutes, Justin spoke. "I can't go without speaking to you or seeing you again," he said.

"Let's hope there's never a reason to," I replied.

"There won't be."

"Where is your dad, by the way?" I asked.

"He's at work, and my stepmom is too."

"Your dad got married again? When did that happen?"

"A few years ago. He said he called to tell me because he wanted me to be his best man. Mom told him that I said I didn't want to. He even sent an invite, but she must have thrown it away before I saw it," he answered.

"I hate her," I said to him. "I hate her so much."

"Me too."

I had never heard him say that he hated his mom before. He had always said that he hated Bill and that his mom made him mad or that he couldn't stand her sometimes, but I never heard him say that he hated her. All of this had changed him. I could see it. Justin had always been silly, carefree, and fun, even with everything he had going on at home, but he was different. It made me sad for him. I hoped it wasn't a permanent change. I didn't want him to lose the fun way he went through life. I hoped that once this was in the past, he could find his way back to happiness again.

Chapter 24

I was lying on my bed, staring at the ceiling and thinking about everything Justin had told me earlier. It was insane that Bill was the person who ran him off the road. It made me hate him even more than I already did. I didn't even think that was possible for me. I wondered if Christy knew and was in on her husband trying to murder her own son. I knew she was awful, but that was a whole new level.

This was all their fault. It's their fault that I thought I lost my best friend, their fault that Justin's life was hell, and their fault that he thought his dad didn't care about him all these years. They could both burn in hell for all I cared. I didn't know if hell was a real place, but I hoped it was only because I wanted them to suffer forever. I hated that I had to leave Justin. I wish I could have brought him to my house and kept him there so I knew he was safe, but it seemed like his dad's house was a pretty safe place for him to be for now.

I stayed there for a few hours, but decided I should probably head home before his dad and stepmom got home. He hadn't told them he'd spoken to me yet, so he planned to tell them over dinner. He said that after he let them know, I could come over any time. It wasn't like he had anyone to talk to because he didn't think anyone would be able to keep the fact that he was alive a secret, other than me.

His dad was the one who suggested he stay quiet and let everyone think he was dead. After Justin told him about the wreck and everything about Bill, he said that to keep him safe, he wanted him to pretend to be dead and stay hidden while he figured some things out. Justin's dad hired a private investigator to look into Bill and find out if he had anything shady going on, so he could put together a case on him.

He hoped they could get him charged with attempted murder for running Justin off the road. He wasn't sure if they could charge him for the child abuse since they didn't have any proof or witnesses. I told Justin that I could be a witness. I'd seen the bruises, and I would gladly testify against Bill in court. He said he'd tell his dad, so he could ask the lawyer if that would be something that could help. I understood why Justin stayed hidden and didn't tell me, but I still wish I could have been there for him through the beginning stages of it all.

I hated that Justin had to go through any of that. His dad thought it was best if he didn't let anyone know he was alive until they had a decent amount of evidence and built a solid case against Bill. He didn't want Bill to know Justin was alive in case that made him try to cover his tracks or hide anything that could be incriminating. If Bill thought Justin was dead, then he'd have no reason to be worried and no reason to hide.

I thought about Max and how I hated leaving him in the dark about everything. I trusted Max as much as I trusted Justin, but I wouldn't tell him without making sure that it was okay with Justin first. He didn't even know about Max yet. Part of me wanted to tell him, but we were talking about so many other things that I didn't know how to bring it up. It would have been weird if I had randomly blurted out that I had a boyfriend. However, another part of me didn't want to tell him yet.

It's not like there was something wrong with it. Justin and I were just friends, always only friends, except for the one night we kissed, and he had stopped that pretty quickly. We both dated multiple people throughout our friendship, so I didn't know what the difference was. Telling him about Max felt different, though. It felt final somehow.

Maybe it was because everyone I dated before wasn't serious. But Max was amazing, and our relationship was serious, or it definitely could be. He wasn't like anyone else I had been with.

I felt guilty that I'd blown off Max, so I sent him a text. I knew he was at work and may not respond right away, but I wanted him to know that I was thinking of him. I knew I'd be a little worried if Max were acting to me how I was currently acting to him, and I didn't want him to worry. He trusted me, and I didn't want to screw that up.

Me: I miss you! I hope you're having a good night at work! :)

His reply came through instantly. He must have been on break or waiting for my text since we'd barely spoken since the day before.

Max: I miss you too. Work is okay. My night would be better if I were with you. :)

My heart melted. Max was so sweet. I wanted him to be with me too, but I was worried that my mom would slip and say something about last night or that I would act weird because I was lying to him. I needed to tell Justin about Max and ask if I could tell him the truth. I decided to text Justin to ask if I could see him the next day. I'd ask him then. But first, I needed to text Max back.

Me to Max: Aw :) Mine would be too. Do you think you could stay over tomorrow night?

If I could get ahead of it and ask him to stay another day, then maybe he wouldn't suggest tonight. I hoped that by tomorrow I'd have the go-ahead from Justin to tell Max as much as was necessary for him to know.

Me to Justin: Could I come over again tomorrow? I want to hear what your dad said about telling me, and I want to talk to you about something.

Max: Of course. That would be perfect :)

Justin: Yeah, I'd love that. Anytime is fine. I'm usually up early.

It wasn't late, but I was exhausted. Not so much physically, but mentally, I was drained. I'd been given a lot of information and found out so many more details about the last year, which was overwhelming. Also, lying to everyone really took it out of me. I hated lying, but I was doing a lot of it. My parents were home when I got back from Justin's, so they asked what I'd been up to all day. I told them I'd gone to an extra yoga class and hung out with Max before he had to work. More lies.

I was already in pajamas. I had showered and changed into them the second I got home from Justin's. I knew I had no energy for anything else, so I planned to go to bed early. I got up, turned off my bedroom light, and climbed back into bed. It didn't take long at all for me to fall asleep.

I woke up to the early morning sun peeking through my curtains. It was always strange for me to wake up early without an alarm. I guess that was what happened when you actually went to bed at a decent time. I rolled over to grab my phone, to see it was seven-thirty. The sooner I saw Justin and got the okay to tell Max, the sooner I could stop lying to everyone, so I dragged myself out of bed.

I texted Justin to make sure that he was up. He texted back quickly and let me know that he was. I brushed my teeth, threw on some clothes and a little makeup, and went downstairs. Mom and Dad were already gone by the time I came down, but Mom left bacon, eggs, and toast in the microwave for me. I scarfed it down and went out to my car. The drive went by quicker this time. It seemed like it was no time before I was pulling into the driveway of the white house, waiting for Justin to open the garage so I could pull in.

I felt more at ease than the day before, and he seemed a little more at ease, too. I guess it was because we'd gotten the hard conversation out of the way for the most part, and now we were okay. I wasn't angry with him anymore, and I hoped he wasn't angry with me for how I reacted. He didn't seem to be, at least. I followed him through the house to the living room again, except this time he sat on the couch facing the television, and I sat down next to him. He leaned back and propped his feet on the ottoman. I folded my feet under me and leaned against the armrest to face him.

"What did your dad say when you told him I knew?" I asked.

"He said that he was glad that I had someone I could talk to now and that if we were able to bring charges for the child abuse against Bill, your testimony would help," he answered.

"I'll do anything to see that man put behind bars, so count me in," I said. "He wasn't upset or worried because you told me?"

"No. I had to recount my whole life since his and mom's divorce, so he knew that you were still my best friend, and how close we were, the same as when we were kids, and he was around. I told him that you'd never tell anyone."

"Of course not. I want to keep you safe, and I want Bill charged just as much as he does," I replied.

"I know you do," he said, giving me a small smile. "I'm really lucky to have you in my life... and death." He finished with a chuckle.

I swatted at his arm. "Stop, but yes. Yes, you are. And I don't want to think about your death anymore. It was hard enough the first time," I said.

"Thank you for being you."

"It's all I know how to do," I replied, and then smiled at him.

"I meant to ask yesterday, did you get the flowers that I sent last year on your birthday from Fiona?"

"I did. They got delivered the afternoon of my birthday," I said as I thought back to that day and how awful it had been. I quickly shook off the memory and returned to the present, where Justin wasn't dead, and everything was crazy but still better than him being dead.

"Good," he said. "I've always been with you on your birthdays, so I hated that I couldn't be there. I was glad I had ordered them in advance, so I could still give you something since your other birthday present got ruined when I wrecked."

"You know I always love the lilies, but getting those last year was tough when I thought you had died the night before. I did keep one, though. I smashed it inside your favorite book," I said.

He smiled. "I really am sorry. I don't feel like I can say that enough for putting you through that."

"It's okay. I understand why you did what you did. It's not like it was for no reason."

"That's true, but still. What did you do for your birthday this year?" He asked.

I thought about it for a second. I didn't make a big deal out of my birthday this year since it was the anniversary of finding out about his accident. It wasn't as bad as I thought it would be. It was the first time that Max and I... I let the thought trail off.

"I didn't do much. I mostly hung out at home all day. Mom and Dad got me a cake and some presents," I said as I reached up to touch the lily pendant that hung around my neck. "We watched Labyrinth, and then I went to the park to watch the sunset. It was nice as it could be, considering..."

"Right," he said. "It sounds like it was a decent day. I wish that I had gotten to watch Labyrinth with you guys. I miss your parents. Is that necklace what they got you?" He gestured to my neck, where I was still touching the pendant.

"It is. It's a lily for you and has your birthstone in the center." It still made me choke up a little thinking about how thoughtful and special it was of my parents to get it for me.

I moved my hand so he could see it better. He reached out, took the lily pendant between his fingers the way I always did, and just stared at it for a second before letting it go. He looked like he wanted to say something, but he didn't. Maybe the necklace and what it represented made him feel even more guilty. I didn't want him to feel bad. It's not his fault that everything ended up this way. He was innocent in all of this.

"My parents miss you too," I continued. "They don't say much around me because they've been trying to tiptoe around the subject of you for my sake, but I know they took it pretty hard, too. Anytime my mom speaks about Christy, she has a disgusted look on her face."

He chuckled. "Yeah, Christy will do that to a person."

"Not even mom anymore?" I asked.

"She doesn't deserve the title. Maybe once, when I was little, but not now. Tracy has been more of a mom to me in the last year than Christy was for the past nine."

I assumed that Tracy was his dad's wife. He didn't tell me her name yesterday when he said his dad was remarried. "Blood doesn't always make family," I said. I felt sad for him because he missed out on what could have been a happy family all these years.

"That's true. Soon, I'll have another family member."

"What? How?" I asked.

"Tracy's pregnant. I'm going to be a big brother," he said with a huge smile.

"That's amazing!" I almost yelled. "Tell your dad and Tracy I said congratulations when they get home today. You'll be the best big brother ever."

"I hope so. It's pretty exciting to have a family that is caring and not dysfunctional. Your parents were the closest thing that I got to experience to that since my parents divorced. Even before they did, I remember them fighting all the time when I was little," he said.

"I'm so happy for you. I know you still have a little way to go before everything is normal with trying to build a case against Bill, but it's not far away. Before you know it, you will have a somewhat normal life again," I said.

"And I can't wait."

We sat on the couch, talking and catching up, and he asked about how school had been and how living on campus was. I told him about my classes and that I was still undecided on my major. I kept conveniently leaving out anything about Max. I said I'd met some people at school, but didn't go into detail. That was not exactly the truth since I'd met Max not long after Justin's accident in a support group, not at school, but something just had me keeping that part of the last year to myself. I asked Justin if he would try and start college once everything came out.

"If I can get in," he said.

"You got in last year, so it shouldn't be too hard to pick up where you left off," I said.

"But I didn't." He looked down at his hands.

"What? We had a whole conversation about what all we were going to do once we got there," I said.

I thought of our conversation just a few weeks before his accident. I was so excited, and we were talking about how great it would be for him to be away from Bill finally. Thinking back, he did seem a little off when we were talking about it.

"I lied. I got my rejection letter, and I was embarrassed and bummed that I'd have to spend another year at home with Bill, taking classes at Briar Glen until I could reapply and hopefully transfer the next year," he said, still looking down.

"Why didn't you tell me? You know you don't have to be embarrassed with me," I said.

"I know, but I was really down because I didn't want to be at home for another year. I never told Christy or Bill either. They probably would have hated that I had to live at home longer," he said. I couldn't imagine how heartbreaking it must be to have one of your own parents not care about you and not want you at home with them.

I reached my hand out and gently touched his cheek as he turned toward me. I looked at him, noticing his boyish features. He still looked the same as when we were kids, but just with facial hair now; his messy hair, blue eyes, and crooked bottom teeth. I had missed his face so much. I brushed his hair back from his eyes, and he leaned into my hand. I stoked his cheek with my thumb. He was just an innocent kid who never deserved all the hell he'd been through.

I knew we were both kids, but my life had been vastly different than his. No matter how much I tried to shield him then, he always had to go home eventually. I wanted to protect him, and I hated that I wasn't able to. Justin leaned in closer, putting his hand on my face, as he brushed my hair behind my ear.

"I missed you so much, Lia," he said softly.

"I missed you too," I replied.

He moved his face forward, kissing me. It felt like it was just yesterday when we kissed last year before his accident. I wanted to throw my arms around him and pull him close to me, but my mind immediately went to Max, and I pulled back. I hung my head down because I felt terrible.

"I can't," I said, not meeting his eyes. "I'm seeing someone."

"I'm so sorry. I didn't know," Justin said.

"It's okay. I'm sorry I didn't say something before." We sat awkwardly in silence for a moment, and then he spoke.

"Was he the guy who was with you at the cemetery?" He asked.

My head shot up, and I looked at him. "What? How did you-" I broke off. I thought back to when Max and I had gone to the cemetery. I felt eerie, like someone was watching me as soon as we got out of the car. It had been Justin the whole time. I remembered the person at the edge of the cemetery that I swore was staring at us, dressed in all black, just like Justin had been when he met me in the park.

"You," I said.

"I happened to go by because I was curious if my mom had gone since it was close to the date of the accident. I wanted to know if she was even pretending to care, but then I saw you there."

224

"I saw you looking at me. I didn't know it was you, but it made me feel eerie, especially because I asked Max if he had seen someone, and he hadn't. I thought I was going crazy," I said.

"I didn't mean to freak you out, but I hadn't seen you in so long, and it took everything in my power not to go over to you," he said.

It was comforting to know that I hadn't been going crazy and that I wasn't hallucinating. It was so strange that he had been that close, and I had no idea. My mind went to the flowers and the card. Had he gone back, and would he have read the card? Maybe that's why he kissed me.

"Did you go to your grave after that?" I asked.

"No, I didn't. After I had such a close call with you being there, I decided that maybe it was too risky to go," he answered.

I let out a sigh of relief. Justin hadn't read the card.

"Is Max the guy you're seeing, the one who was with you?" He asked.

"Yeah, we've been dating a little over a month, but we've been friends for about a year."

"A year?" He asked curiously.

I knew the timing must have seemed odd for Justin, considering that just over a year ago was when he wrecked. "I started going to a grief support group after your accident. I met Max there, and he was there for me a lot while I was having a hard time. He was in the group because his girlfriend had passed away a few months earlier from cancer."

"That's terrible," he said.

"Yeah, it was easy to talk to him because I felt like he understood what I was going through. We'd both lost somebody that we loved."

"I'm glad you had someone to help you while I was gone," he said.

Every time I brought up how hard of a time I had this last year, he always looked so sad. It was awful, but none of that mattered now that he was back. I wished that he would stop feeling guilty for it. "I've been lying to him the past couple of days, and I feel terrible," I said. Maybe this was my opening to ask if he minded if I told Max.

"Why have you been lying to him?"

"He was supposed to come over the night I met you in the park. I honestly thought the note was from him and that he had some surprise planned, but once I met you and got upset, I lied and told him I was in bed. He would be able to see that something was wrong, and I couldn't tell him what it was. I didn't even know anything, just that you were back," I said. "Then the next day, I blew him off because I was worried mom would say something to him about me going the night before because she thought I was with him too, so it would have been a mess if she mentioned it around him and he found out that I was lying the whole time."

"Why didn't you tell him what happened?" He asked.

"You didn't want anyone to know," I said to him.

"If you trust him, then I trust your judgment. You can tell him, so you don't have to keep lying." So, I didn't even have to ask. If I had known that it would be that simple, I would have brought it up the day before, or I'd like to think I would have. I wanted to, but for some reason, I had been hesitant. Maybe I didn't want Justin to feel like I replaced him with Max since he was gone, or I didn't want the door closed on possibilities of what Justin and I could be now that he was back. But I couldn't think about that right now. I needed to think about how I was going to tell Max.

Chapter 25

The whole drive back, my mind was racing with what had happened. Justin had kissed me, and I wasn't quite sure how I felt about it. Guilty was one emotion because I felt like I had betrayed Max. Not only had I been lying to him, but I kissed someone else. I wasn't sure if I should leave that detail in when I told him that Justin was alive. If it didn't mean anything and there was no reason it would happen again, I could leave it out and let everything be normal without hurting Max.

The thing was, I wasn't so sure that it didn't mean anything. I stopped it because it wasn't fair to Max, but if I weren't with Max, I don't know if I would have stopped it or not. My mind was all over the place. I cared about Max so much, but Justin had been there my whole life. We had been through everything together; he was my best friend since birth. When I kissed Justin last year, I had been so embarrassed when he stopped it. I thought he didn't think of me that way, but maybe it was just the timing. There were so many things to consider and not only mine but also other people's feelings to consider.

I didn't know how I wanted to tell Max, or what exactly to tell, or what to leave out. It was too much to think about. The last thing I ever wanted to do was hurt Max. I couldn't stand the thought of hurting him. Maybe if I had more time to think and get my thoughts straight, I could figure out what to do. I'd taken in more information in the past three days than my brain could handle while still making rational decisions.

Once I got home, I texted Max that he could come over whenever he was ready. I made myself a sandwich and ate quickly. I was ready to see him because it had been days, and I was so used to seeing him that the last few days had felt like forever. But I was so nervous at the same time because I knew the conversation we had to have. I knew I had to tell Max the whole truth, even if it made me uncomfortable. I couldn't keep anything from him. He deserved better than that.

About thirty minutes later, Max was knocking on the front door. I forgot to unlock it when he told me he was on the way, so I walked to the door and pulled it open. He was standing there, dressed in light blue jeans and a dark grey t-shirt. He smiled as soon as he saw me, and my heart fluttered. I was so happy to see him, but the pit in my stomach grew because I knew he wouldn't be this happy for long.

"Hi," he said as he came inside.

"Hey," I said, smiling back at him as I shut the door.

When I turned back, he was right there. He pulled me into a hug, and I felt my body relax into his. It was my natural reaction to Max, no matter what was going on in my head. "You look beautiful," he said, looking at me before he brought his lips down to meet mine.

I'd missed Max's lips. They felt as perfect and soft as they ever did. I wrapped my arms around his neck and pulled him closer. I didn't want to break from that perfect moment because I worried he might not want to kiss me again once he knew I'd kissed someone else. I relished the moment for as long as I could before I pulled back. "Thank you. You look handsome too, but that's nothing new." I gave him a grin.

He kissed the top of my head. "Thank you. I missed you."

"I missed you, too." The nerves set in as we both went quiet. I knew I couldn't hide the fact that something was going on in my head from Max. He could always tell, so I figured I might as well spit it out instead of dragging it out longer than I needed to. I took a deep breath and let out a small sigh.

"Is something wrong?" Max asked.

"No. Well, yes. Not wrong, but there is something that I need to tell you," I answered. I could feel him looking at me, but I didn't want to meet his gaze. "Do you want to go sit in the living room?" I asked. My parents weren't home, so I thought we could have this conversation downstairs instead of in my room.

"Sure," he said.

I turned to walk to the living room, still not looking at him. He followed behind me, and we sat on the couch in our usual spots—me, at the end where the chaise lounge was, and him right next to me. I finally looked up and saw that his eyes were full of worry, his brows drawn in anticipation of what I was about to say. I hated this. I wished that I could leave out the part about the kiss. That would have made this a million times easier. If I knew that it meant nothing, then maybe I would spare that detail, but right now, I couldn't one hundred percent say that it didn't. No matter how much I cared about Max, I still felt something for Justin. When I thought he was dead, it didn't matter, but now that I knew he wasn't, it was different.

Max was waiting for me to speak, but I didn't even know which part to start with. I didn't know if I should say that Justin was back, or how I found out he was back, or what. I figured the beginning was probably the best place to start, so it all made sense of how I even found out.

"The day after dinner with our parents, I got a letter. It told me to come to the park at nine that night. I initially thought it was from you and that you had some surprise or something planned," I started.

"I didn't leave a letter here, and that was the day I went to the movies with Devon," he said.

"I know. I thought that you telling me that you were going to the movies with Devon was some way to make me think you weren't planning something, so I'd be surprised," I continued. "So I went to

THE GHOST OF YOU

the park, and I waited. I heard someone walking up behind me and assumed it was you, but it obviously wasn't." Max nodded, urging me to continue. "This is going to sound crazy, but when I turned around, it was Justin standing there."

Max's eyes went wide, and he looked confused. "Your friend who died in the car accident?" He asked. The look went from confusion to pure shock.

"Yes," I said. "When you called me that night, and I didn't pick up, it was because I was there. I told you I was in bed because I didn't know what else to say, and I feel terrible about lying to you. I could barely believe it myself, and he didn't want anyone to know, so I just lied." I watched Max's face carefully. He still looked shocked. "At the time, I didn't know how he was back or what he'd been doing for a year, so I wouldn't have had any explanation to tell you. I wanted to find out what happened before I said anything."

"So this is why you've been avoiding me the last few days?" He asked. He didn't seem angry when he asked, just curious. I knew that he would notice that I was acting weird. I instantly felt guilty that he thought that I had been avoiding him for some unknown reason.

"It is. I hated not telling you, but I needed to wrap my head around it. That night, I left before he could tell me anything. I was upset, angry, and so confused as to why he would pretend to be dead and let me go through hell, so I told him that I couldn't talk about it yet," I said. "I went home, took a bath, and went to bed. I hated telling you not to come over, but you would have seen how upset I was, and I didn't know what I would tell you was wrong."

"I understand. That would be a big shock to anyone. I don't understand what would make a person do that, but I can't imagine how hard that must have been for you to find out after the tough year you've had." He reached his hand out to place it on mine. I wrapped my fingers in his for what might be the last time. This was the easy part, shocking but still manageable compared to what else I had to tell him. "I yelled at him that night. I felt so bad about it. I had missed him so much, but finding out that I struggled so much and he wasn't even gone made me angry," I said. Max rubbed the back of my hand with his thumb. He had a sympathetic look on his face. My heart sank. I couldn't hurt him. I just couldn't.

"Did you find out why he did that?" He asked.

"I did."

I explained everything to Max about the wreck that Justin had told me. He already knew how bad Bill and Christy were from what I had told him before, but he was still surprised when I said that Bill was the one who caused Justin to wreck. I told him about Justin's dad and stepmom and how they were working on building a case against Bill before Justin could let everyone know that he wasn't dead and why he kept me in the dark so long. I said how scared Justin was and how he didn't know what to do.

"That's insane," Max said after I finished telling him everything.

"It is. It was a lot to take in, but I understand why he did what he did now."

"Yeah," Max said. "It seemed like he didn't really have a choice."

"I've felt horrible lying to you the past few days, but I needed to find out what happened and let it sink in, you know?"

"I completely understand. You don't have to feel bad about that. It's a crazy situation," he said.

I looked down at our hands; our fingers were still intertwined. Now came the tough part, the part I was trying to put off for as long as possible. I could feel a lump in my throat rising. I swallowed it down before I looked back up at Max to speak. "There's one more thing that I need to tell you."

Max's expression was neutral now. "What is it?" He asked.

I took a deep breath and tried to calm my now jittery nerves. "You know how I told you I went over there again this morning?" I started.

"Yeah," Max said, looking a little confused. I'm sure he had no idea where this was going.

"When I was there, we were talking about his mom and everything, and it got a little emotional," I said. Max was looking at me, his expression unreadable. "It was a weird moment, and we kissed." I waited for Max to say something, but he was still just looking at me, maybe processing what I had said. "I stopped it," I went on. "I told him I couldn't because I was seeing someone."

He took a deep breath and let out a sigh. "Did it mean anything to you, or were you just caught up in the moment?" He finally asked, his voice sounding a little shaky.

"I don't know," I said, looking down. He pulled his hand back from mine, and I knew I had messed up. My hand felt cold at the loss of his touch, so I folded my hands together in my lap.

"You don't know?" He asked, a slight edge of irritation in his voice. "I know you had feelings for him before, but do you still?"

"I don't know," I said, still looking down. "I mean, I thought he was dead, so how I felt didn't matter." I felt the lump rising in my throat again, and the tears pricked at my eyes. I heard him take a deep breath, and I peered up at him. His cheeks were burning red, and his eyes looked glassy.

He finally spoke after a couple of seconds. "What do you want to do?" He asked, his voice still shaky.

"I care about you, but…" I trailed off.

"But?" he asked, waiting for me to finish the sentence. I looked up and saw a few tears running down his cheeks. He wiped them away quickly but didn't meet my eyes.

"Max, I'm sorry," I said.

"What are you saying? Are you breaking up with me?" He asked. He still wasn't looking at me, but I could see the tears in his eyes, which made the tears in mine fall even faster.

"I don't know what I want," I said as my voice cracked. "I'm so confused right now. Maybe I just need some time," I said.

"Time? To decide if you want to be with him or me?" Max asked.

I could hear the hurt in his voice, and it broke my heart. Max was the last person in the world that I ever wanted to hurt. He'd been my rock when I didn't think I'd make it through, and the one constant good thing in my life for the last year. I didn't want to lose him, but was it selfish of me to try to hang onto him when I wasn't sure what I wanted? Max stood up from the couch.

"I think I need to go," he said.

"Please don't leave yet," I pleaded.

"I don't know if I can sit around and wait while you decide who you want, Amelia. I care about you so much and want you to be happy; I truly do. But I don't think that's fair to ask me to do."

"It's not, and I'm sorry. I don't know what to do right now. My head is all over the place. I didn't want to hurt you, but I didn't want to keep this from you either. I'm so sorry." My tears were coming full force now. "I don't want to lose you." I reached out for him, but he pulled back out of reach. He backed up, walked around the couch, and headed for the front door, but I followed after him quickly.

"I think I need some time to think about all of this. You take whatever time you need, but I can't promise I will be here when you decide what you want," Max said with a sniffle, his eyes red from crying.

I felt horrible, my sweet Max. I hated being the thing that caused his tears. He reached for the door handle, and then he was gone. I stood there staring at the front door. I hated this so much. The one person who was always there for me and whom I could always count on, I had hurt. I hated myself for that, but I couldn't help how I felt.

I went to my room and crawled into bed. I didn't eat lunch. I wasn't even hungry. I was just sad. I had a text from Justin asking if I was coming over the next day, and I wanted to, but I was still thinking about Max and how hurt he looked before he left. I wanted to be excited to see Justin tomorrow, but at that moment, I just wanted to cry, sleep, and maybe cry some more. I have had my heart broken before, but this time I was on the opposite end, and it still felt just as awful. I didn't want to break up with Max, but I needed to figure out my feelings for Justin and if there was anything to them.

I had to tell Max what happened to be able to do that. I would never cheat on him while I figured it out. I couldn't do that to Max or anyone, for that matter. It wasn't fair to ask him to wait for me to figure it out, but it also wasn't fair to him if I kept dating him when I possibly had feelings for someone else, either. I felt like it was a lose-lose situation. There was no perfect solution where no one got hurt. Someone would be hurt no matter what I did, and I hated that. I didn't like hurting people, and I didn't like being the bad guy. I sent Max a text telling him how sorry I was, but he didn't respond. I didn't expect him to, and I didn't blame him for not responding, but that still didn't make it hurt any less.

Chapter 26

I woke up feeling a little better, still sad, but I knew I had to push through the day. I had to figure out what I wanted. Max deserved a definite answer sooner rather than later. That was if he would even speak to me by the time I made my decision. He still hadn't texted me back, which was understandable. I probably wouldn't want to talk to me either. But Max had been such an incredible and comforting presence in my life, so knowing I may never have that again was hard to accept.

I finally texted Justin back when I woke up to let him know I was coming over. I felt like we needed to talk about him kissing me and what that meant for us. I needed to know if he was caught up in the moment because he had missed me and it was an emotional time, or if he actually felt something for me. I also felt like I needed to tell him I remembered the night at my house when we kissed, since he didn't read the card I put on his grave. I didn't want any more words left unsaid.

I wanted everything I felt out there, and I needed to figure out what was best for us. Not only for me, but for Max and me, just for everyone involved in my life. I hated hurting people, especially those I cared about so much. None of this was easy, and it had my head all jumbled. I needed some clarity. I wanted to let go of everything around me for a few minutes and just be in the moment. Thankfully, I had yoga soon, so hopefully, I would be able to ground myself and calm my mind for a

THE GHOST OF YOU

little while.

After yoga, I went home, took a quick shower, and headed to Justin's. The whole drive there, I was trying to decide how I wanted to start the conversation and what I would say. The drive seemed like it got shorter every time. I didn't even need my GPS since it was a relatively simple route to memorize. There was another car in the driveway when I pulled up, so I texted Justin that I was outside.

Seconds later, Justin walked out of the front door. I rolled my window down and asked if it was okay to park where I was since the garage was blocked. He said it was fine, so I got out and walked up the driveway to meet him on the porch. He walked down to the end, where a swing hung, and sat down, so I followed after, sitting down next to him.

"Is someone else here?" I asked curiously.

"Yeah, my dad is home. He said the private investigator had some more information and wanted to come over and show my dad what he found."

"Oh wow, I wonder what it is," I said, looking at Justin.

"I don't know, but it must be something good because dad said that the PI told him that I shouldn't have to be stuck in the house much longer with what he's found," he replied.

"When is he coming over to show your dad everything?" I asked.

"He should be here anytime. I think Dad's lawyer is coming over, too. Dad said that he would be able to advise us on the best course of action to take with everything."

That was amazing news. Justin was so close to being able to go back to a normal life, and I was so happy for him. Hopefully, Bill would be behind bars soon, and if we were lucky, maybe Christy too. I wanted nothing more than for Justin to be able to live his life again and finally be happy, especially now that he had his dad, stepmom, and a baby sibling on the way. It would be perfect for him, and I couldn't wait.

Two cars pulled up at almost the exact same time. One was a sleek black Audi sedan, and the other was a black Mercedes SUV. They both exited their cars and nodded to one another. The one in the Mercedes wore a tailored grey suit and carried a briefcase. The other wore jeans and a t-shirt, and he was carrying a cardboard file box. I assumed the man with the suit and briefcase was the lawyer. The front door opened, and Justin's dad, Alan, stepped out onto the front porch.

He looked down the porch at us. "Amelia! I haven't seen you since you were a little girl," he said, giving me a huge smile. "How have you been?" He asked.

I smiled back. "I've been well, other than…" I gestured to Justin and around.

He chucked. "Right. Hopefully, everything will be straightened out and back to normal very soon."

"I hope so."

The men were coming up the porch steps as Justin's dad waited by the door. They both nodded their greetings to him as they approached, and he opened the door and ushered them inside. "Let's see what you've found," I heard him say as he shut the door behind them.

"Well, that's exciting," I said to Justin.

"I'm really curious what they've found out," he replied.

"Do you need to go in there with them? I can sit out here and wait."

"Oh, Nah, not yet. Dad's going to get all the details from the PI, and they're going to discuss the best options. Then I'll go in so they can tell me the gist of what they found and see what I'm comfortable with doing," he answered. "Did you tell your boyfriend about everything yesterday?"

"I don't think he's my boyfriend anymore, but yes. I did," I said.

He looked at me with wide eyes. "What do you mean? What happened?"

I told him everything Max and I had spoken about, and what Max said, and how he understood why I lied. Then, I told him how I told

Max about the kiss.

"Oh no, Lia. I'm sorry. I didn't want to cause any problems for you. I feel like I've already caused enough," Justin said with a weary expression.

"It's okay. It's not your fault, it's mine," I said, shrugging.

"Well, I kissed you, not the other way around."

"I know, but it wasn't the kiss that upset him. I think he could have let that go," I said.

"Then, what was it?" He asked.

I bit my lip, suddenly feeling nervous. "He asked if it meant anything and if I still had feelings for you." I looked down at my hands. "I said I didn't know and that I was confused and needed some time to think about everything."

"Still had feelings?" He asked with a raised eyebrow. I had never told him, but I thought he might have known since I kissed him. I figured that would have given it away.

"Yes, still. You had to know that I did before." I looked over at him.

"I didn't know. How would I? You never said anything about it." He looked confused.

"I kind of figured you knew since I kissed you that night," I replied.

"You remember that? I thought you didn't, so I assumed you had just kissed me because you were drunk," he said, surprised.

"I remembered. I was just embarrassed because you stopped it. I thought you didn't feel the same way," I answered, letting my shoulders sag a little.

"I did feel the same way, but I didn't want to go any further while you were drunk. I wanted you to be sober and sure of what you were doing." He sounded relieved.

"Did?" I asked.

"Did. Still do, I think."

"I get what you mean. That's why Max got upset. I couldn't give him much more than an 'I don't know' because so many emotions are going through me right now. I like Max, but I've always loved you, and you kissed me. My mind is so all over the place that I can't tell what I'm feeling for anyone anymore," I explained. Justin put his arm around my shoulder and hugged me close to his side, stroking my hair.

"It's okay. I understand that it's all a lot. I didn't mean to make it more confusing by kissing you yesterday. I wouldn't have if I knew you were dating someone," he said.

It wasn't his fault. He had no idea about Max. It was my fault for not telling him. I think I would be confused either way. I had always felt the same about Justin, or at least in recent years, but I only acted on it once, and then I thought he died, so I didn't worry about the feelings I had for him because it didn't matter anymore. When I thought he was dead, the only thing I was worried about was how much I missed him and how sad and empty I felt. His coming back made those feelings resurface.

He had always been my best friend, so I didn't even know how it would be to have an actual relationship with him. Did I have real feelings, or was it normal to develop a crush on someone who had always been there for you and whom you cared for so deeply? I didn't even know if we would work as a couple. We had been around each other our whole lives, so you'd think it would be a no-brainer, but it wasn't. Max and I started as friends, too, but I hadn't grown up with Max.

I rested my head on Justin's shoulder. I wasn't sure what else to say. Part of me wanted to test my theory, just kiss him and see how we felt about it afterward. I wanted to see if there was anything to our feelings or if we were feeling this way because emotions were high with him coming back after a year and everything else going on. I felt like I owed it to myself to try, especially since I had possibly ruined what relationship I had with Max already. I picked my head up from his shoulder and turned to look at him. He gazed back at me.

I leaned in, nearly closing the space between our lips, when the front door swung open. I jerked back immediately, and we both turned to see Justin's dad standing in the doorway, his head still turned, looking into the house, speaking to one of the two men who had gone inside earlier. He stopped talking and stepped outside onto the porch, looking toward us before he spoke.

"Do you want to come inside and see what all we've found on Bill? I think you'll be interested in this," he said to Justin.

"Sure." He stood up and walked toward his dad, while I stayed seated on the swing.

"Amelia, you can come inside. You're welcome to be a part of this, too, since you know everything that has happened," Alan said to me.

The two men were sitting at the table in the formal dining area with papers splayed across the table in all directions, nearly covering the whole thing. I had no idea what I was looking at, but I sat down in a chair next to Justin. His dad sat down across from us. Justin's dad relayed to us everything they found, and the PI, whom I now knew as Philip, filled in any important details Alan missed. The lawyer, Bruce, told Justin about his options and how they could proceed with bringing a case against Bill.

Bill had been laundering money through the car dealership he owned, according to a former employee whom Phillip was able to track down. He left with some bad blood between him and Bill, so he was more than willing to tell the PI anything he wanted to know. The ex-employee said that once in a back room, he'd opened a crate that he thought had new displays for the dealership and saw a ton of guns, but he wasn't sure what kind they were. He also told Phillip that Bill had a terrible gambling problem and that he would hold poker games with shady clientele and take money from the business account to place his bets when he ran out of his own.

Philip looked into Bill a little more after that and found that about a month before Justin's accident, Bill had taken out a hefty life insurance policy on Justin. Phillip believed that Bill was broke and trying to get rid of Justin to collect the life insurance before he had to file for bankruptcy. He figured that between Bill's illegal dealings and the gambling, he had gotten into some hot water and needed a large amount of money quickly. They weren't entirely sure of Christy's part in any of it, but Bruce made sure to let Justin know that if they tried to take Bill down, it was possible that his mom could go down with him, too.

Justin said that he didn't care if his mom went down too at this point. I knew that Christy helped at the car dealership, and I wondered how much she knew. I was curious if she knew about Bill's gambling or the money laundering, or if she was helping Bill go broke with all of her unnecessary spending. She'd always been like that. Justin's dad was a doctor, and sometimes I wondered if one of the reasons they divorced was because of how much money she spent.

Bruce told Justin that it may be more difficult if he wanted to try to bring a case against Bill for child abuse, since there wasn't any evidence, and since he was legally an adult now. But he said they could use the abuse in the attempted murder case to show that this was a pattern for Bill to harm Justin. Bruce asked me if I was comfortable with being a witness on the stand during the case. Although it was a little scary, I wanted to take the stand and look at Bill in his smug, stupid face when I testified about what I had seen him do to Justin.

There was so much information to take in that it made my head spin. I couldn't imagine how much this must be costing Justin's dad between the private investigator and the lawyer, but I was so happy that he was willing to do all of this to get justice for his son. I admired him for it. He reminded me of my own parents because I knew they would do the same thing. I thought of them and how they would react to the news that Justin was okay. My parents always thought of him as their second child because we were always together, so his accident was tough on them, even though they tried to hide it and stay strong for me. I couldn't wait to tell them that he was okay.

After Bruce and Phillip told Justin everything he needed to know, we went upstairs to Justin's room. They still had other things to discuss with Justin's dad, and they were trying to figure out how to find more evidence that Bill was the one who ran Justin off the road. They said they worried Bill would try to say that Justin didn't remember correctly because he had hit his head in the wreck, so they needed to find a way to get more concrete proof. They were so close to the end, but they still had to tie everything together before they let anyone know that Justin was alive.

His room upstairs was bright, and there was a huge window that let in so much sunlight that I bet made it impossible to sleep once the sun came up. The white walls made the room even brighter as the sun reflected off them, and his bed was queen-sized with a navy blue and white striped comforter and pillow shams. It didn't look like Justin, but I guessed that was because it was a guest room before he got there. Maybe he would make the space more his style once everything was settled.

He walked over to the bed, plopped down on one side, and grabbed the remote to turn on the TV. I walked to the other side and climbed on, scooting until I was in the middle of the bed, so I was closer to him. He looked over at me and then moved my way until our arms were touching. It felt awkward, like we were both tiptoeing around something, and maybe we were. We were trying to figure out how to act around each other now that we knew about each other's feelings. It was so odd.

Justin picked a random show and put the remote on the bedside table. He chose a cooking competition show. Those were always a good option when you had no idea what to watch. I looked over at him as he turned to face me. I brought my hand up, brushing my fingers lightly against his cheek, before running them through his hair. He closed his eyes, took a deep breath, and leaned into my hand. I leaned forward and pressed my lips against his. He brought his hand up, gently placing it on my face as he moved the other to my waist. He kissed me back, and the butterflies in my stomach went wild.

I wrapped my arms around his neck and twisted my fingers into his hair. He deepened the kiss. My lips parted as he ran his tongue along my bottom lip. It felt like something that was a long time coming, but I couldn't stay focused. It was probably because of everything we'd just found out and how new everything was. It was overwhelming, but I wanted to enjoy the moment and not overthink it too much.

I opened my eyes to peek at Justin; his ocean blue eyes were closed, his long lashes fanned out. Seeing him helped take my mind off everything else. He was so gorgeous, so how could it not? I closed my eyes again and pulled my body closer to his. I let my hands roam over his body, losing myself in the moment.

Chapter 27

I t had been about a week since I told Max how I felt about everything. It took him four days before he would speak to me at all, and even then, it wasn't much. He responded to my message to let me know he was okay, but that was the extent of it. He didn't keep a conversation going by any means. I missed him so much that I could barely stand it. I understood why he wasn't talking to me, but I hadn't gone this long without talking to him since we first started being friends last summer.

I was so happy once he finally messaged back, even if it was only something short. I was glad that he was okay, and I hoped that he might come around as time passed. I thought about Max all the time and desperately wanted us to go back to how we were. He had always been so sweet and caring, and I hated not seeing or speaking to him. There were a couple of times that I considered showing up at the restaurant when I thought he would be working, but ultimately, I decided against it. I knew that he needed space, but I missed him beyond words.

Justin and I had been hanging out almost every day, but that never really kept my mind off Max. I thought that it would, at least a little, if I had feelings for Justin the way that I thought I did, but it didn't. Things between Justin and me had been fine, or a little less than fine, I guess. We got along like we always had, but everything had been more awkward. The first day, I thought it was because we had a lot on our minds, but it seemed like every time we were alone or tried to be intimate, it felt off. I hadn't let anything more than kissing and a little exploring hands happen because it didn't feel right to try to take things any further with him.

I loved Justin, but the past week had me wondering if maybe I was wrong in thinking that the love was more than just love between friends. Justin and I had always been great friends, so I guess I assumed that it could be more. But it felt strange and unnatural, for me at least. And that was the total opposite of how it had always felt with Max. It seemed like Max and I transitioned from friends to dating effortlessly. It felt like a natural progression that was supposed to happen when it did. There was no awkwardness there. Maybe there was shyness at first, but that comes with any new relationship.

I had a pit in my stomach from missing Max all week, and I didn't think it was fair to Justin to keep trying when I knew it wasn't working for me. I needed to tell him, but I hated to hurt anyone else. I had already lost Max, and I didn't want to risk losing Justin too, but I couldn't continue to pretend that it didn't feel weird to me. Justin deserved the truth the same way that Max had. I was starting to think that maybe I didn't need to tell Max anything to begin with. I was starting to think I was just caught up in the moment and thinking of old feelings and how much I had missed Justin. He and I were meant to be friends and be there for each other, but we didn't work romantically.

I lay on my bed, mulling over everything that was going on in my head. I was supposed to see Justin later, and it was probably best to tell him how I was feeling before it went any further. It wasn't long before he would be coming over, and I needed to get my head straight and figure out what I wanted to say. I loved and cared about him so much, just not in the way I thought I did, and I hoped that he would be okay with that.

My phone vibrated next to me, and I assumed it was Justin letting me know he was on the way. I picked it up and was surprised by the name on the screen. It was a text from Max. My heart fluttered when I saw the message was from him. I almost couldn't believe it. This was the first time in a week that he had sent me a message that wasn't just a short, one-word response to a question I asked him.

Max: Hey. Do you think I could see you sometime today or tomorrow? I would like to talk to you in person.

Me: Of course! Today would be perfect.

He didn't have to ask me twice. I was just happy that he wanted to speak to me, and I wanted it to be as soon as possible. I did want to talk to Justin first, though. I thought getting that conversation out of the way first would be better, depending on what Max wanted to talk about. Maybe he just wanted to talk to me like when we were friends, but I was desperately hoping that he wanted to talk about us. I needed to tell him that I didn't have romantic feelings for Justin and that I was just confused. Justin's coming back had thrown me for a loop, and I didn't handle it well.

Max: What time works for you?

Me: Around five would be good.

Justin had to be back home at five because his dad had another meeting with the private investigator and lawyer to discuss a few more details. They had found out more information, and it looked like they had a pretty solid amount of evidence against Bill. Justin would find out what new information they had found, and then they would have the go-ahead to go to the cops to let them know about Bill and that Justin was alive.

The next day, after I had gone to Justin's when the PI and lawyer were there, I asked Justin if I could tell my parents that he was alive because I knew how happy they would be. He cleared it with his dad, and they said it should be fine since they were so close to telling everyone anyway. My parents were shocked, to say the least. My mom cried, and my dad almost did. I explained to them everything that had happened after the accident, and told them about everything Bill had done to Justin.

To my surprise, my parents told me they had known or had an idea that it had happened at least once. They said that one time, when Justin was over swimming when we were kids, they noticed some odd bruises on him and got worried. Mom said they went to Christy and told her what they had seen, and she had brushed it off. My parents told her that if they ever saw another bruise on him, they would call CPS. That was when the falling out happened between my parents and Christy. That was why they always seemed to hate her, too.

I had no idea they had known about it since we were kids. Mom cried even more when I told her it went on the whole time. She didn't know because she never saw any more bruises on him, so she thought Bill had stopped after she and my dad threatened them. They just made sure that he hid the bruises better. I knew the bruises were there, but he was always careful to be covered up if he was around my parents. I wish I had told them about it, and then maybe Justin could have been living with his dad the whole time and never had to go through any of it.

The day after I told them, Justin came to the house to see my parents for the first time. It was risky since his mom and Bill were right down the street, but I had a pretty good idea of when they came and went since I had been avoiding them the whole summer, so I made sure he came when they wouldn't be home. I always had Justin pull into the garage where no one could see the car. It also helped that Justin's dad had gotten his car windows tinted as dark as possible within the legal limit.

My mom sobbed when she saw him and hugged him so tight that I worried she was going to suffocate him. Justin just let her squeeze him and hugged her back. He knew how hard it had been on them as well. My dad gave him a quick hug and had to go to the garage for something immediately after. I think he just didn't want anyone to see him cry.

My dad was a crier, even though he liked to pretend that he wasn't. He was a big softy and always had been, whether he admitted it or not.

My phone buzzed twice. One message was from Max, and the other from Justin.

Max: 5 works. Should I come to your house?

Justin: I'm about to turn on the road now.

Me to Max: Yeah, if that's okay with you!

I got up and went downstairs. Justin always let me know when he was turning on my road so that I could open the garage for him. I took the steps two at a time and hurried into the kitchen and to the door that led out to the garage. I opened it, stepping into the garage, as I hit the button for the door. A couple of seconds later, Justin was parking, but just as I pressed the button to close the door, Christy drove by. She turned, looking into the garage directly at me as she slowed down and threw up a small wave. I desperately wanted the garage door to close quickly.

I held a hand up, motioning Justin to stop, so he didn't get out of the car until the door was fully shut. Once it finally touched the ground, I felt a sense of relief. That was too close. She wasn't usually home at that time. I didn't know what was different today, but that meant we would have to be even more careful when it was time for him to leave. He opened his car door and got out.

"What happened?" he asked.

"Your mom drove by just as the door was shutting," I answered. "I was worried that she would see you."

"That was really close."

"No shit."

We headed inside, stopping in the kitchen to grab water and chips before going to my room. Justin raced me up the stairs like he always used to do, and won, just like he always did, unless I cheated and got a head start. I was out of breath when I plopped down on my bed next to him. He had already grabbed my remote and was turning on a background noise show since he knew that we'd probably end up talking through it and not paying attention anyway.

That part felt natural, and the same as it always had. Justin and I playing around, racing each other up the stairs, hanging out in my room, watching TV, and eating snacks; none of that ever felt strange or awkward. The awkwardness came anytime we tried to do anything more than that. When we kissed or tried to do anything further, it was off and made everything feel wrong. This was the part I had missed so much, having him here, being able to tell him secrets or have long conversations about our lives and what we wanted to do when we got older. I needed his comfort when I was upset or his advice when I was indecisive. I wanted to be his ears when he needed to vent or a shoulder when he needed someone to lean on.

I just didn't think I could be his girlfriend, no matter how much I wanted that at one point. I needed to bring it up, but I wasn't sure how. "I need to tell you something," I said, as I turned to face him.

"What's on your mind?" He asked, looking away from the TV to me.

"I care about you, and you know that I love you, but I feel like it's been weird between us this last week, like we're maybe trying to force something that isn't working," I said, hesitantly. I was worried he might look hurt, but he didn't. He almost looked relieved.

"I'm really glad that you brought that up," he replied.

"You felt it too?" I was so glad it wasn't just me.

"I have. It was like every time we kissed, it was nice, don't get me wrong, but it felt unnatural," Justin said.

I let out a sigh of relief. "That's exactly how I felt. I couldn't get into it the way I wanted to."

"I completely understand. I felt the same way. I wanted to, I really did, but it just wasn't there," he said.

I let out a laugh. "So, friends?"

"Best friends," he answered, smiling at me. I wrapped my arms around him, hugging him tightly. He hugged me back and rested his head against mine. This was how it was meant to be, and I was so happy that it was mutual. He pulled back from the hug.

"Hey, you are a great kisser, though," he said playfully.

"I appreciate that. You're not so bad yourself," I answered with a smile.

"So, tell me more about Max," he said as he wrapped his arm back around me so I could lay my head on his shoulder.

I told him that Max had barely spoken to me all week and that he finally texted earlier, wanting to see me. I also told him how much I liked Max and how much I had missed him all week. I filled him in on our friendship over the past year, and how it evolved once we came home for summer break. I told him how much Max had been there for me when I thought he was dead. I told him what I knew about Max's girlfriend, Vanessa, and her friend Ari, and what she had said to me when I met her right before we came home for break. I told Justin that I was sure he would like Max, and he said he thought so, too. It was so nice to be with him like we used to, without the extra pressure of trying to force a relationship.

After I told Justin all about Max, I realized I had completely forgotten a significant detail; that he had dated Max's brother for a while. I knew Devon was single now, so I thought it would be nice if they could at least catch up and talk once all of the craziness was over and Justin was free to be out in public again. I sat up and grabbed my phone. I went to Devon's Instagram to double-check that he hadn't reunited with James in the past week, since I hadn't spoken to Max. As far as I could tell from his Instagram feed, there was no sign of James. He had even deleted all of the pictures that he used to have of them.

"I completely forgot to mention that you may have seen Max because you dated his brother."

"Who's his brother?" Justin asked.

"Devon. Tall, slightly curly brown hair, hazel eyes, ridiculously long eyelashes, tan skin," I said, trying to jog his memory.

A small smile formed on his lips. "Ah, I remember."

"I bet you do. He's too hot to forget," I said playfully.

"Well, if he's Max's brother, then Max must be pretty hot too," Justin said with a chuckle.

"He definitely is," I agreed. I liked talking about Max with Justin without it being weird. It just reaffirmed that being best friends was the best thing for us. He was an amazing best friend, and I knew he'd be an amazing boyfriend to someone else, too.

"You know, Devon is single right now," I said, raising an eyebrow at him.

"Oh, is he? I'd love to catch up with him sometime, but I think I need to get to where I don't have to be kept a secret anymore before I try to date someone."

"Fair enough," I said. "It would be pretty hard to date someone when you can't be seen in public."

"Exactly."

We talked and watched TV until it was time for Justin to leave. He had to be back at five, and he knew that Max was coming over, so he made me promise to text him and let him know how my talk with Max went. I didn't want another close call with Christy, so I looked outside to see if I could see her car. I couldn't, so it was either in the garage or she had left again. When he left, he drove a little quicker to get out of Cape Falls and back to his dad's. He definitely didn't want to risk meeting his mom on the road.

I didn't have long before it was time for Max to come over, and I was so nervous because our talk did not go well the last time, and ended in him leaving upset. I hoped that would not happen this time. I went back upstairs and decided to put on a little makeup and a cute dress. I knew how I looked didn't make a difference, but I thought that maybe if I looked better, I'd feel better and be more confident and less anxious. I hadn't even realized it was already five until I heard the doorbell ring.

I ran down the stairs too quickly, nearly tripping, and then had to stop at the bottom for a second to catch my breath. My heart was racing, but it was only partially from running down the stairs; the other part was from the nerves. I took a few slow breaths to calm myself before going to the door. I pulled it open, so excited to see Max, but it wasn't Max. It was Christy, of all people. Seeing her face disgusted me even more than it usually did. I wasn't sure why she had come by, but I assumed I was about to find out.

"Hey?" I said, a little confused.

"Hey! I just wanted to stop by and see how you were doing," she said with a huge smile. Her smile didn't light up her face like most people's did. It made her look untrustworthy, but I guess that made sense for her.

"Um, I'm fine," I said as I looked past her to see Max pulling into the driveway.

"That's good. I was just curious how you have been holding up with everything. I know your birthday must have been tough this year, too." She was looking past me, into the house. She looked like she was looking for someone, or maybe just being nosey. You never knew with her.

"Yeah, it was. My parents aren't home if you were looking for them," I said as I eyed her suspiciously.

"I wasn't. Just wanted to stop by. Did you guys get a new car?"

"Huh?" I said, confused why she was even asking that, and then it clicked. She had seen Justin's car in the garage earlier when she had driven by.

"I saw a car in the garage earlier when I passed by, so I thought that maybe you had gotten a new car," she said as she glanced behind me again. Max had gotten out of his car and was right behind her now.

"Oh, that was me," he answered, and I looked at him. "My brother had my car, so I drove my mom's car over here earlier." She turned to Max. She hadn't realized that he had walked up behind her. She must have been too preoccupied looking into the house behind me to notice him pulling up.

"Oh," she said. "I guess I'll get going. I just wanted to check and see how you were." She turned and walked back to her car, giving me a small wave.

"Alright," I said, turning and rolling my eyes. I moved aside so Max could come in, and then I shut the door behind me and locked it.

"Was it Justin?" He asked. The question made me nervous because I didn't want him to think I was messing with him by having Justin here, and then telling him he could come over right after, but I didn't want to lie either.

"It was. She's not usually home, so I thought it would be fine, but she drove by right after he pulled into the garage," I answered.

"I figured," he said, but he didn't seem upset. "I thought it might help to just say it was me so she would stop asking."

"I appreciate that. Thank you."

"Anytime," he replied, giving me a small smile.

"How have you been?" I asked. We were still standing by the front door, so I started toward the living room, and Max followed.

"I've been all right," he answered. "Just working at the restaurant and hanging out with Devon." I knew it had only been a week since I had seen him, but a week felt like a lifetime when you were used to seeing someone every day. "How have you been?" He asked.

"Oh, I've been okay," I answered as I sat on the couch. Max sat down next to me, but not too close. He made sure to maintain a little distance. I could tell he wanted to say something, but he seemed nervous, too.

He placed his hands on his lap and looked at me. "I wanted to talk to you and apologize about the last time I was here," he started.

"You don't have anything to apologize for. I completely understand

THE GHOST OF YOU

why you were upset," I interrupted.

"But I do. It wasn't fair of me to get so upset the way I did. I should have been more understanding because it was such a crazy situation. That would mess with anyone's head. I was your friend before I was anything else, and I should have been there for you like a friend would have instead of getting upset and leaving."

"But, it's okay. I get why you reacted the way you did. I don't blame you at all," I said, feeling even more guilty than I already did. He cared about me so much that he was apologizing for how he reacted when I hurt him. I was the one who had hurt him, so it was completely rational for him to be upset with me.

"I blame myself, though. It wasn't okay. I knew you had feelings for Justin before, and that doesn't just go away. Finding out that he was okay must have brought on such a rush of emotions that I couldn't imagine feeling. I want to still be your friend no matter what. I want to be here for you, and I don't want you out of my life," he continued. "I love you, Amelia. And it would be harder not to have you in my life at all than to see you with someone else."

My face grew warm at his words, and I knew my cheeks had to be bright red. Max was perfect. He was more than I could have ever asked for and far better than I deserved. I was so happy that I felt like my heart could explode into a million pieces. I wanted nothing more than to have Max in my life. I wanted him as more than a friend. I wanted him in every way and never wanted to be without him. He made my days better, and he always put a smile on my face. I never had to question if he cared for me or if he would be there for me because he always made sure I knew, ever since we first started being friends. He had my heart, and there was no question about that anymore.

"I love you too," I said with a huge smile, before I leaned forward and planted a kiss on his lips.

He wrapped his arms around me and pulled me into him. It was

254

fireworks when my lips touched his, just like the first time we kissed. It always felt like the first time with Max, and I loved it the same way that I loved everything that had to do with him. He pulled back for a second and looked at me.

"So, you two aren't together?" He asked.

"No," I said, shaking my head at him with a smile. He smiled, pulled me back to him, and pressed his lips against mine. I felt the kiss change. His body was warm, and his hands moved from my waist to my hips, and then to my thighs. He wrapped his arms under my legs and stood up. He carried me up the stairs and to my room, all without our lips breaking contact. When we got to my room, he kicked the door shut behind him, walked over, and lowered me down on the edge of the bed, bending down where he could still kiss me.

His hands slid up my dress and tugged it up and over my head. He stood up and pulled his shirt over his head while I unfastened his belt and pants, tugging his jeans down. He slipped his shoes off and then stepped out of his pants. I looked up at him, noticing every muscle and how they flexed as he moved. I had missed him, in general, but I had missed this part too. He was the most attractive man I had ever laid eyes on, and it had been difficult not to be around him for more than one reason.

I moved back onto the bed, and he climbed up next to me. I positioned myself on top of him, my legs on each side of his hips. I bent down and kissed his lips as he ran his hands up my back. He found the clasp for my bra, and it was off. Soon, our underwear was on the floor with the rest of the clothes, and then Max and I were wrapped up in one another in a moment that felt so right that it was undeniable that Max was the person for me. He was who I needed, and I knew he felt the same way.

Chapter 28

I woke up feeling amazing. Everything felt like it was back to how it should be, and I knew everything would be okay. Max was still sleeping, and I didn't want to wake him. I slowly got out of bed and got dressed. He hadn't planned on staying the night when he came over yesterday, but after finding out that Justin and I weren't anything more than friends, he had changed his mind. After we made up, I explained everything to Max, how I felt about everything, how it didn't feel right, and that Justin felt the same way I did.

He said he understood why I had been confused and apologized again for how he had reacted, to which I told him there was no need. He told me that it was nearly impossible not to talk to me, and it made me happy that he had missed me just as much as I had missed him during our time apart. Maybe going through this minor hiccup helped solidify our relationship even more. I never doubted that Max and I should be together until Justin came back, but there wasn't a doubt in my mind about it anymore.

I quietly opened the door to my bedroom and slipped out. I went downstairs and into the kitchen. Mom was standing by the counter drinking coffee, and Dad was sitting at the bar flipping through his notebook from work. They both looked at me when I came into the kitchen. "So, I take it that you and Max made up?" Mom asked with a grin.

"We did," I answered, grinning back. I was so happy to have Max back that it was impossible not to smile.

Last week, Mom had noticed that Max hadn't been around at all, so she asked me if something was going on. I ended up telling her everything about how I thought I felt about Justin and how I felt about Max. She told me that she could see why I would feel that way for Justin, considering I had grown up with him. He was who I had always been closest to and most comfortable with, but she also said that she could tell how happy Max had made me and how it was different from how I seemed with Justin. She did the motherly thing and said to go with what my heart felt was right, and now I had.

"I'm happy that you got everything figured out," she said before taking another sip of her coffee.

"I am too."

I got out the pancake mix, eggs, and bacon. I wanted to try to make breakfast before Max woke up. He was always making me breakfast or going to get me breakfast, so I wanted to do something for him for a change. Mom walked around the bar and sat next to my dad so I could have the kitchen. It didn't look like they had eaten yet, so I made enough for all four of us. They watched as I cooked and asked if there had been any updates with Justin or if he or his dad had any idea when they were going to go to the police. I told them they weren't exactly sure yet, but it would be soon.

I already had the pancakes and bacon on the plates when Max came walking down the stairs. His eyes were still sleepy, and his hair was tousled all over his head. I'd found a pair of pajama pants he left in my drawer for him to put on last night, and they hung perfectly on his hips. He looked so good that I almost wanted to say the hell with breakfast and run back up to bed. Maybe absence really did make the heart grow fonder. He walked over to stand at the bar next to my parents. "Something smells amazing," he said.

257

"Amelia decided to make breakfast this morning," my mom said. "It's so good to see you, by the way," she added, patting him on the shoulder.

"It's good to see you guys too," he said, smiling at her.

"The eggs are almost done, then we can eat," I said to them.

Mom, Dad, and Max all complimented me, even though it was just boxed pancake mix, and you couldn't really mess that up. I loved them for it, though. When we finished eating, I took everyone's plates to the sink. I had to fight mom to let me wash the dishes, but she finally gave in, and she and dad went to the living room, while Max came over to help rinse and dry.

I bumped into him with my hip, and when he looked down at me, I smiled. He smiled back and leaned down to give me a quick peck on the lips. I bit his lip, and he pulled back, raising an eyebrow at me. I gave him a quick wink and went back to washing dishes. It didn't take long with both of us, and when we finished putting the last dish away, we headed back to my room.

Max didn't have to work, and I was happy that he didn't have to leave. He could spend the whole day with me if I wanted him to. I checked my phone and saw a text from Justin. I had quickly told him last night that Max and I were good, but didn't give any details because Max was still with me, and I wanted to have all of my attention on him.

Justin: Just wanted to see how you were today. And I'd love to officially meet Max sometime soon if he's okay with it.

I looked over at Max. He was lying on my bed, stretched out, with his attention on the TV. I wanted him and Justin to meet, too. They were the two most important people in the world to me, other than my parents, and it would make me so happy if they could be friends too. I felt sure that they would get along. I hoped my little confusion didn't mess up that possibility. I knew it hadn't on Justin's end because we mutually agreed that we didn't work as a couple, but I hoped that Max would be open to it, too. From what he said yesterday, before he knew that Justin and I were not together, I thought he would.

Me: I'm good. How are you? Did you find out any new info yesterday when you got home? And I would love for the two of you to meet.

Justin: I'm good. We did find out a few new things. I'll fill you in when I see you. Let's plan something. You know I'm always free.

I climbed up on the bed next to Max, and he held his arm out so I could snuggle up next to him. I lay my head on his chest, breathing in his scent that I had missed so much. I really loved this boy, and it felt so nice to be able to think that and not run from the thought as I would have a few months ago. It felt nice to be open to love someone and not have that crushing feeling of grief taking up every part of my brain and heart. Having Max as my boyfriend and Justin as my best friend was all I needed. I was complete. They were the two halves of my heart, and I felt so lucky to be able to have them both in my life at the same time.

"Would you ever want to meet Justin?" I asked Max, tilting my head up to see his face.

"Of course," he answered. "He's your best friend and someone who has always been such a huge part of your life, so definitely."

"Oh, good," I said. "I wasn't sure if you would because of everything."

"No, I'm not worried about that. Even if you had been with him, I still would have wanted to meet him. I was fully prepared to just be your friend if that had been all that I was able to do yesterday," he replied.

Max was the most understanding and compassionate person I had ever met. I can't say that I would have been able to do the same thing so easily had the situation been reversed. I would have been pretty heartbroken. But if it were just friends or not in my life at all, I would probably make myself find a way to deal with it so I didn't have to completely lose Max either. It made me love him even more.

"You're perfect," I said to him.

"Far from perfect, but thank you," he replied.

"No, thank you."

"For?" He asked.

"For being you. For being so caring and so wonderful to me."

"I don't need thanks for that. I love you, so of course I want you happy," he said.

"Well, you didn't always love me, so you're just a nice person. You've always been amazing to me, even before you said you loved me yesterday," I replied.

"I think I always did love you, though. I just didn't tell you until yesterday," he said as he looked at me, his expression soft.

My heart squeezed in my chest. Maybe I had loved him a lot longer than I wanted to admit to. I was just too afraid to admit my feelings. I was happier with Max than I had ever been with anyone I dated before. I had told past boyfriends that I loved them when they said it first because I thought I had to say it back, but I never meant it. I didn't know what that felt like in a relationship. My only experience with loving someone that wasn't my family was Justin, and maybe that's why I had gotten confused and thought I had feelings for him. While I love him and Max both so much, it is in different ways.

"I love you too," I said as I moved up to place a kiss on his lips.

"I could listen to you say that all day," he replied.

"Oh, really? Well, I love you," I said as I kissed his right cheek, "I love you," his left cheek, "I love you," his forehead, "I love you," his nose.

He smiled and then moved his hands to cup my face. He pulled my lips down to meet his. He kissed me slowly, moving his mouth gently on mine. I felt his tongue trace my bottom lip, and I sighed. He carefully switched places with me, moving me so that I was lying on my back and he was over me, his lips never leaving mine in the process. I wrapped my arms around his neck and wished that I could keep him like this in bed with me forever. He ran his hand softly down the side of my body, and I shivered. He pulled back, giving me a knowing smile, and then crashed his lips back into mine.

CHAPTER 28

Once Max and I finally found our way out of bed for the day, we showered and started getting ready. Max told me that Devon wanted us to come eat at the restaurant with him because he had missed me this past week, too. I missed him almost as much as I had missed Max. I'd gotten used to seeing Devon a couple of times a week, whether at the restaurant when I'd stop by or just hanging out with him and Max when they were both off work. Max was ready before I was, but I wasn't far behind. I blow-dried my hair and raked a brush through it. I didn't think it was an occasion for lots of makeup, so I opted for concealer, mascara, and a little lip gloss, and then we were on our way.

When we got to the restaurant, there were so many cars in the parking lot, as usual for The Pancake House. We got out of the car and walked up the sidewalk to the front doors. Max held the door for me, and I stepped inside. There were a couple of people waiting on the benches at the front. Steph was at the hostess stand and came out from behind it to wrap me in a big hug as soon as she saw me.

"Amelia!" She nearly yelled as she threw her arms around me. "I haven't seen you in over a week! Where have you been?" She asked excitedly. Judging by her question, Max hadn't told anyone about what had gone on with us.

"Oh, you know…" I started.

"She had a lot of family things going on," Max interrupted. I was glad because I wasn't sure what to say.

"Oh no! Is everything okay?" She asked with a worried expression as she pulled back from our hug.

"Oh yeah, it's fine. It's nothing bad," I said, hoping to ease her worry.

"So you'll be back around here again?"

"Of course," I answered, and she smiled.

"Good! It's so good to see you," She said to me, and then turned to Max, "Devon is at a booth in your normal spot."

"It's not good to see me?" He asked jokingly. Steph smiled and rolled

261

her eyes at him.

"You work here. I see you all the time. Seeing Amelia is the treat," she said to him playfully.

We walked into the dining area and zigzagged through tables and chairs full of people eating and laughing. When Devon saw us, he waved and stood as we got to the booth. He threw his arms wide and pulled me into a hug the same way Steph had. I hadn't realized that staying gone for a little over a week would warrant such a fuss when I returned. I wrapped my arms around him, squeezing a little.

"I miss you!" He said, pulling back and looking at me. "You look like a different person."

"It's barely been over a week," I said as I smiled at him.

"Well, it feels like a year." He retook his seat, and Max and I followed suit, sitting down across from Devon.

"So, tell me. What's new?" Max and I exchanged a look. I wanted to tell Devon because I knew he liked Justin and would want to see him, but I couldn't say anything yet. "Why are you guys looking like that?" He asked suspiciously.

"No reason," Max and I said in unison.

"Hm, I don't believe you, but I'll let it go for now," he said with narrowed eyes.

I gave him an innocent smile. "How have you been?" I asked.

"I've been okay. I taught an art class down at the arts center last week. I'm considering making it a weekly thing. It was a lot of fun," he answered.

"That's amazing!" I exclaimed. "I'll come and take a class one week if you do."

"I would love that. It would be nice to have a familiar face in the crowd. It wasn't bad last week, but I was nervous since I didn't know anyone who was taking the class."

"I bet so. I couldn't teach. I'd be petrified," I said.

Devon told us more about his art class and how if he made it a weekly thing, he was thinking of doing themed classes for holidays and even small competitions. He had so many great ideas for it, and I knew it would be something my mom would love to hear about, so I told Devon that he had to come over soon and have dinner with my parents and me. We all ordered and ate our food slowly since we were talking the entire time. It was so nice to see Devon and see him excited about something. I was worried about him after his breakup with James, but he seemed to be bouncing back just fine.

After we finally finished eating, I got up and went to the bathroom. Once in there, I took my phone out of my shorts pocket to check it because I realized that I had never responded to Justin's earlier text. I thought that maybe now would be a good time, as ever, to see if Max wanted to meet him since he was off and we didn't have any plans for the rest of the day. I texted Justin back quickly, asking if he'd be free in about thirty minutes and if it was okay to bring Max to his dad's. He replied quickly that he didn't mind, so I washed my hands and headed back out to the table.

Max was wiping down the table while Devon gathered our plates, utensils, and cups into his arms when I returned. "Can I help with anything?" I asked.

"Nope, we've got it," Devon answered with a smile as he headed back to the kitchen with our dishes. A busboy came by with a plastic tub on his way to clear a table and asked Max if he was finished with the rag. Max nodded his head and handed it to him as we waited for Devon to get back so we could walk out together.

"Ready to go?" He asked as he came out of the kitchen before turning to walk back toward the front of the restaurant. We shook our heads and followed after him. When we passed by the hostess stand, Steph waved at us and told me that she had better see me again in a few days. I assured her I would be back soon, and then we were out the door.

263

Devon gave me a big hug again before we parted ways, and Max and I walked to the car.

Once we were inside, I turned to him. "How would you feel about meeting Justin today?"

"That's fine with me," he answered.

"Okay, I thought we might as well since you're off today and he's always free," I replied.

"I'm good with that. Where are we meeting him?" He asked.

"At his dad's house in Kingsland. You know he can't go anywhere in public, and with the close call we had with his mom yesterday, I don't want to risk him coming over again. Plus, she thinks his car is your parents' car, so it would be weird if your car and his car were at my house at the same time," I explained.

"That's true. Give me the address, and we can head there now."

I gave him the address to put in the GPS because, although I could get there on my own, I wasn't great at remembering to tell people when they needed to turn and which road to take. It wasn't long before we pulled into Justin's dad's driveway. Justin came out the front door as soon as we parked, and gave us a big wave as we got out of the car.

"Hey, you," I said to Justin.

"Hey! You must be Max," Justin said as he held his hand out to Max.

"And you must be Justin," Max said with a smile, taking Justin's hand and shaking it.

"Firm handshake. I like it," Justin said, and turned to hold the front door open for us to walk through. Once inside, I walked to the living room and sat on the couch facing the fireplace. Max followed and sat down next to me. Justin plopped down on the other couch, sitting where he was turned to us.

"It's nice to finally meet you," Max said to Justin, breaking the silence.

"Likewise," Justin answered. "Lia told me so much about you, and I couldn't be happier for you guys."

"Thank you. I've heard a lot about you, too. I'm so sorry about your situation. I can't imagine how tough that all is," Max said sympathetically.

"It's been something, but it will hopefully be back to normal soon," Justin replied.

"Speaking of that," I interjected, "What new stuff did you guys find out?" I asked.

Justin relayed everything the PI had told him and his dad the day before. They talked to some homeowners around the area before the bridge that Justin ran off of, and a few of them had cameras in their yard and were able to pull up old recordings from the night that Justin wrecked. They let Phillip watch them over, and they saw a black SUV on a couple of them just a few minutes before the time that Justin had wrecked. They could see it was a black Chevy Tahoe, and Phillip was almost positive that it had to be the one Bill was driving.

Phillip went to Bill's dealership and pretended to be a customer, and asked if they had any Tahoes because he was in the market for one. Bill showed him one that had a few thousand knocked off the price because it had minor damage to the front left bumper, which would line up with how Justin said he ran him off the road. Phillip told Bill he'd be back next week to get the Tahoe if he'd hold it for him. He gave Bill a little cash to ensure he didn't sell it before then. Phillip and Bruce told Justin's dad they felt they had pretty solid evidence. They thought they'd be able to get Bill charged for insurance fraud at the very least, but more if they could get the ex-employee who told them about the money laundering and gambling to testify in court.

It was good news, and I was so happy for Justin that all of the craziness with him having to stay hidden was so close to an end. I couldn't wait for him to be able to get back to a normal life. After Justin told us about everything they found, he and Max started talking about football and other guy things that I had no interest in. It seemed like they were hitting it off pretty well, which made me happy.

I didn't even mind that I had no idea what they were talking about as long as they were getting along. My two favorite people being friends made my heart beam. Max and Justin talked so long that we were still there when Justin's dad and stepmom came home. They ordered takeout and told Max and me to stay for dinner. We ended up having such a great time. Justin's dad seemed to like Max, too. But to be fair, it was hard not to like Max. He was a charmer, not because he was trying to be. He was just a great person, and anyone could see that.

Chapter 29

I t had been four days since Max, and I had gone to Justin's house, and the two of them were already texting each other almost as much as they texted me. We also had a group chat between the three of us. They hit it off much better than I could have ever expected, and I was so happy about it, except when they teamed up to pick on me in the playful way they did. Once Devon knew that Justin was alive, he could be added to the group chat and, hopefully, side with me against the two of them.

Max had spent the night with me every night since, and I was not complaining. I never wanted him to leave, but I knew his parents liked seeing him when they were home. I also made sure to go by the restaurant to see Steph so she wouldn't yell at me the next time I came in for going too long between visits. I visited Justin a couple of days, while Max was working, but Max went with me when he got off work early one day. I think he enjoyed hanging out with Justin as much as I did, and I knew Justin felt the same. He texted, telling me how great Max was, as if I didn't already know, and how he was so happy I had met him.

Max was at work, and I was lying on the couch watching TV until it was time for my yoga class. I had considered taking another class or two a week, so I would have more to do. I would have gotten a job, but the summer was more than halfway over, and I'd have to be back at school soon, so it was a little late to apply anywhere. It was almost time to start on my summer reading list for school, so at least that would take up a decent portion of my time. I didn't start at the beginning of the summer because I was a quick reader and wanted the books to still be fresh on my mind when school started. I heard my phone ding and assumed it was either Max or Justin, so I picked it up to see which one.

Justin to the group: It's time! Dad and I are on the way to the police station now. Phillip and Bruce are meeting us there!

The message took me by surprise, and I jumped to my feet, unsure where I was going. I couldn't believe it was finally time and that this would all be over soon. The trial and everything would take a while, but Justin's hiding and having to pretend that he was dead would be over by the end of the day. This was amazing, and I was so excited, but nervous for him. I wondered what they would do, if they would come and arrest Bill right after, or if it would take a couple of days? I wasn't sure exactly how everything worked, but I couldn't wait to find out.

Me to the group: OMG! I'm so excited for you! Fingers crossed that everything goes well! Please, please keep me updated!

Justin to the group: Will do!

I didn't know what to do with myself. I couldn't just sit back on the couch and do nothing. I was anxious about what would happen. I looked out the living room window at Christy and Bill's house. Both of their cars were home, which was very odd for the time of day. I wondered if something was going on. Had they been tipped off or something? I hoped not. I noticed that Max hadn't replied to Justin's message in the group and thought he must be busy at work. I hoped he would have a break soon to check his messages. I knew he would be excited, too.

I texted my yoga teacher and told her I wouldn't make it to class. I was antsy and needed to do something, but I also didn't want to leave the house and possibly miss seeing Bill get arrested. I paced back and forth from the living room to the kitchen. I opened the pantry, looking for something to snack on. I wasn't hungry, but I didn't know what else to do with myself. I thought about maybe taking a swim since I hadn't gone swimming since before Max, and I had our little break, but I wouldn't be able to see out to the front if anything happened.

I went upstairs, grabbed one of the books from the summer reading list, and plopped down on the window seat in my room with the curtains open. I had a perfect view of Christy and Bill's house, and I wouldn't miss anything. I had to keep reading and rereading each page because my mind was so all over the place that it was hard to focus on the words. I hadn't retained anything and would likely have to read it all for a third time.

I checked the time on the message that Justin had sent earlier. It had been about an hour, so he should have been at the police station already. It only took about thirty minutes from his dad's to Cape Falls. I didn't know how these things worked, but I thought that they would probably be talking to the police by now and telling them everything. I wondered if the police would go by the dealership, assuming he would be there. I sent a quick text to Justin telling him that both his mom's and Bill's cars were home so that he could let the police or whoever know.

I went back to reading and tried to keep my mind focused on the book this time. I had no idea what was going on in the story, though. I couldn't recall one line. It was impossible, but I kept trying because I was going to go crazy waiting if I didn't do something. After a few minutes, Justin texted me back a thumbs-up. I guess he couldn't text much since they were inside, and he wanted to let me know that he got the message about Bill. I hoped that I was right and Bill was home and didn't just drive a new car or something. My phone dinged again with another text. I checked it, and this time it was Max.

Max to the group: Bro! That's amazing! Let us know what's going on as soon as you know something!

Max sent another text a second later, but this time to me and not our group. He asked if I was home and if I had seen anything going on at their house. I told him that I was home and nothing had happened yet. He said he wished he were with me. I told him it was pretty boring staring out of a window and waiting, but I'd let him know as soon as anything happened, and that I might even try to get a quick video. I had wanted this man in jail since we were kids, and I would revel in watching it finally happen.

Another thirty minutes passed, of me reading my book, and getting nowhere. I knew these things took time to plan, but I was impatient. They had so much proof of all the terrible things Bill had done, not only to Justin but in general. From the insurance fraud, illegal poker games, money laundering, and whatever was up with the guns that the ex-employee had seen. What more could they possibly need? Maybe it took a while to explain all of the evidence, and then they probably had to wait for a warrant for his arrest. I could be sitting and waiting for hours. I probably should have just gone to yoga, so I would have had something to make the time pass quickly.

I went to my closet and grabbed my yoga mat. I unrolled it and set it in the middle of my floor. There was no reason I couldn't do yoga in my room by myself. I had taken enough classes that I knew a few basic things I could do to pass the time. I made sure to leave my curtains open, so I could still see out to Christy, and Bill's just in case, though. I thought that some stretches were a good place to start. I sat on my mat and put my legs out in front of me, stretching over them to grab my feet. I did a few more twists and stretches on the floor before I stood up.

A Sun Salutation was an easy sequence that I remembered, so I decided to do a few rounds of it. It did calm my nerves and made me feel a little less anxious, but I had to do a few more rounds before I felt like I had burned off enough of my antsy energy. I finally sat back down on the window seat and picked the book back up, flipping back to the beginning. This time, when I tried to read, I absorbed what I was reading without my mind constantly racing. Yoga helped a lot with that, and I was grateful. I probably needed to start practicing at home on days when I didn't have class.

I had finally gotten lost in the book when I heard my phone ding twice. I didn't realize that it had been almost two hours since the last time I had checked it. There were two messages, one from Justin to our group and one from Max to me.

Justin to the group: They got the warrant for Bill and are about to come and get him. We called the dealership to be sure he wasn't there first. When we asked to speak to him, they said he wasn't in today, so they will be on their way to their house soon!

Me to the group: I'm sitting by the window waiting!

Max to me: I got off a little early, so I'm heading to your house now.

Another message came through from Max right after.

Max to me: I'm hurrying because I want to get there before the cops are on the road. See you in a few.

Me to Max: I'm up in my room. Use your key and come in.

I had given Max his own key since we were back together. It would be easier, so he could come in whenever and not wait for us to come to the door. I knew The Pancake House was closer than the police station, so I hoped Max could make it here before everything went down. If I was anxious before, the feeling had tripled now. It wasn't a negative, anxious feeling, but an excited, anxious feeling. It was the kind you got when you knew you were finally getting something you really wanted. I had wanted to see Bill get in trouble for so long, and I couldn't believe that the day was finally here. Granted, I didn't realize it would take Justin faking his death for it to happen, but the result was still the same and what we all wanted.

Max wasn't joking when he said he was hurrying because it only took a couple of minutes before he was pulling into my driveway. He was out of the car and through the front door so fast. I heard his loud footsteps as he ran up the stairs, and then my bedroom door flew open. He came over to stand next to me at the window. He was out of breath, so he paused with his hands on his knees, trying to take some deep breaths before he could speak. When his breathing finally slowed to normal, he sat on the window seat next to me.

"You meant it, huh? I've never seen you get to my house from work that fast," I said to him with a chuckle.

"I said I was hurrying," he laughed.

"Well, you didn't miss anything. I've been by this window for hours now."

We both sat, looking out the window. Neither of Christy's nor Bill's cars had moved, and I hadn't seen either of them come outside the whole time I had been here. I didn't know if they were even awake. If not, they would be once the police were there. I wondered why he decided not to go to work today. Maybe he was sick. Being that evil had to make you sick sometimes. I realized I hadn't told my parents, and I had promised to let them know when Justin and his dad finally went to the police. I shot them a quick message saying that the police should be coming by to get Bill anytime now. They both said they hated that they were at work and had to miss it.

Seconds later, I heard sirens and knew this was it. I saw one, two, three cop cars flying down my road. The first pulled into Christy and Bill's driveway; the other two stopped on the edge of the road in front of their house. All three cops jumped out of their cars and walked to the house. Just as they got to the front door, three more cops and a SWAT van pulled up, parking in the middle of the road before officers in full gear with helmets, vests, and rifles got out. All the officers except the three on the porch had their weapons drawn and pointed at the house. I saw four officers go around to the back of the house. I was in shock at the number of officers who showed up.

I knew Bill was into some bad stuff, but it was just him and Christy at the house. I didn't think he was dangerous enough to warrant all of that, so there had to be more to it than we knew. I saw the officers on the porch banging on the door, but no one answered. Max stood beside me, mesmerized as we watched the commotion. I looked up and saw what I thought was someone peaking out of the curtains of a second-floor window. They were home, and they were awake. They just didn't want to answer the door. Bill knew that he was in deep shit. The officers banged on the door several times before retreating to the yard. A couple of the SWAT officers went to the van and pulled out a battering ram.

Five SWAT officers walked onto the porch. Two held the battering ram and swung it hard, making the front door fly open. The other three had their weapons up and went inside. The two dropped the battering ram and followed behind them. I waited, hoping they would get Bill without too much of a fight. I saw someone pass an upstairs window again. Then I heard gunshots ring out from inside the house. My heart leaped into my throat. I wanted to know what was going on. I didn't care about Bill's safety, but I didn't want anyone else hurt because of him. I heard a few more gunshots, and then silence.

Justin's dad's car pulled into my driveway, and I jumped up from my seat and hurried down the stairs to the front door. Max came running behind me as I flung the front door open, ran down the steps, and threw myself into Justin's arms. He hugged me tightly, and I felt tears sting my eyes. It was over. Justin was free to be back, and he would finally get justice for the hell Bill had made his childhood. I was so happy for him. I pulled back, looking at him, and he had tears forming in his eyes, too. I glanced over to where Max and Justin's dad stood and was sure their eyes also looked a little glassy.

There was so much commotion outside that I noticed most of our neighbors were either on their front porch or peaking out of their windows. I knew they had no idea what was going on. They were probably shocked that perfect Christy and Bill had all these cops swarming their house. I couldn't imagine what they must have thought was going on. Just then, a news van pulled onto our road and parked across the street from my house, and a reporter and cameraman jumped out, going as close to Christy and Bill's house as the cops would allow. I wondered what was taking them so long to come out and if something terrible had happened.

I saw an ambulance rush down my street. It pulled up behind the SWAT van, and two paramedics jumped out, grabbed a gurney, and headed inside the house. It was only a couple of minutes later, and they were coming out. One of the SWAT officers was lying on the gurney. He sat up slightly and waved to his fellow officers. "I'm fine!" I heard him say to everyone. I could see a little blood on his arm, but other than that, he did look fine. Had Bill shot at the guy? I wouldn't put it past him, but that was crazy. Hopefully, another charge in the long list of charges already stacked against him.

Max, Alan, Justin, and I all stood on my front lawn looking down at the house. We were waiting for them to bring Bill out. Justin had his arm draped over my shoulder, and Max stood next to Alan. He looked over at me and gave me a smile. I smiled back before turning back to the house. It was a few minutes later when they finally emerged. First came one SWAT officer escorting Bill with his arms cuffed behind his back, and then came Christy, a second officer holding her with her arms cuffed behind her back, too. They both had their heads hanging down. They looked up as they came down the front porch steps, probably curious to see if the neighbors were watching.

They scanned their eyes across the houses, but both stopped when they saw us. Christy and Bill's eyes went wide, and their jaws fell open so far that I was worried they'd trip over their bottom lip coming down the porch stairs. They both stared, mouth agape, like they'd seen a ghost.

With Justin here, they probably thought they had. Bill's face turned red, and he struggled against the officer, but the officer tightened his grip and told him to cut it out. Christy looked shamefaced for a second, but then it turned to anger, and she yelled, "Why would you do this to us? This is why I didn't want you to begin with. You're an embarrassment."

Anger flared through me like a wildfire. How dare she say that to Justin? It took every single ounce of self-control I had not to march over there and hit her right in front of all those officers. It also helped that when I started to take a step, Justin tightened his arm around my shoulder and whispered, "It's okay," to me. Then, I heard Bill yell out, "You fucking brat!" right before the officer holding him shoved him into the back of one of the many police cars on our street. They put Christy into another car and slammed the door shut on both of them.

We stayed on the front lawn, watching as more officers entered the house. Two more went back to the cars where Christy and Bill sat, and they got inside and cranked the engines. We watched as they backed up and drove up the road toward my house. Christy and Bill scowled at us as they passed, and we could see that they were both saying something, but we couldn't hear them through the glass. I gave them both a smirk and a little wave as they drove by, making them even angrier than they already were. It was such a satisfying sight to see both of them in the back of a cop car, angry because they got caught. Justin was finally getting justice, and there were no words for how happy I was to witness it.

Chapter 30

Five Months Later

"Hey, can you grab me a Sprite?" I called over to Justin, who was walking into the kitchen. I was on the couch, lying back with my feet across Max's lap, and I didn't feel like getting up. Justin returned a minute later, carrying a big bowl of popcorn and a Sprite. He sat down on the couch between Max and Devon and handed the Sprite to Max to give to me. I opened it, taking a long, throat-burning sip before handing it back to Max to sit on the table.

"Thank you," I said, smiling at him.

"Of course," he said, shaking his head at me.

"Are you going to start the movie or not?" Devon asked, playfully impatient.

"I am, I am," I said as I grabbed the remote and pressed play.

Max and I were home from college on our winter break, so I told him that we all needed to watch Home Alone together. It was one of my favorite Christmas movies, so it was a must-watch every year before Christmas. Justin had always watched it with my parents and me every year, and now we got to continue the tradition with Max and Devon. I looked over at Justin. He had his arm draped around Devon's shoulder, and Devon was snuggled up next to him.

I remembered the day that Devon found out that Justin was alive and how shocked he had been. He couldn't believe it at first. He was a little annoyed that we didn't tell him sooner, but once we explained everything, he understood. Seeing them together made me so happy because I knew how perfect they both were for each other. I had missed them so much during our fall semester while Max and I were at school. Thankfully, it was only a two-hour drive, so they came up on some weekends, and Max and I came home on others. We made sure we didn't go too long without seeing each other.

It had been about five months since Bill and Christy were arrested, and the four of us were living our best lives. My parents hated that they had missed all of the action while at work, but they were happy to know that Christy and Bill were behind bars. "Good riddance," my dad said when he got home from work that day. Good riddance, indeed. They went to trial quickly because the police had been building a case against Bill for some time before Justin and his dad ever went to them.

They just didn't realize that it was Bill that they were building a case against. They had arrested so many people over the past few years, who kept getting caught with illegal guns and a lot of cash on them. They assumed there must have been a prominent dealer in town or nearby. Whenever Justin and his dad brought everything they found to the police that day, they put two and two together. They got a search warrant for the car dealership and Bill and Christy's house, and found so much stuff that went beyond just the guns. That was how Bill managed to fund his and Christy's extravagant lifestyle. A few people from the department were fired and charged as well because, since Justin was alive, there was no body, which meant that someone signed off on something they shouldn't have. Christy and Bill assumed he had drowned and gotten washed away in the river, and Bill wanted the insurance money quickly, so they paid off the coroner to create a death certificate and sign off on everything because they didn't want to have to wait for his body to be found. It had been a closed-casket funeral, so no one had any idea.

It came out on the news the next day about the arrest, and it said Christy was the one who had shot the cop when they were all in the house. She also wasn't innocent in Bill's illegal dealings either, so on top of shooting a cop, she was also charged with money laundering and insurance fraud. She was the one that had helped Bill alter his books from the dealership. It came out that all of their stuff went so much deeper than any of us had realized. Justin and his dad just helped police get to the bottom of a case they'd been sitting on for over a year.

Bill was charged with money laundering, insurance fraud, bribery, importing, and selling illegal weapons, and he was also charged with attempted murder for what he had done to Justin. Christy had a lesser sentence than Bill, but from what the judge said, it would be a long time before either of them could even qualify for parole if they were able to at all. It was the perfect ending. Their house went up for auction, and a sweet couple with two small children got it cheap and moved into it a couple of months after everything happened. Justin wasn't sad to see the house go because so many of his memories there were terrible anyway. When we found out that someone had bought the house, he told me he hoped they would have much better memories there than he had.

Right after the initial craziness of everything had died down, Justin took my suggestion and reached out to Devon. Devon was ecstatic, to say the least, and Max and I were too. Justin seemed to be returning to his old self, and I believed that Devon had helped that process along. Devon brought out the fun side of everyone. He was so lovable and someone I'd consider one of my best friends, next to Justin. They were the perfect pair, and I'd never seen Justin so happy. I kept my fingers crossed that this relationship was for the long haul.

Max, Devon, Justin, and I all planned to head to Europe as soon as Max and I were home for the summer and stay for at least a month. We had so many places to explore, and it made my heart full that I could do these things with the three people I loved most in the world. It's funny how life changes. Sometimes it throws insane obstacles at you that you are sure you'll never get over, but when you finally do, you come out the other side a whole new, better version of yourself. I felt whole again, having Max, having Justin back, and now Devon and all of the other friends I had met through Max.

I may have gone through hell for a year thinking that my best friend was gone, but that was nothing in the grand scheme of things. I'd do it over a million times if I knew that in the end, my best friend would finally get the justice he deserved. He got his abusers behind bars, a family that loves him, a new baby sister, a wonderful boyfriend who adores him, and he got new friends in the process, too. All I ever wanted was for Justin to be safe and happy, and he finally was. And I couldn't ask for anything better.

ACKNOWLEDGEMENTS

Writing this book has been such a journey for me, and one of the biggest goals that I've wanted to accomplish for a long time. This isn't the first story I've ever started, but it is the first I've ever completed, and that makes it so special to me. What began as a dream I had one night turned into a full-blown novel with characters I love and a love story that made my heart melt. This was a process over several years with many long breaks because of overwhelm in life, and many, many bouts of writer's block, and along the way, there have been so many people who were there through it.

First and foremost, I want to start with my husband. Syd, you are incredible and have been my number one fan (even though you don't read), cheering me on, encouraging me to write, and also keeping the kids occupied while I write, even when you've been busy, too. I love you, and I don't think I could have gotten through this book without you. I also want to thank my children. They are a huge part of my motivation. Going for your dreams and putting yourself out there can be incredibly scary, but I wanted to do that to show them that they can and should reach for their dreams, too, no matter how scary it may seem at first. I love you more than anything, my BooBoo and Bug (Not their real names, obviously).

I also need to thank my very first reader ever, Jasmine. Calling you a friend doesn't seem like enough at this point. You are family. I love you so much, and you've always been so supportive of my writing, even when it was just my random fan fiction. You've read the things I've written at their very roughest first draft and still complimented them, and I appreciate that so much. That helped me keep going more than you know.

Augusta, we have been friends, almost like siblings, for twenty-five years, which seems so crazy to say because we're basically still teenagers, right? But you've listened to me yap about my writing and book ideas and really just everything on the phone for hours, and been supportive of anything I said I wanted to try. I love you and thank you so much for being there to listen.

Marina, you have been such an amazing person in my life, and I will always be thankful to BookTok for bringing us together. It's so funny to have met a random stranger from making TikToks about books and click the way that we did. You've been the best book-reading partner and so supportive when I told you I was writing my own book. I appreciate you taking the time to beta-read this book for me when I know how busy you are. I love you, and I'm so happy to have you always cheering me on in everything I do.

Axia, thank you for being one of the first readers of this story. Our weekly writer meetings, which turn into yap sessions about kids, life, yoga, etc., have been something I look forward to every week. It has been so nice to have another friend who writes and stresses about writing the same way I do. Bouncing ideas off each other and working plot points out with another person's brain has helped me so much more than you know. I love you and always appreciate your feedback.

I also have to give a shoutout to Alison, my therapist. Thank you for encouraging me when I was afraid to keep going, not just with the book, but with everything in life. You've heard about every grueling step of my publishing process, and it was so nice to talk out my frustrations about it. I also have to say thank you for being there as I worked through my own anxiety disorder, much like my main character. I've come a long way, and I know that is in part because of you.

I could keep going until the acknowledgment section is nearly as long as the book, so I will try to wrap it up, but I still have some thanks to go around. Another huge part of my journey as a writer is my Papaw. He started reading to me before I could even remember, and kept reading to me long past the time when I could absolutely read books myself. He fostered my love of reading, which inspired my desire to write. He always made sure I had books, and that was one thing he never minded buying for me. He bought me a copy of my favorite book at fifteen years old, and I still have that copy at thirty-two, seventeen years later. It has a cracked spine (which I usually consider a crime, but it's been read A LOT), and it is very well-loved, which brings me to my next thanks.

Thank you to Sarah Dessen. You have no idea who I am, but I am a huge fan, and your work inspired me so much. Your characters are so relatable, especially to a teenage girl. Even now, into adulthood, I can still relate to not only the main characters but also the adults in the story, as well. I found your books in my high school library as a freshman, and I was hooked. That favorite book with the cracked spine my grandpa bought me is 'The Truth About Forever.' Your books and your characters' relatability made me want to write stories that made people feel what the characters are feeling, and relate to them on the level I always did while reading your books.

This last thank you is a huge, all-encompassing one. Thank you so much to my family, friends, acquaintances, and anyone who has ever been supportive of me and the things I create. I love you all. This would be insanely long if I named everyone who has ever been supportive of me, so I promise I'm not forgetting you, I'm just trying not to add twenty extra pages to the book. If you've ever shared a post of mine, said you were going to purchase my book, liked a TikTok, or followed me on social media, thank you. Every bit of support counts, and I appreciate it beyond words. And last, a big thank you in advance to my future readers. I hope you enjoyed my book and look forward to more things from me, because there will definitely be more coming. Your support means the world, and I couldn't do it without you all! I love you, I love you, I love you!

XXXX(All kisses)

About the Author

Summer Nicole is a brand new author whose need to create stories stemmed from a huge love of books at a very early age. She loves how great stories can bring people together and create community. She is a mom to two wonderful girls who make her want to achieve her dreams to show them that they can, too, and wife to a wonderfully supportive husband (even when she's freaking out about literally everything). When she is not writing, she can be found reading, spending time with family, doing yoga, or crafting.

You can connect with me on:
- https://summernicolewrites.com
- https://www.facebook.com/authorsummernicole
- https://www.instagram.com/summmmernicole
- https://www.tiktok.com/@authorsummernicole
- https://www.threads.com/@summmmernicole

Subscribe to my newsletter:

✉ https://summernicolewrites.com/contact-me

www.ingramcontent.com/pod-product-compliance
Lightning Source LLC
Chambersburg PA
CBHW050030120726
47903CB00006B/1979